Beautiful Scars

Breathless

Book One

of

The Beautiful Scars Duet

Jenni Chris

ISBN: 979-8-218-67751-0

Cover Designed by Jenni Chris

Published by: www.jennichris.com

First edition 2025

This book is dedicated to those of you with indestructible hearts.

The ones who have lived through fire and learned how to breathe in the ashes.

The ones who know what it's like to live in the aftermath, the almost, the echo of what came before, and still, somehow, believe in a maybe someday.

It's dedicated to anyone who's ever tripped over their own heart while gathering its broken pieces, uncertain if, or how they'll ever fit together again.

If you've ever craved the kind of love that stays with you—imperfect and messy, but willing to try again and again—this is for you.

So, take a breath, relax and let me tell you a story.

Content Notes

This book contains some heavy themes and scenes that carry a lot of emotional weight throughout.

If you have any doubts and would like to see a content list please check my website:
jennichris.com/contentnotes

How It Started

CHAPTER ONE

SUNNY

TWO HUNDRED AND TWO steps.

That's how far I am from freedom. Or at least as close to it as I ever get—my spot under the old maple tree in the backyard.

Just keep moving. One foot in front of the other.

My body screams with each step, but I've gotten good at ignoring pain. Practice makes perfect, right?

When I finally ease myself down onto the grass, I close my eyes. The late afternoon sun paints the inside of my eyelids brilliant red, touched by the black shadows of leaves catching the wind. It's almost peaceful out here. Almost.

As soon as my head hits the grass, the tears start. They trail down my cheeks and pool in my ears before sliding out and soaking into the ground underneath me. I don't bother wiping them away. What's the point?

This soft patch of grass is as far from the house as I can manage or dare to go right now. I'm exhausted. Broken. Unfortunately, the thing I really want to get away from is myself—not exactly a distance problem.

A groan escapes from deep in my chest as my mind starts playing its favorite game of 'let's-see-how-much-more-she-can-take-today'.

The movie projector in my head rewinds and whirs to life, replaying every single sickening moment of the last few hours on an endless loop. The shudder that rips through me lights up every bruised and aching part of my body, making me want to throw up.

Silently, I begin measuring and counting each breath.

One...

Steam curls around me as I rest my head against the shower wall. The hot water running down my back feels like heaven—a rare moment of peace with the house empty. Mom's at the club, Garrett's at his meeting. It feels good to be able to relax.

Exhale...

And, two...

My favorite purple towel is still warm from the steam when I wrap it around myself. The citrus lotion I bought with Mom's stolen change feels like a small, but delicious rebellion as I smooth it over my skin. Through the window, I can see that it promises to be a perfect afternoon. Perfect to sit under the tree and read a while—pretend for a few hours that it's normal for me and not a luxury.

Exhale...

And, three...

The front door slams open while I'm working on getting the comb through my damp curls. Something crashes downstairs followed by the distinct sound of glass shattering. My heart stutters, then races. It has to be Garrett. He's home early. Too early. My hands shake as I grab for my clothes, trying to move silently despite the panic rising in my throat. I manage to step into my underwear. 'It's okay, it's going to be okay,' I whisper, even though I know it's a lie. It's as far from okay as it can be and I know it.

Exhale...

And, four...

The bathroom door bursts open—and I realize too late I forgot to lock it. Stupid. Garrett fills the frame, swaying, his bloodshot eyes crawling over my skin. The stench of whiskey and cigarettes erase the sweet citrusy clean smells of lotion and soap.

"Special surprise for you, Princess." His fingers dig into my wrist. "Been avoiding me, haven't you?" One twist forces my arm up behind my back until something pops in my shoulder. My fingers go numb and the towel falls.

Exhale…

And, five...

He marches me down the stairs and into the kitchen. The cracked, dirty linoleum smacking into my knees when he forces me down. "Look at me, girl," he slurs, pressing his boot under my chin. Tears burn behind my eyes, but I blink them back and swallow them down. He doesn't get those. They're mine.

The belt whips free with a harsh hiss—leather against denim. He folds it in half, testing it with a loud snap that makes me flinch.

Exhale…

And, six...

Step. Snap! Step. Snap! Each moment stretches out—pulled tight like a piece of string ready to break. When he stops in front of me, sweat beads on his forehead. The first strike is brutal—catching me across the top of my bare thighs without warning. I crush my lip between my teeth to stay silent. Through the pain, I see him tapping the belt against his leg, his other hand moving across the bulge in the front of his jeans—

The sound of someone clearing their throat above me yanks me out of my head. My eyes fly open, heart slamming against my ribs. I shriek—a small, choked sound—and try to scramble backward but fail miserably. My muscles scream at the sudden movement.

A figure towers over me, blocking out the sun. Too tall. Too big. My vision swims as I blink against the blinding light, desperately trying to focus. As the shadows shift, details emerge. A guy, maybe my age or a little older. Long legs covered in dark denim. Shoulders broad enough to block out the sun.

I can't see his eyes at first, but the harsh, angular lines of his face send panic racing through me. He shifts his weight, and I start calculating how fast I can get to my feet if I need to.

When he shoves his hands in his pockets, I notice something odd. He looks almost, uncomfortable. Which makes zero sense given *he's* the one who invaded *my* space.

"Damn, you're a lot more," he pauses, like he's choosing his words carefully, "nervous, than I thought you'd be. I didn't mean to scare you." His scowl deepens, like I've somehow personally offended him.

"You know, you'd be so much prettier without all those tears."

The words hit me like a slap. The fear evaporates, distilling itself down into anger. I welcome the shift—angry is safer than scared. I stare up at him, mouth open, momentarily stunned by his audacity.

What the actual fuck?

"Umm, thanks? Yeah, it sucks. Who...?" I take a deep breath before continuing. This is ridiculous.

"You know what? Never mind. I don't even care who you are. Fuck off. Get the hell out of here and leave me alone."

"I just..." He looks down at me, his scowl deepening. For a moment, discomfort becomes unsure. But it only lasts for a moment. Before I can object he collapses onto the grass next to me with a frustrated sigh. My body tenses at the sudden movement, but I force myself to stay still, cautious. He stretches his long legs out alongside mine, brushing thick dark hair from his eyes. "I meant, I've seen you around and I think you're pretty. It's a shame to see you doing anything to ruin it."

"Ruin it," I mumble, tasting the bitterness of the words. Because obviously, that's my biggest problem right now—not being pretty enough for this random asshole.

I push myself up, trying to hide how much it hurts, and study him. Is this some kind of sick joke? I start gearing up for a fight—God knows I've had enough practice today—but then his eyes meet mine.

A slow, warm smile spreads across his face, and something in my chest gives just a tiny bit. A tiny bit of space that gives me some room to breathe, which in turn causes my anger to deflate a little, which somehow pisses me off even more.

The tears are drying on my cheeks as he cocks his head, studying me right back. His eyes are the most intense shade of emerald green I've ever seen, and they pin me in place. I try to speak, to tell him exactly where he can shove his opinions, but words fail me. For the first time in my life, I'm speechless. My mouth opens, closes, opens again—nothing comes out.

"You shouldn't do that either. That thing with your mouth. Makes you look like a fish." His smile fades. "Also, you know it's kind of rude to not at least try to smile when you meet someone for the first time."

Me. Rude. The guy who invaded my space, insulted me, and is now telling me to smile is calling *me* rude. Un-fucking-believable.

"I'm Levi. We just moved into the house behind yours." He holds out his hand like this is a social engagement or something and I'm not sitting here trying to keep myself from falling apart.

At least that explains how he knew I was out here. I can see the surprise flash across his face when I don't take his hand or introduce myself. He looks like the kind of guy who doesn't get brushed off very often. My indifference and anger seem to throw him off balance, leave him uncertain. Good. Maybe he'll go away.

He pulls his hand back, letting it fall into his lap. "That's okay. You don't have to tell me your name. I'll find out what it is eventually." His voice comes out strong, sure. Apparently, his ego's big enough to give him a quick recovery.

"I've got time. For now though, I've got to call you something." He rubs his chin, where a thin layer of stubble is starting to show. "I think I'll call you Angel. You know, like the fish."

The words that just left his mouth absolutely crack him up. In seconds, he's laughing hysterically, eyes wet with tears. I, on the other hand, am not amused. In fact, I'm the exact opposite of amused.

"I. Am. Not. A. Fish." The words leave my lips slowly, separately, through gritted teeth. I ball my hands into fists and press them hard into the grass at my sides. Never in my life did I imagine those words would come out of my mouth.

"So, uh, thanks for stopping by, but I gotta get back to what I was doing—you know, that whole being ugly and not smiling thing. So, I think it's time for you to say goodbye, *Levi*."

"You *think*? Well now, that doesn't make it sound like you're so sure that's what you really want, *Angel*." The emphasis on the last word causes a cocky smirk to turn up the corner of his mouth.

I want to smack the smile off his face. I've had enough of this bullshit. Slowly, painfully, I get to my feet and come to stand in front of him. There's not a spot on my body that doesn't throb or ache, but there's no way I'm going to let him see it. I'm more than ready, more than capable of pulling this jerk to his feet and dragging him out of my yard if I have to, regardless of what condition I'm in.

Before I can even start to put together a plan, the screen door leading from the house out to the second story deck crashes open.

CHAPTER TWO

SUNNY

"THERE YOU ARE PRINCESS. Thought you could sneak out on me, huh?"

The words come out slurred as Garrett stumbles out the door and onto the rickety wooden deck. The rotting wood sags under his weight. His face is red and flushed, twisted into a deep, angry grimace leveled directly at me.

My stomach drops, and my heart follows right after threatening to pound it's way out of my chest. Even it wants to escape.

Suddenly, the problem of the guy stretching out on my lawn seems incredibly small and insignificant. All the anger I was feeling drains away. It's replaced by icy-cold, mind-numbing fear.

At his best, Garrett's a sadistic, perverted prick. But, on days like today, when he's been drinking and has gotten a good taste of my pain, he's so, so much worse.

I know because it's not like anything that's happened to me today is a one-off. I wish I could say it was, but it's not. It didn't come from some mistake my mom made this one time. Garrett is only one mark sitting on a timeline filled with errors in judgement that she can't ever seem to correct. He's not the first and probably won't be the last to see *me* as the icing on a very fucked up cake.

Garrett staggers forward, stopping at the top of the steep stairs leading down into the yard. "Aww, you didn't think I was done with you did you darlin'? I just needed a little break. Now, why don't you send your *little friend* home and get that sweet little ass of yours up here so we can finish what we started?"

"I...I... uh..." I stammer, unsure of what, if anything, I can say to make this better.

It was a desperate choice I'd made when I chose to come outside. There are strict rules to the games Garrett likes to play with me—the first being, no early outs. Everyone stays until he wins. I'd only broken that rule once before and paid the price dearly.

Apparently not dearly enough because here I am again.

I'd needed some fresh air though. I was desperate. I'd waited until he passed out on the couch before dragging myself to my feet and stumbling into the bathroom. Standing in front of the mirror, I forced myself to look—to inventory the damage.

Bright red stripes the width of his leather belt crisscrossed the pale skin of my chest and stomach. Deep purple and black bruises were starting to form in the shape of hands and fingers along my arms, ribs, over my hips and down the insides of each thigh. It occurred to me, as I stared at my reflection, that each time was getting worse.

As I stood there, staring at my reflection, something clicked. I could see everything, big picture and clear as a bell.

Eventually, there'd come a time when there would be no coming back from it, from him, because there'd be nothing left of me. Nothing left to hurt. Nothing left to take. And nothing left to try and piece back together.

One day, I won't be able to get back up.

That thought—that moment of perfect clarity—was suffocating. It felt like I was being buried alive. I had to get outside and put some space between me and what I saw in the mirror. I'd been desperate enough to break his rules, to risk everything to breathe a few mouthfuls of air that didn't smell like him.

I'd hedged my bets and lost. It was that simple. Usually when Garrett passes out, he's down for hours. Sometimes less, but he'd been so wasted when he got home I was sure my mom would be back before he woke up.

Not that I had any grand illusions about her rushing in to save me. She's proven time and time again that she won't help anyone, including me—unless there's something in it for her. She's selfish, but predictable. After her shift at the club, good night or bad, she always comes through the front door with 'gifts' for her and Garrett. A fresh bottle of liquor in one hand, a little plastic baggie of white powder or pills in the other.

I've never asked how much those 'gifts' cost her because I don't want to know.

They aren't exactly conventional weapons, but they do the trick. As long as I stay quiet and out of the way, I'm invisible, forgotten.

Right now though, there are too many minutes taking up the space between now and when she gets home to do me any good.

My feet are heavy, planted in the grass. I'm trying urgently to will them to move, but, they're frozen. With every second that ticks by, I can see Garrett becoming more tense, more angry. I shudder when he licks his lips, and steps down a few stairs. I can see all the ways he's planning on showing me how badly I fucked up written all over his face. My heart is pounding so hard it hurts.

"Now!" The word is a sharp, whip crack sound that causes the muscles deep inside my belly to clench. My cheeks catch fire, and a lump settles firmly into my throat making it hard to breathe. I know that from where Levi is sitting, on the grass behind me, he's got a perfect front row seat for all of this.

I'm so focused on Garrett and trying to get my body to work, that I don't even notice Levi get to his feet until he's standing next to me. Reaching out, he places a hand on my shoulder. It's unexpected and

I startle, jerking away from him with equal amounts of surprise and pain.

As I pull away, one of his fingers catches on the sleeve of the loose-fitting shirt I'm wearing. The fabric slides off my shoulder and down my arm a bit. I shrug it back up as fast as I can, but the look on Levi's face tells me it's too late. He's seen the swollen, dark marks in perfect finger-shaped lines that cover my skin.

He yanks his hand back like he's been burned. When I turn to face him, his brows are furrowed and there are deep creases lining his forehead. His mouth is turned into a deep frown. When he finally raises his eyes to meet mine, I see all the questions people have had over the years but never, ever ask painted in his expression. His face colors as all the pieces start sliding into place for him.

After stealing another quick glance at Garrett, I drop my eyes to the ground and stare at my bare feet, wiggling them nervously into the grass. My shoulders slump and my face burns. I wish with all my heart the ground would just open up and swallow me whole.

I'd never be that lucky though. When I lift my eyes again, the look on Levi's face has transformed from one of concern into one of pure venom. His eyes are narrow slits as he turns his head to zero in on Garrett with laser focus and intensity.

"Is that from him? Did he do that to you?" His voice is harsh and low and he leans in close, speaking through gritted teeth.

He doesn't wait for me to answer. "Don't you dare take even one step towards him. Not until you answer me, Angel."

"You need to get out of here. Please don't do anything. It'll only make things worse. Please. Just go. It's not—*I'm* not worth getting hurt over," I plead.

Out of the corner of my eye I see Levi hesitate. He looks from me, to Garrett, and back to me again, taking full measure of the situation. He inhales deeply and exhales loudly before squaring his shoulders and giving a small nod, like he's answering a question only he heard.

Taking a step forward, he places himself between me and Garrett. "Stay behind me." His tone is steady, even and calm.

"Whoa, Princess, looks like you've found yourself a little wannabe hero." There's a flicker of something in his eyes when he looks at Levi. He hesitates, narrowing his eyes and setting his jaw before continuing.

"And here I thought I'd been keeping you plenty busy. Guess I'll have to make more of an effort." He lowers his tone and chuckles before continuing.

"Listen. Kid. I don't share." I can hear the cruelty in Garrett's voice as he directs his attention to Levi. The silence stretches between them.

"This has nothing to do with you. Why don't you run on home to your asshole daddy where you'll be safe. I'm sure he's waiting for you."

Levi remains silent and solid in front of me, perfectly still. I keep my gaze focused on his back—watching the tiny muscles in his neck and shoulders twitch with each breath he takes. I count the freckles that dot the smooth surface of the skin on his neck and arms. I may not know exactly how any of this is going to play out, but I do know that it won't end well. Not for him and definitely not for me. It never does.

"C'mon kid. I got no beef with you. Let her by. The longer she stays down there the worse it's gonna be. For both of you." Garrett's voice is taking on a hard, angry edge as he speaks.

"Don't make me come down there and get her. Trust me, it's easier for everyone if she gets. Her ass. Up. These fucking stairs." He slams his meaty hand down on the railing, emphasizing each word. The rotting wood shakes with each smack. His patience is gone.

Levi takes another deep breath before speaking. His voice comes out cold, emotionless. "She's not going up those stairs and you're not coming down here to get her. *You* should go back inside and sleep it off while you still can." The threat hangs in the air.

My entire body starts to tremble when I hear Garrett start to laugh. It's a wicked sound—one I've heard too many times right before things go completely sideways.

Levi has no idea what Garrett is like when he's well and truly pissed. There's no way either of us are going to leave this back yard in one piece. We're both totally fucked. Levi just doesn't know it yet.

"Alright. Have it your way kid."

The instant I hear the stairs creak as Garrett moves down another step, Levi lowers his shoulders and charges forward with a loud, low roar. By the time Garrett registers what's happening it's too late—the alcohol's made him too slow—Levi's already on his way up the stairs. He drives his shoulder hard into Garrett's leg right as he takes his next step down. There's a loud crack as his knee takes the full force of the impact. He flails wildly, forced off balance.

Levi quickly gains his footing and takes advantage of Garrett's precarious position by slamming his body into him. Hard. Garrett's full weight falls against one of the railing's weak support posts. There's the sound of splintering wood as it gives way and the entire section of railing tears away from the stairs. Garrett lets out a loud howl of pain and surprise as he falls. He lands with a sickening thud on the broken pieces of wood and hard ground.

Levi takes his time walking down the fractured stairs to meet me where he left me standing.

"You okay Angel?"

I nod, trying to wrap my mind around what's just happened. "I'm good." My voice comes out shaky. My eyes are glued to Garrett lying on the ground. He's pissed, and moaning in pain, but he's not getting up.

Slowly, I let out the breath I was holding. I should feel so many things right now, but all I'm feeling is relief. I know it won't last, but I'll take it. "I'm good," I repeat.

"Come with me. I want you to hear this," Levi says. "It's okay. I got you." Reluctantly, I follow him.

I wince with every step as we walk over to the spot Garrett's lying, clutching his leg, writhing in pain. Levi lets go of my hand and squats down beside him. "I need to make sure you hear me, you stupid piece of shit." He pauses, waiting until Garrett turns to face him. "If you ever lay so much as a finger on her again, I'll find you wherever you are and slit your goddamned throat in the middle of the night. Do you understand me?"

"Fucking little ungrateful bitch!" The words hiss from his lips, part agony, part anger. "You have no idea who you're fucking with, kid! You're both gonna pay for this!" Garrett sucks in a breath, his eyes darting back and forth between both Levi and me.

"Talk to me, not to her." The calm in Levi's voice is disturbing. His face is expressionless as he watches Garrett rail against him. "I'm thinking you didn't hear me. Let me make sure I have your full attention when I say it again."

Levi stands and takes several long strides out into the yard. With a look of determination, he plants his feet, takes a breath, and pushes off, building up speed. He delivers a kick to Garrett's ribs hard enough to lift his body and move it several inches. Garrett curls into himself gasping for air. Levi repeats the action two more times before squatting down again, gritting his teeth and asking, "Do I have your attention now? I said you'll never touch her again. Ever."

Garrett's breath is ragged and uneven. He's lying folded up on his side groaning every time his chest moves. He nods his head and breathes out a soft 'yes'.

"Angel? Look at me." Levi stands and takes his phone out of his pocket, getting ready to dial. Before his fingers push the buttons he looks at me, his expression serious. "I'm going to call an ambulance for him, but first, you and I need to get our stories straight. Okay? That's the only way this is going to work."

I nod my head slowly, keeping my eyes on the ground. I'm trying to ignore the raspy breathing and gasping coming from the spot in front of me. "Yeah. Okay," I respond.

"I came over to introduce myself and we were sitting out here talking. He was drunk, came outside, leaned on the railing, it broke, and he fell. That's it. That's everything."

There's a long pause. "Look at me Angel, I need to know you got it. I know you can do this. That's the story. No more, no less. Now, repeat it back to me."

My voice is shaky and breathless. "You came over to introduce yourself. We were out here talking, Garrett came outside, leaned on the railing, it broke, and he fell. I...I think he was drunk."

"Atta girl." He smiles broadly as he very gently reaches out to tuck a loose strand of hair behind my ear.

"He'll never hurt you again," he says. His eyes search mine, his brow furrowed.

If only I could believe those words.

CHAPTER THREE

LEVI

RED, WHITE AND BLUE flashing lights flood the neighborhood. Standing on the sidewalk that cuts through Angel's yard, I scan the houses lining the street. Gawking faces with wide, curious eyes peer out from every half-closed blind and curtain edge. Everyone loves a good tragedy. I may be new to this neighborhood, but people are people, and they're the same everywhere. Especially in crappy neighborhoods like this one, where everyone only pretends to mind their business. Privacy has its limits—it usually ends right where the yellow tape starts.

By tomorrow, those faces pressed to the glass will have called or texted every friend or relative they have. They'll spread their opinions and make guesses about what happened like it's their job. By tomorrow night, it'll be so far ground down through the rumor mill no one could recognize the truth if they tried.

Good news for me, but not so much for Angel. She can kiss her privacy goodbye. I think she's going to be the subject of conversation for a while, like it or not.

To me, it seems like a small price to pay to be rid of the scumbag being loaded into the back of the ambulance, but to Angel? I'm not sure how she's going to feel about it.

I get the feeling she's no stranger to any of this though. Hell, if she went through half of what I'm thinking she did before I showed up, not to mention everything that came after, and she's still holding it together? The girls got some guts. She's standing there calmly on the curb—not a hint of anything that would give away what happened today. Before or after I showed up. Respect.

"So, you're telling me you have no idea how Mr. Coleman ended up with those tread marks on his side. Is that correct, son?" The question rips my attention from Angel. It comes from the tall, skinny cop standing in front of me, and for a minute it throws me. I didn't consider that I'd probably left marks on the guy.

Fuck. What a rookie mistake.

The cop has one eyebrow cocked and is staring down at my size 13 boots. He knows the answer. The real answer. The hint of a tight smile at the edges of his lips and the tone of his voice tell me that much. He's just waiting for me to incriminate myself.

He thinks I'm just a stupid kid. But I know that the fact he's even standing here asking me instead of cuffing me and hauling me in for formal questioning means that for whatever reason, he doesn't really care about my answer. I breathe a tiny sigh of relief—confident I've got nothing to worry about. At least from him.

I'll admit though, I'm not sure he'd be as generous if he knew how hard it'd been to stop myself. I'd wanted nothing more than to grind that asshole into the ground. It took everything I had in me to stop kicking once I started. I don't think I would've if Angel hadn't been standing there watching.

"No, Sir. Like I said, I've never met the man before," I reply, trying to sound as sincere and respectful as possible. Cops eat that shit up. "We just moved here." A lesson pounded into me from my father about dealing with cops—less is always more. *You can't poke holes in the truth, son,* he always used to say. Short, sweet and with as much honesty as possible is always the way to go.

"Ah well. We know Mr. Coleman, and his," he pauses and his eyes dart to the spot where Angel is standing, "habits. He enjoys pissing off the wrong people and tends to do it often. His condition and the fact that he's refusing to talk to us isn't surprising. Thank you for your cooperation. If we need anything else, we'll be in touch." The cop smiles widely at me and offers me his card. I take it and tuck it into my pocket. Who knows, maybe it'll come in handy someday. The guy reaches out to shake my hand before stepping away. I take it too. Now *that* is something I'm not used to.

Common sense is telling me that I should let myself take the win and get out of here. Consider what I did my good deed for the day and let the karma coin drop. The sane, rational voice in my head is begging me to just forget this girl, forget this house, forget all of it.

And that little voice is right. The last thing I need is the kind of trouble all of this could bring me, bring my mom. I didn't get yanked out of the middle of my life, dragged from one side of the country to the other only to end up in the kind of situation we risked everything to keep me away from. I'm tired of running. The last thing I want to do is pack up and leave another place. As much as I hate it here, I hate moving even more.

Too bad for me though. What I want simply isn't in the cards. Right as I take a step to leave, I see the cop take a couple steps closer to Angel. He seems like a decent enough guy. The look on his face is full of pity and what looks like genuine concern. Reaching out, he places a hand on her shoulder and squeezes gently.

Angel's reaction is immediate and big. She recoils and gasps, an expression of intense pain twisting her face. Now, my rational brain knows this guy's only trying to comfort her, offer some support in a difficult situation. But, my other brain, the ancient caveman one that seems to be running the show today, is imagining the sound of each of his fingers breaking, bone by bone.

I don't know for sure what happened to Angel today before I showed up, or what her life is normally like. Today could've easily been a one off. One small, fucked up little blip on the radar screen of an otherwise perfectly normal life. And if it wasn't, it's not like I should care. I don't know her. Life is hard and sucks sometimes for everyone. I'm a neighbor. That's it. I don't even know her real name for Christ's sake.

But, wishing I was stupid doesn't make me stupid. I saw and heard enough to know that sometimes for everyone, is all the time for her. It makes my blood boil to think of everything that was behind what that asshole said this afternoon. People like him, like my father, are cut from the same cloth. Thinking they can own people. Do whatever they want and never face any consequences.

But I'm not letting myself off the hook. I've got plenty of anger leftover for myself. I don't know what happened to me when I walked into that backyard. I hadn't planned on being such a dick. It's not like I walked over there with the intention of making her angry or upset. In fact, I spent the last three weeks camping out on my balcony watching her. And, when I wasn't watching her, I was looking for her and wishing I was. I'd spent a good portion of that time thinking of what I'd say when the time came. All that rehearsing and planning only to have my brain freeze up on me as soon as I walked through that gate.

I'd wanted to introduce myself. That was all. To be fair though, I was seriously *not* prepared to find her the way I did. It caught me off guard. Those deep, hitching breaths and perfect pink cheeks wet with tears made everything come to a grinding halt. Everything including my heart. The shock made me stupid, and I regret it. I *will* find a way to make it up to her. Eventually.

I wish I didn't, but I can relate to everything that cop is feeling right now. I'm sure it's close to the same way I felt when I touched her and got that same response. It's obvious he feels bad—he's falling all over himself apologizing. It's obnoxious.

As if she can feel me watching, and hear what I'm thinking, she turns her head and fixes me with those big brown eyes of hers. She takes a thick section of honey blonde hair and twirls it nervously around her fingers. Then, as if I didn't have it bad enough already, she offers me a sweet, wide smile that lights up her entire, beautiful face. My heart rattles in its cage, and I have to remind myself to breathe.

Who am I kidding? I can't walk away from that. From her. I'm not going anywhere anytime soon. I sigh deeply and go take a seat on the cracked, concrete front step to wait.

Once the doors of the ambulance close and it pulls away from the curb a few minutes later, Angel's entire body relaxes. It's not until the very last patrol car turns the corner and the last of her neighbors slide their curtains closed again, that she finally turns to look at me. She seems as surprised as I am that I'm still here. Making her way slowly from the curb to the front porch, she wraps her arms around her body, hugging herself tight.

I move over and pat a spot on the broad concrete step beside me. She looks at me with her head tilted, studying me silently, weighing her options. Eventually, she lowers herself down to sit, wincing slightly once or twice and making a pointed effort to not touch me.

And so, we sit together. Both of us still and quiet, lost in our own thoughts as we watch the blue summer sky fade into twilight. It's not until the streetlights flicker on and the cool night air is filled with the sound of crickets that she finally says something.

"I suppose you're still here because you think I owe you something for what you did today." She sighs and it's as if her entire body deflates. "It was stupid, you know. Garrett could've killed you. He's dangerous." Her eyes stay fixed on the ground in front of her, focused on the spot where the overgrown grass meets the concrete. "It was sweet though. In a dumb, fucked up way. No one's ever…"

Her voice fades as she starts wiggling her toes against the sidewalk. Her hands slide down her calves and I can feel how nervous she is. She lowers her voice to almost a whisper and her hands tremble as she continues.

"Don't fool yourself though. You didn't really save me from anything. He'll be back, meaner and more pissed than ever. It'll be worse for me then." Taking a long, slow, deep breath in, she holds it a moment before closing her eyes to exhale.

I don't know what to say to that. I keep my mouth shut, unwilling to risk making any of this worse than it already is.

"Did you mean what you said to him. At the end?"

I meant every single word of what I said to the prick. It would bring nothing but pleasure to erase him. Still, it takes a minute for the weight of the question to settle and to formulate an answer that doesn't make me sound insane…

But, I'm not quick enough. Before I can answer, she's on her feet, dusting herself off. As she turns to walk up the steps, I want to say more. I want to answer her and take away the doubt I see clouding her eyes, but I'm stuck on mute. I'd say just about anything to keep her here next to me a little while longer. I want to say something that will reassure her and coax one more of those heart stopping smiles out before she leaves me sitting here wishing I'd done even more things differently.

She turns and lifts her eyes to mine. Her expression darkens and the next words out of her mouth hurt my heart. "It's okay, I know the answer. You bought me some sleep and time to heal and that's more than I had before you showed up."

"Angel, I—"

"Look, I have no idea why you did what you did or if it was even for me really. I don't want to know your reason, because I don't care. You need to know though that I have nothing I can give you. *Nothing* to offer you." She raises her chin and smiles at me sadly, lowering her tone. "At least nothing you'd actually want. It's probably best if you don't come back here again. You need to stay away from me. Garrett's right you know, I'm not worth it."

With that, she takes the few short steps up, opens the door, steps over the threshold and disappears inside. The faded wooden screen door slams shut behind her and I find myself staring at the empty space she left behind, wishing she'd come back. I sit like that for several minutes, going back over the past few hours, before getting up to start the short walk home.

I'll give her the space she's asking for. I'll give her the time she wants. I've got time. I'm patient.

To a point.

I turn and look over my shoulder one more time before leaving.

Oh, but you have no idea, Angel. You are exactly what I want. You're more than worth it.

CHAPTER FOUR

Sunny

THE HOURS RIGHT BEFORE dawn are the worst. The silence is deafening. It leaves too much space for my mind to wander and get lost in. The memories get bold, sharpen their teeth, and tear me apart—one small piece at a time.

It's been a while, but there used to be a time I could lay here and calm the monsters, minimize the damage. Convince them to go back to sleep and leave me alone a little longer. I used to be able to dig down under all the dirt and filth I'm buried in and find a few good parts of me left. Pieces that weren't ruined and broken. But now? I think they're all gone. If there were any left I don't think I'd be so disappointed to wake up every morning.

Mom had a meltdown when she got home and Garrett wasn't waiting for her. She'd come bursting through the front door, all giggles and blown pupils, party favors in one hand, bottle in the other. She's nothing if not predictable.

Her expression had gone from ecstatic to shocked to downright pissed in a matter of seconds. I told her the same story I gave the cops about what happened. She's smart though. Even fucked up she's smarter than most cops.

Halfway through my story, her lips twisted and her eyes narrowed into slits. She could see I was lying. I prefer honesty but am smart enough to know that lies have their place. I don't do it often, but I can be good at stretching the truth. But not to the woman standing in front of me. She's a human lie detector when it comes to me.

She didn't call me out on it though. Instead, she went into the kitchen, cracked open the new bottle of whiskey, poured herself a shot, and marched off to her room.

When she came out, she was wearing fresh clothes and muttering to herself about what a selfish prick Garrett was before storming out. She's at the hospital now. The good news is that while she doesn't believe the story now, she will eventually. It's easier that way, which is just how she likes it.

I've been lying here staring up at the ceiling trying to breathe through the suffocating tightness in my chest that makes me feel like I'm dying with no luck. Logically I know I'm fine, but my pounding heart and the thoughts racing through my mind are doing their best to convince me otherwise.

I know my mom. There's no way she's sticking by Garrett while he heals. It's not in her nature. She's not a ride or die. She's loyal to herself. Period. Full stop.

It's not that she doesn't know how to show compassion or empathy. There was a time I remember her being a good mom. A time when we were happy. But then, it all changed. Now, she only shows that side of herself when someone's watching. If there isn't an immediate payoff for her efforts, she doesn't make them. She'll only do uncomfortable for so long.

It occurs to me that maybe I'm more like her than I want to admit because I can't help but wonder what all of this means for me. I know it's a fucked-up way to think, but even as evil as Garrett is with me, I know what I'm in for with him. I know what to expect. Usually, I'm not such a fucking idiot and can sidestep the worst. What happened today was my fault. I knew better.

I'm fairly certain though that there are more real live human monsters out there in the world. Ones with sharper claws and much bigger appetites than Garrett. Not to mention better imaginations.

I meant what I'd said to Levi when I left him sitting on the front step. He didn't save me from anything. Not really. He gave me a momentary break, a pause. I'm thankful for it—I mean I'll take it, but I know it won't last. It never does.

Mom had Garrett moved in before Dad's side of the bed was even cold. Before anyone could even ask if he was dead or just... gone. That's how Mom operates—she's incapable of being alone. When Garrett takes off for one of his "business" trips, she always finds someone to fill the temporary space. That someone is usually worse, never better.

I know there's no way she'd get away with the things she does if she weren't so beautiful. Years of addiction have done little to take away from her looks. It's a distraction—how she hides the absolute disaster she is underneath it all. No one sees it, until it's too late. She's a force of nature—she destroys everything and everyone she touches. I'm just collateral damage. Nothing more, nothing less.

Yesterday, in the backyard, when I watched the calm resolve of decision-making move across Levi's face, I knew there was no way he'd be able to protect me. I'd truly believed he was on a suicide mission. He'd been so confident—so solid and unflinching as he stood his ground. What he did opened the door, a tiny crack, to something I hadn't felt for as long as I can remember.

For a brief moment, there was a barely noticeable wingbeat in the center of my chest. A tiny flutter that asked me to consider that maybe someone saw something in me worth protecting. Something worth saving.

It was a ridiculous thought, an impossible thought. I've learned that girls like me don't get heroes. We don't get noticed enough to be rescued. Our lives are too messy. Too dirty. Too painful. I'll never be mistaken for anything other than what I am. What Garrett has made me. Not in this lifetime at least.

But, for a moment, I knew what it *would* feel like if things were different. It felt good. It felt warm and safe and weird. And, I liked it.

That is the real reason I told Levi to leave and stay away. I'm not ready to let go of that feeling yet. I want to wear it a little longer. And, if he'd stayed...

Well, if he'd stayed, we'd have started talking. Which can be dangerous.

I know how it would go. Nothing big at first. Surface questions meant to hold the space between us and keep us dancing around what'd happened. Eventually though, he'd start asking questions I didn't want to answer, couldn't answer. Of course, I'd end up unable to stop myself from asking some of my own. Then, after we both were a little more comfortable, I'd ask the big one. Why? Why did he do what he did for me?

As I was standing on the curb watching the ambulance pull away, I'd gone through every answer I could think of to that question. I decided that I'd rather send Levi away and keep guessing, than risk having that tiny, fluttering beat of hope crushed inside my chest.

If nothing else I've learned over the past few years that hope can be cruel. It makes you weak at times you can't afford it. It makes you want things you have no business asking for, and no right to think you could have. Worst of all, it makes you start to believe in impossible things. Things like maybe there is someone, with a perfect smile and beautiful green eyes, who isn't afraid to risk everything for you.

I wake up, choking on the scream stuck in my throat. Inside my chest my heart is pounding so hard it hurts, and I'm covered in a thin sheen of sweat. A deep shiver runs the length of my body even though it has to be close to a hundred degrees in my room.

I sit up, trying to focus my eyes and gulp down a raw, gasping breath. I let out a low groan as the room starts to come into focus and my head clears. There isn't an inch of my body that doesn't ache and throb. I can't remember ever feeling this bad before—and that's saying something.

A loud, *thud, thud, thud* coming from downstairs hammers its way into my skull turning the dull hammer strikes into icepicks. I lay back down, stare up at the ceiling, and try to ignore it. No one ever knocks on our door. Ever. Even the guys in suits carrying bibles seem to know to stay away.

If I ignore it, it'll go away.

A second series of hard knocks is followed by a third before I decide that whoever it is, isn't leaving. I roll out of bed, fighting back tears once my feet hit the floor. I would never have thought it would be possible for *every single part of me* to hurt this bad.

I trip and almost kill myself trying to make it down the stairs. By the time I get to the door, I'm irritated, and positive my head is going to explode any second. The clock in the living room says it's almost 5:00. In the afternoon. Which means I've slept almost eighteen hours. No wonder I feel like shit.

I yawn and stumble to the door. My plan is to crack it open, get rid of whoever it is, and then get back to bed as soon as possible. But the loud crack and shooting pain that runs up my leg when I stub my toe on the door frame is the last straw for me. Now, I'm pissed. At the door. At my toe. At whoever can't take the hint and leave like a normal person.

Instead of cracking it open to peek out, I yank it open, stand there with my hands on my hips and manage to croak out, "What the fuck do you want?"

I stand there in horror when I realize it's Levi. I watch the smile slide off his face as he takes me in.

I'd rolled out of bed in my pajamas—a pair of boy shorts and a tank top. Great for sleeping in, not so great for hiding in. My cheeks catch fire as he looks me up and down knowing full well what he's seeing.

My skin is a mosaic of bruises and welts and bite marks. I went over all of it last night in the mirror when I got out of the shower, but I know they always look and feel worse the next day. Judging from his shocked expression and the anger flaring in his eyes, it's bad. Maybe even a little worse than it feels.

"Hey, uh, Angel," he says sheepishly. His eyes stay fixed on my bare thighs where the damage is most concentrated.

His gaze is so intense, it's a struggle to keep from trying to cover myself with my hands. But, I don't. I refuse to hide. He's the one showing up where he's not wanted and doesn't belong. It would be pointless now anyway. He's already seen it all.

I don't give him a chance to say anything else. "Look. I appreciate what you did for me yesterday. I do. But I told you. You need to stay away from here. Away from me. I have nothing for you." I lean over slightly, wincing at the sharp pain from a spot near my ribs and tilt my head to catch his gaze. I lock on to his eyes and drag them up from my legs to my face as I stand straight again. "Nothing," I repeat.

"I needed to check... I wanted to be sure—"

Fuck. Of course. How could I be so stupid?

A cold rush of panic floods my chest. My breath catches and my fingers twitch against the doorframe, ready to slam it shut before he can voice whatever threat he came here to make. I should have known better. I should have known this was coming.

"I'm not a snitch. I promise. I won't tell a soul what happened yesterday. As far as my mom, the cops, and everyone else knows it all happened exactly the way you told me to say it. You don't have to worry."

The words rush out of my mouth. Desperate. As soon as he started talking, it dawned on me how important it might be that I convince him of everything I just said. He doesn't know me, doesn't have any reason to trust that I won't say anything. I feel nauseous.

He took Garrett out. Put him in the hospital like it was nothing. Of course he wants to make sure you aren't going to say anything to anyone.

A scowl etches his face. "No. Wait. That's not—that's not what I meant. That's not what I'm here for." The words are gentle when he speaks them even though his brow is furrowed and his eyes are hard.

I feel like I'm on the verge of falling apart in front of him and there's nothing I can do to stop myself. Every muscle in my body is wound tight to the point of pain.

"Let me start over." I watch as he draws in a deep breath, holds it and exhales slowly. He closes his eyes as the air leaves his lungs, and when he opens them again a small smile tips up the edges of his mouth and his eyes have softened.

"I wanted to stop by and see how you're doing, make sure you're okay. Yesterday was," he pauses and I can tell he's weighing his words out carefully, "a lot. I came by earlier, but there was no answer, and then I saw your mom leave and..." He stands there in the doorway and jams his hands in the pockets of his jeans. "Angel. I'm not going to hurt you. I'd never hurt you."

"Oh." I stand there looking at him with a stupid, blank look on face unsure of what to say next. The knot in my stomach stays firmly in place, but the tension in my jaw and my shoulders drains away.

A full minute passes, before he speaks again. "So, are you?"

"Am I what?" I feel like I missed something.

"Okay," he chuckles.

"I'm fine." It's not quite a lie. I *will* be fine. Judging by what I saw in the mirror last night, it's going to take a while, but I'll be okay. Eventually. I always am. Even though I feel like an idiot, and my body aches and my head feels like it's getting squeezed in a vice, I offer up a big, wide, toothy smile as proof.

His expression turns serious as his eyes travel down my body and back up again. "Right. Um, I think we might have different definitions of 'fine'."

He raises an eyebrow not taking his eyes off me, but the judgement and disgust I'm expecting to see written on his face isn't there. It feels like he's waiting for a response, but he doesn't push, doesn't say anything else. The words sit between us, heavy and awkward. I swallow hard. Obviously, he doesn't believe a word I've said even though he doesn't say it. It's irritating.

I shift uncomfortably, wiggling my toes, digging them into the worn wooden floor. He's not the first person to have seen evidence of what my life is like. Most people don't have the stomach for it though—I think it makes them nervous—as if bruises and pain are contagious or something. My mom ignores them completely. She has since the day Garrett moved in with us. If she doesn't acknowledge them, she doesn't have to ask questions she doesn't want the answer to. My friends, at least the ones I used to have, couldn't handle the *heaviness* of seeing and knowing. There are a lot of things I blame them for, but that's not one of them. I wouldn't want to deal with it either. Not if I had a choice.

But Levi? He's not looking away. He's looking right into the center of it all and *not* flinching. I've never had anyone stare so openly and see so *much* of me—with no trace of guilt or pity or contempt. He's just... looking. And somehow, that's harder and more disturbing than any of the reactions I've gotten before. I don't know what to do with it.

"Really. I'm fine. Or, I will be. I've been through worse." Again, a half-truth. I've never been through anything that comes close.

Now it's his turn to stand there with a stupid, shocked look on his face not knowing what to say. After a long moment he responds.

"You don't have to lie to me Angel." He hesitates, his tone low and careful as he continues. "What I mean is, you don't have to be 'fine' if you're not. I've seen enough to know that…" He trails off, like he's searching for the right words, then lets out a long sigh.

I open my mouth to argue, to tell him he doesn't know anything about me, but the words won't come. They stick in my throat and I have to force myself to swallow over the lump they make.

"Look, I just wanted to check on you. You don't have to do anything with what I said," he says quietly. "But I'll be around if you need… anything." He takes a step back, hands still stuffed in his pockets, watching me with a gaze that sees so much more than I want him to.

I want to tell him to go, to leave me alone and let me pretend this never happened. But somehow, I can't find it in myself to push him away again. I don't have the energy or the desire.

Instead, I nod stiffly, feeling his stare as he takes me in one last time before turning to leave. Right before he steps off the porch, I hear him murmur, almost to himself, "I meant it when I said I'd never hurt you."

I close the door, leaning against it. Part of me wants to laugh at the absurdity of what just happened, but the other part—the one that feels small and raw and exposed—aches.

Chapter Five

Levi

"Welcome to the team, man. You killed it out there today."

I grunt in response and take a sip of my beer. The words come from Ryan, one of my new teammates. The last thing I'd wanted to do was get stuck playing football again, especially for a crappy, broke team like the one here in Easton Creek. Everything from the faded bleachers to the ragged, weed-filled end zones screams disappointment. I know I'm supposed to try to blend in as much as possible, but holy hell, why does it have to be so hard?

It's been a little over three years since my mom and I left my father. Three long years, since we packed a few bags, closed a couple bank accounts and left in the middle of the night. Four moves later and the places we land keep getting worse. Mom insists we need to do everything we can to not draw attention to ourselves—the less visible we are, the harder it will be for him to find us. She's fooling herself, and I don't have the heart to tell her so.

My father is as smart as he is ruthless. He has a long reach and I have no doubt that he knows exactly where we are. It wouldn't surprise me if us ending up in this hell hole was his idea. He's a master at pulling strings and getting exactly what he wants. To him, the world is a chess board and everyone, including us, is nothing but a pawn.

The only reason we're still here and not back under his roof and under his thumb is because, for now, for whatever twisted reason, our being here serves his purpose. This taste of freedom? It only exists because he's seen fit to grant it to us. It's not going to last forever.

Rolling my shoulders, I stretch my neck groaning at the loud pop when it cracks. My muscles ache from the try-outs and the hours of practice after. It's been a while since I played—but thinking about all the time and energy I'm going to waste playing for a team like this one is what really hurts. But, here I am. The new quarterback. Lucky me.

Ryan is leaning against the wrought iron railing running along the balcony outside my room. He's been nursing the same beer for the past half hour and it's driving me nuts. Not that I want to get the guy hammered, but it has to be warm and undrinkable by now. He doesn't seem to notice though—he's too busy checking out the view from up here. You can see all the way to very edge of town.

This house—our house—is three stories which makes it the tallest in the whole neighborhood, and almost the whole damn town. It's ridiculous. I don't even want to know what kind of mental gymnastics my mom performed to make it fit into the whole 'not drawing attention to ourselves' idea. As she told me, "*We might've been forced to downgrade but there's no reason to settle for less than the best. Even if it's only the best of the worst.*" And this place, this town, and from what I've seen so far, the people, are definitely the worst.

My bedroom is on the top floor, by itself. There are double doors that open out onto the balcony. When I saw it, I hadn't been above using guilt to get my way and make sure this part of the house was mine. It's private and quiet and gives me plenty of space to call my own. I love having a bird's eye view of everything. Especially Angel's backyard.

I take a swig of my beer, the bitter taste not doing as much to distract me as I'd hoped. It's been a little over two weeks since I stood on Angel's porch wanting to check on her, and I can't seem to let it go. Every time I close my eyes, I see the violence that covered her skin—as if someone had taken a paint brush and covered her in the ugliest shades of purples and blues and yellow-greens. But it's not just what I saw—it's what it all meant.

Each one of those marks told a story of pain and fear and things I don't even want to put a name to. It's no wonder she thought I'd come over to keep her quiet.

And the way she stood there—trying so damn hard to convince me she was fine… Every nerve in my body still feels raw, unsettled. Nothing seems to help.

I force myself to stare at the peeling paint on the outside of the house, my knuckles turning white around the bottle neck as I try and resist the urge to look over at Angel's house.

I'm doing my best to stay away from her. Doing my best to do as she asked. But I don't see it lasting. I don't think I'll be able to keep it up much longer.

I take another sip of my beer. Ryan is right. I didn't do too bad today. Especially for a guy who hasn't gotten more than a few hours of sleep a night in the past couple of weeks.

"Thanks, man, I —"

"The party tonight was a good idea. The guys'll come around eventually, it's gonna take a little time is all. Zack on the other hand..." he pauses to take another sip of his beer, "He can be a real dick sometimes, and he holds on to things forever. You need to watch your back around him."

I nod. I get it. It has to suck to be the top dog for most of your life only to have a new guy come in and steal your thunder senior year. I wish I could tell him to just take it. He can have it—I don't want it. I never did.

"Damn! I didn't realize you lived behind *her*." Ryan lets out a low whistle and turns his full attention to the yard directly behind me. "She may be fucked up, but damn, I could get used to a view like that."

I come to stand next to him and follow his eyes down to the spot they're glued. I see exactly what he's talking about. Walking carefully down the broken steps leading to her backyard, Angel is balancing a full plate of food and a can of soda on top of a thick book she's holding like a tray.

It's good to see her out. This is the first time I've laid eyes on her since that day at her house. Long, sand colored waves fall carelessly over her shoulders and frame her perfect heart-shaped face. Her nose is scrunched up—crinkled in intense concentration.

She's fucking adorable.

I'm pretty sure none of that is what drew Ryan's attention though. It's probably the same thing that I can't drag my eyes away from. Today, Angel's wearing a pair of tight denim jeans that hug her full hips and thighs in a way that look as if she's been poured into them. Her thin black T-shirt is obviously a size or two too big for her, but she's knotted the bottom of it at her side to adjust the length. The knot sits at the dip of her waist and pulls the cotton material tight over her full breasts.

Out of the corner of my eye, I see the look on Ryan's face and anger flares in my chest. My jaw clenches so hard it's a wonder my teeth don't crack. He's looking at Angel like she's his next meal. I can't tear my eyes away from her either, but she's not for him. She's for me. Only me.

When she gets to the bottom of the stairs, she looks up, and her gaze finds mine. Her lips curl into a small, shy smile and she tips her chin to me. I can't help it—a smile takes over my entire face in response.

Her smile fades into a deep scowl when she notices Ryan gawking at her. With a stiff gait, she makes her way to a spot under the tree and lowers herself with a grimace to the ground. Her back is to us. An intentional cold-shoulder.

"So. You know Angel?" I casually turn my back on the girl sprawled out on her lawn when it becomes obvious she's not going to turn around again. I work to keep the edge out of my voice.

"Angel? Who's…?" Ryan runs his hands through his hair, chuckling when he realizes who I'm talking about. "Oh, you mean Sunny. She's something else, isn't she?" He takes another swig of his hot beer. "But, she is definitely *not* an angel. Where'd you get that from?"

"Nowhere," I mumble and shrug. The image of the outrage on Sunny's face when I called her Angel flashes in my mind and I have to force myself not to laugh. "Yeah, she's something else alright. She seeing anyone?"

Ryan laughs. "Um, no. Well, not exactly. Sunny doesn't... Sunny isn't... "

I can tell Ryan's thinking, weighing out his next words carefully. Too carefully. He tips the bottle and swallows the last of his beer. Setting the empty bottle on the table, he takes a seat in one of the cheap wicker chairs.

"Sunny doesn't what? C'mon man, spill." The words come out tightly controlled. Do I know I'm too invested in this girl already? Yes. Yes I do, but no one else needs to.

"Well, Sunny's...um, different. I know she's amazing to look at, and she used to be a lot of fun to hang out with, but, seriously man, keep your distance. She's trouble. And not the kind it's fun to get into."

Taking the chair across from Ryan, I think about going in and getting us another beer. But, I begin peeling the label off my beer instead, waiting for him to continue. As if I don't already know that Angel—Sunny—is trouble. On the day we moved into this place, I'd stepped out onto this balcony and all it took was a few minutes of watching her under that stupid tree with her nose in a book and I was hooked.

Without knowing anything about her, including her name, I'd been willing to risk everything to help her. And even after everything was said and done, and all I got out of it was a warning to stay away, I'd do it again in a heartbeat.

The stupid piece of shit had it coming. I saw those bruises on her arm and it was like holding a lit match to gasoline. One look into those big, brown eyes and I don't think there's anything I wouldn't do for her.

Yeah, I have no doubt that she's trouble. Big trouble. I'm just waiting for Ryan to tell me how truly and deeply fucked I am.

"Huh. What's her story?" My eyes settle on her, and I take a deep pull on the bottle I'm holding. *Easy boy, not too anxious.*

"She's been through a lot the past few years," he says. He's lost in thought for a moment as he rolls his empty bottle along the edge of the table. "All of us pretty much grew up together. Sunny was always cool as hell. Everyone loved her."

"But, then, her dad disappeared. And things kind of fell apart for her. And her mom." Ryan looks out, his attention still focused on Sunny.

"What happened to her dad?" I ask.

"No one knows exactly, but people talk. Rumor has it he pissed off the wrong people." When he continues, his voice is laced with a tinge of sadness. "It destroyed Sunny."

"After that..." Ryan trails off, taking another sip. "Her mom moved that guy Garrett in and started dancing out at The Foxhole." He glances at me. "You been out there yet?

I shake my head, jaw tight.

"Yeah, well, it's a dump. Brings in the worst kind of people." His voice turns razor-sharp with disgust as he scuffs his feet against the weathered deck. Leaning back, he tilts his face to the sun, eyes closed tight. "But Garrett? The things I've heard about what goes on in that house—" he breaks off, jaw clenching. "He's the worst of the worst. Everyone knows to stay out of his way."

I nod and pick at the pieces of sticker that didn't come off, trying to remember to breathe. My heart feels stuck in my throat.

The worst of the worst. Fuck.

"Zack is the one and only guy who ever asked her out. They went to the movies. Garrett showed up halfway through and threatened to kill Zack right there in the theater. Caused a huge scene and dragged Sunny out like he owned her or some shit." Ryan shakes his head. "He's a sick bastard."

My grip tightens around the bottle. If I'd been there... *he wouldn't have walked out with her.*

Ryan opens his eyes and looks at me. He must see something on my face that concerns him. Frowning, he holds up his hands in front of him. "Hey, don't go getting all pissed off. Sunny's been through a lot, but it's not like no one's tried to help her," he says defensively. "She doesn't want anything to do with anyone and I don't blame her."

Ryan whistles through his teeth, "But damn, she's easy to look at, right? Maybe now that Garrett's out of the picture for a while, I'll—"

"Don't." The word is out of my mouth before I can stop it, a low warning rumble in my throat.

Ryan pauses, glancing at me. "Whoa, calm down, man. Didn't mean anything by it."

I clench my jaw, turning away from him, and stare down at Sunny again. She's sitting under the tree now, reading, completely unaware of the conversation going on up here. She's oblivious to the fact that now, more than ever, I'm determined to make sure she knows I'm here for her. That she never has to worry about anyone hurting her like that ever again.

Ryan stands up and walks over to the railing again. I stand up, and again, it takes every ounce of control I have not to slam my fist into his face. My glare burns into his back, but he's too busy drooling to notice. I turn away before I do something we'll both regret.

"Listen man, I gotta get out of here and get ready for tonight. I'll be back about eight." Ryan hands me his empty bottle and grabs his backpack off the table. "Look, I didn't mean anything. I'm gonna say it again though. Forget about Sunny. There will be plenty of girls here tonight who can't wait to get their hands on the new guy," he says with a chuckle.

I don't answer him, but silently lead the way down the stairs, through the kitchen and hold the front door open for him. "See ya later, man." The words slide out between gritted teeth. As Ryan heads out the door, I finally let out the breath I didn't realize I was holding.

I take my time heading back inside, stopping in front of the refrigerator and grabbing a fresh, cold beer and twisting the cap off. I take a deep draw off the bottle trying to cool down. Once I feel like I can breathe a little easier I head upstairs to hit the shower. I'm definitely not in the mood for a party tonight. But it's the best way to find my way in and make it easier to stay here for a while.

I'm halfway up the stairs when my mind locks on to a single, unshakeable truth that's as solid as the ground beneath my feet. Sunny's going to be mine. She just doesn't know it yet.

Chapter Six

Sunny

I can't sleep.

The music coming from the back of the house is too loud. The bass is thumping hard enough to rattle my bedroom windows. It's annoying. I've been tossing and turning for what feels like hours and can't get comfortable. The harder I try to ignore the noise and forget that there's a party, the louder it seems to be. It's impossible.

I keep telling myself that I don't care—whatever happens on the other side of the fence is none of my business. I'm talking but I'm not listening. The problem, as much as I don't want to admit it, is that somehow Levi's managed to find a way inside my head.

I told him to stay away. Several times. And I meant it. Every. Single. Time. His answer? A white slip of paper slid under the front door this afternoon. An invitation. To the party at his house tonight along with a promise to keep his distance. If that's what I wanted.

The whole thing is irritating, but impossibly sweet. Two words I seem to use to describe the things he does more than any others when I think about him.

He's ridiculous. He has no idea what he's asking from me, or what he'd be setting himself up for. If he did, there's no way he'd have invited me.

That stupid slip of paper is still sitting on my dresser. I haven't thrown it away—yet. It's the first time in forever that someone's actually thought about me and it feels wrong to just throw that away.

I keep thinking he has to know though. There's no way he doesn't understand by now how awful it would be if I showed up. I saw him with Ryan. If he's hanging out with someone on the football team, it means he's *on* the team. Those guys only hang out with each other. It's like they're in some sort of weird, exclusive cult. Which is a good thing, mostly, because it makes it easier to stay out of their way.

I can't imagine that no one's rushed to spill every single last one of the gory details of my life. There's nothing any of the people I know are on the other side of that fence love more than making sure I know my place. And stay there.

The whole thing could easily be a way for him to stroke his ego a bit and feel good about himself. Offer up a pity invite to the sad, loser girl with the shitty life and no friends. Like I'm some sort of charity case..

I haven't gotten the impression he's like that though. My gut tells me he means everything he's said. But it's not like I know him and I definitely know better than to read too much into anything.

But here I am, lying in bed like an idiot, unable to stop my mind from wandering over the fence and into his backyard. To him. I catch myself wondering what he's doing over there. If he meant what he said about keeping his distance unless I changed my mind. I wonder if he's thinking about me, hoping I'll show up.

Of course, there *is* another option. One I try to slam the door shut on before it can take hold. Maybe the reason he invited me was a trick. A joke. Maybe he heard the rumors and it changed his mind about me. Maybe he picked a side and I'm not it.

One more reason to not show up.

The idea of him surrounded by other people—normal people who aren't scared of their own shadow—creates a hollow ache in my stomach that feels like too much. I tell myself that I feel this way because he made me feel safe. That it was one time, and nothing more. I know I'm being stupid for letting someone—a stranger—take up this much space in my head.

But the ache doesn't go away, and I hate myself for caring about any of it.

Flipping over on my stomach, I press my face into the pillow and squeeze it over my ears. It doesn't help. Nothing helps.

Finally, with a groan, I kick the blankets off and sit up. No real point in lying here pretending anymore. Dragging myself out of bed, I throw on some shorts and a T-shirt and pad down the stairs. When I get to the back door, I open it quietly and step outside. The music and laughter are even louder. I close the door behind me with a soft click as I step out onto the deck. The last thing I want is to be seen. Talk about humiliating.

It's a beautiful summer night, with only a small sliver of moon and a sky full of stars. I take a deep inhale when the cool night air hits my face. It smells of fresh cut grass and cigarette smoke. I walk over to the stairs leading down to the lawn and take a seat on the first step.

From up here I have a good view into Levi's backyard. People are spilling out of the house into the yard where they cluster into small, tight, cliquey groups and sip drinks out of red plastic cups. Soft white lights are strung up between the trees casting a soft glow over the entire yard. The steady hum of conversation is punctuated with sharp laughter and soft giggles. The whole scene looks like something out of some cheesy teen movie. It's ridiculous. And beautiful.

I'd never admit it out loud, but I'd give anything to be a part of it.

It looks like anyone who's anyone is there tonight.

Everyone but you. I grind my teeth.

My gaze drifts over the groups, scanning the faces until—there he is.

Levi.

He's standing at the edge of the porch, leaning against the railing with his arms crossed. He's wearing a plain white T-shirt and jeans that fit him perfectly. A cluster of girls, obviously hanging on his every word, surround him. I get the feeling he's used to being the center of attention. It explains a lot. He's wearing a smirk and from here it looks like he's holding court—effortlessly commanding the space around him like he was born to it.

But even from this distance, I catch a few little tells that maybe he's not as comfortable as it would seem at first glance. His fingers drum restlessly against the wooden rail, and he keeps moving his head like he's scanning the crowd. It seems like maybe he's going through the motions, playing a part that doesn't quite fit.

I should go back inside. I should turn around and go to bed. There's nothing for me out here. None of this is for me.

But I don't.

I stay. I keep watching like some awkward masochistic peeping tom—telling myself I don't care, when obviously I do. Even I'm not that good of a liar.

My breath catches in my throat when his eyes find mine through the darkness. Despite the dark, and the distance, his gaze zeroes in on me. I can feel it.

It was like he knew I'd been sitting here all along. He straightens a little, the smirk on his face fading just enough to make me feel like I've been caught doing something wrong. I freeze. For a second, I think about standing up and running back inside where I belong.

But again, I choose to stay.

I don't move. And neither does he. Not until he hands his cup off to the guy standing next to him without even looking. His eyes are still locked on mine when he starts across the yard.

He disappears briefly behind the fence before popping up over the top of it. My heart beats frantically while I try to ignore it.

I don't *want* him to come over. I don't want to talk to him. This isn't part of my plan. I should be inside, tucked into bed, asleep. I shouldn't be *here*.

Before I know it, Levi is standing at the bottom of the stairs, looking up at me.

"Are you spying on me?" His voice is low, but teasing.

I try to shrug, but it comes off as a jerky, weird twitch instead. "I couldn't sleep." It's not a lie, but it's not the entire truth either, which seems to be all I'm capable of with him.

He doesn't respond right away. He just stands there, watching me with this intense gaze that feels like he can see right through me. After a second, he starts up the stairs. When he gets to the top, his eyes move over me, stopping at my bare legs. Even though the bruises have faded into pale sickly yellow dots, I'm glad it's too dark to see much. I don't even bother spending any time regretting choosing shorts over pants.

Levi tilts his head slightly as he speaks. "You know, you could've just come over."

I snort. "Yeah, that would've gone over *so* well. Besides, it's not really my thing."

His eyes and his voice soften as he lowers himself down to sit on the stair below mine. "It's not really my thing either."

"Yeah, I could tell. You looked pretty miserable. I mean surrounded by gorgeous cheerleaders falling all over themselves for you. Yuck. Who'd want that." I laugh and crinkle my nose.

He laughs, and it's a really great sound. A really great one.

"Well, I'm here with you and not over there with them, so..."

My snarky comment dies in my throat and I'm not sure what to say. A comfortable silence settles between us. We sit on the stairs, together, watching as the party gets louder and more obnoxious, until my eyes get heavy, and I can't help the yawn that escapes.

Levi stands and stretches. "I suppose I should get back. Even though they seem to be doing fine without me."

"Yeah. Mom's going to be home soon and I try to avoid her knowing I'm awake. I need to get to bed."

Levi offers his hand to me, and I stare at it for a full minute before taking it and letting him help me to my feet. "Thank you." I say the words as I turn to head inside. "Goodnight Levi."

"Goodnight Angel." He smiles and turns to leave. Almost as an afterthought, he adds, "You could've come tonight. There's no way I'd have let anyone mess with you. You know that, right?"

I don't answer him, but damn it, I *do* know that. I hate that I know it, but I do.

CHAPTER SEVEN

Sunny

LAST NIGHT, AFTER LEVI walked away, I told myself I wouldn't think about him anymore. I'd let his words settle into the back of my mind and stay there, untouched. I have more important things to deal with.

There are seven places Mom hides money in the house. Eight if you count the tampon box under the bathroom sink, but Garrett found that one last month. I check them methodically—the loose floorboard in the hall closet, the hollow curtain rod in the spare room, behind the baseboard in Mom's closet. Most are empty. No surprise there.

Mom's still passed out at the bottom of the stairs where she landed last night. I'd covered her with the old afghan from the couch, but she hasn't moved since. The house is quiet except for her soft snoring and the hum of the ancient refrigerator that holds nothing but ketchup and beer. My stomach cramps, a sharp reminder that I haven't eaten since yesterday morning.

I find twenty-three dollars stuffed inside an old boot in the hall closet. Another twelve folded into the pages of her high school yearbook. The real prize is wedged behind the loose brick in the fireplace—two crumpled fifties that must have been forgotten about.

"I'll pay it back," I whisper into Mom's ear as I stuff the money into my pocket. We both know I won't, and that she's too gone to hear me say it, but the lie makes me feel better. Besides, she'd give it to me if she were awake. Maybe.

I check my phone—ten 'o' clock. It's the perfect time to hit the store. All the moms who go shopping after dropping their kids off at daycare or summer camp are finished, and the lunch rush isn't for another hour.

The Food Xpress on Marshall Street is having a sale on chicken. If I hurry, I can get there and back before Mom wakes up. Before she remembers why she was crying last night. Before she starts detoxing and looking for the money she needs to keep herself even.

I grab my backpack, the one with the broken zipper that I've sewn shut three times now. A hundred and thirty-five dollars. It's more than I expected to find. Enough for real food, not just ramen and mac and cheese. Enough to hide some away for next time.

"I'll be back soon," I call over my shoulder as I walk out the door, knowing she wouldn't care even if she were awake.

The morning air is thick with humidity as I step outside. I make sure to lock door behind me before I stop and count the money one more time, planning out each purchase in my head. We need real food, but I need to be smart about it.

The Food Xpress parking lot is even emptier than I expected. Perfect. I grab a cart and head inside.

The fluorescent lights make everything look harsh and washed out. The sale items are always in the back, making you walk past all the expensive stuff first. I head there first, not letting myself get distracted.

I do the math in my head as I walk through the store filling up the cart. Weighing cost against all the other considerations. Chicken is on sale, good protein. Rice is cheap and filling. Frozen vegetables are better than canned. Mom's voice whispers in my head, working as a guide. There was a time, not that long ago really, when she cooked dinner for dad and I and did all the shopping.

Mrs. Roberts is working the deli counter. She used to live next door, but moved not long after Garrett moved in. She pretends not to recognize me, but I know she does. I used to help her in her garden every day in the spring. It's better this way though—less awkward. Her eyes are kind behind her thick glasses.

"Half a pound of turkey," I say, keeping my voice steady. "And half a pound of the ham, please."

She nods, her movements efficient as she works. I watch the numbers on the scale. I pretend not to notice when she hits the button, prints off the sticker and then adds a few more slices of meat to each package. I thank her. She nods.

I'm comparing prices on pasta when I hear the whispers. Two women, cart parked at the end of the aisle, looking at me like I'm some sort of freak.

"I'm telling you that's her," one says, not being nearly as quiet as she thinks she is.

"I heard..." the other starts, but I tune them out.

I grab the cheaper pasta and move on. I can guarantee that anything they've heard isn't nearly as awful as the truth. Their words won't fill the fridge, keep my mom sober or make Garrett disappear for good. So, does it really matter?

At checkout, I count out exact change, ignoring the disdain on the cashier's face. My fingers don't shake as I zip the money into the inside pocket of my backpack. They used to, but I've gotten past it.

The plastic bags cut into my fingers as I push through the automatic doors. The humidity is like a wall when it hits me, and I adjust my grip.

"Sun-ny."

My stomach drops at the voice. Zack Thompson leans against his truck, surrounded by his usual group of friends. Of course. Because this day needed to be even harder.

I keep walking, eyes forward, arms steady despite the heavy bags.

"Hey, I'm talking to you." Zack pushes off his truck and comes to stand in front of me, blocking my way. "What's wrong? Too good to say hello to an old friend?"

The laughter from his friends makes my skin crawl, but I don't let him see it. Don't give him the satisfaction of a reaction.

"Come on, Sunny baby." He takes a small step forward, standing over me so close I can feel his breath over my hair. "Don't be like that. We used to be friends, remember?"

I keep my eyes focused on the concrete behind him. Eight steps to the sidewalk where there will be eyes and traffic and safety. Seven if they're big steps.

"I heard Garrett's going to be gone for a while," his voice drops lower, meant just for me, "Might be fun to try something new."

My breath stops and my mind goes blank. Shame burns hot in my chest, mixing with something else. Something that tastes like rage.

"Leave me alone Zack," I say quietly, still not looking at him. The bags are heavy in my hands, the plastic cutting deeper. "Move."

"Or what?" He steps closer, and his friends' laughter dies down, sensing a shift. "What are you going to do if I don't? There's no one to tell Sunny. No one to step in and save you."

I finally look up at him. Really look at him. And something in my expression makes him take a small step back.

"No," I say, my voice steady and clear despite my hammering heart. "But he'd find out wouldn't he. He's not going to be gone forever Zack. He'll be back and then what? How long did it take your nose to heal?"

His face flushes red. One of his friends snickers but is quickly silenced by Zack's glare.

I sidestep around him, my movements deliberate. Not running. Not afraid. Even though my heart is trying to beat its way out of my chest.

"You're nothing but a whore, Sunny," he calls after me, but his voice lacks conviction. "Garrett's dumb little whore."

"Maybe," I say, not turning around. "But I'm still too good for you."

I keep walking so I don't see Zack's face when my words hit. I do know they landed in the right spot by the roar of laughter, and the way he yells at everyone to "shut the fuck up."

I make it to the sidewalk, then the corner, then another block before my legs start shaking. The plastic bags dig into my fingers, cutting off circulation. My chest is too tight. I try to swallow the lump in my throat, but it won't go down. I keep walking. One foot in front of the other.

I wish sometimes I were even half as brave as I pretended to be.

CHAPTER EIGHT

LEVI

THE SMELL OF GARLIC and tomato sauce hits me as I push through the front door to Mario's. I'd rather not be here, but it'll probably do me some good to get away from the house for a while. I've been trying to give Sunny her space, but it's getting more and more difficult.

The place is packed, mostly with my teammates and what seems like half the cheerleading squad. Their voices bounce off the brick walls and mix with the tinny sounds coming from the ancient arcade games in the corner. It's annoying, loud, and does nothing for my mood.

I slide into a crowded booth, the vinyl seat sticky against my bare arms in the summer heat. Zack holds court from the opposite side, lounging back with his arm draped over a cheerleader who looks like she'd rather be anywhere else.

"Do these freshman girls get hotter every year or what?" Zack's eyes are laser focused on a table of girls who are obviously way too young for him to be looking at the way he is. His voice carries over the din.

A memory surfaces—hits me hard out of nowhere. *Standing in the doorway of my father's office, frozen, as he pushed his barely out of high school secretary up against his desk. He had the same look on his face as Zack does now when he told me to leave. He pulled me aside later. Clapping me on the shoulder, he'd leaned in like he was about to reveal one of the world's greatest secrets.*

"Son, men like us don't get to be where we are by hesitating. We see something we want, we take it. Don't ask, don't apologize. It's who we are. It's what separates us, puts us on top."

I grip my water glass harder, forcing myself back to the present.

"Jesus, Zack, that's Sarah's little sister you're talking about," Ryan says from beside me, his voice tight, tinged with disgust.

"Even better." Zack winks, reaching for his soda. "Remember how Sarah was before she graduated?"

A few guys laugh, but it's strained. I watch them avoid eye contact, pushing pizza around their plates. No one wants to challenge him, but that doesn't mean they like it. Zack doesn't notice though, he's too focused on the girls sitting at the other table. He's clearly mistaking the silence around him for admiration and approval. That can be dangerous.

"So, new guy," he turns his attention to me, eyes glinting. "How you liking being QB? You settling into it okay? Must be quite the change from... where was it you said you were from again?"

"I didn't." I keep my voice neutral, even as my pulse picks up.

"Gotcha. Working the mysterious stranger angle. I'll tell ya a secret though." He leans in a bit, with a smile plastered on his face that doesn't quite reach his eyes. "The girls around here? Let's just say, you're working too hard if you're working at all. They don't need all that." He stops to shove half a slice of pizza in his mouth. His eyes flit around the table as he chews. "You sure managed to impress Coach though, and most of these losers. Some of us put in years for our spots. Earned it, you know?"

The way he emphasizes 'earned' makes my jaw clench. It's the same tone my father used when he'd talk about 'earning' things. It screams entitled. Asshole.

"Sounds like you're having a little trouble letting go," I say, matching his stare. "Maybe I'm not the one who needs to worry about settling into their new… position. I hear the bottom isn't so bad once you get used to it."

A few guys snicker. One of the linemen smirks into his drink. Even Ryan looks down at the table, trying to hide his grin.

Zack notices. His shoulders tense, jaw tightening as his face flushes red. His grip on his soda tightens like he's imagining throwing it in my face.

He opens his mouth—probably to say something stupid, something threatening—but before he can, the waitress approaches. She can't be more than sixteen and seeing how much she's struggling with the tray she's carrying, she's pretty new to the job.

"Welcome back, sweetheart." Zack's voice drops to what he probably thinks is a seductive tone.

She starts setting down pizzas, trying to ignore him. My stomach turns as Zack leans forward, deliberately sliding his finger down her arm as she works. She jerks away from him.

"Come on, don't be like that," he says when she steps back. "I'm only trying to be friendly. When do you get off? I could take you out. Show you a good time."

"Don't be difficult, dear." My father's voice, smooth as oil. *"Most women would kill to be in your position."* The memory of my mother's face, tight with fear and forced politeness, makes me grip the edge of the table.

"She's not interested," I say, the words coming out harder than intended.

"What's your problem?" Zack's attention snaps to me. "White knighting for some random piece of—"

"My problem," I cut him off, "is sitting here watching you act like some entitled prick. No one here owes you anything, Zack."

The table goes silent. Even the cheerleaders seem to sense the shift, their chatter dying down.

"Oooo, big words from the new guy." Zack leans forward, all pretense of friendliness gone. "You might want to watch yourself. You don't know how things work around here yet."

"Oh, I think I've got a pretty good idea." I stand up, tossing some cash on the table. The rage is building, familiar and dangerous. If I stay, I might do something I can't take back.

"Running away?" he calls after me.

The jab hits hard. Harder than it should. My hands shake as I dig my keys from my pocket, and push through the doors. Memories of midnight escapes and my mother's tears threaten to overwhelm me. It was a mistake to come tonight.

In my truck, I grip the steering wheel until my knuckles turn white. The engine's rumble does nothing to drown out the echo of Zack's words, my father's voice. Three months we've been here. The longest we've stayed anywhere is a year. Just long enough to start feeling normal before something happens and we have to take off again.

I watch through the window as Zack returns to holding court, already acting like nothing happened. He's laughing, surrounded by people who smile and nod while silently cringing. It's disgusting.

As I pull out of the parking lot, my father's words from that day in his study come back to me. *"Son, you'll learn. The world, and everything and everyone in it belongs to men like us."*

I press the accelerator harder, trying to outrun the sick feeling in my gut. The streets blur past as I drive aimlessly, through unfamiliar neighborhoods. My thoughts drift to Sunny, wondering if she's out on her deck tonight. The image of her sitting there is a sharp contrast to the chaos in my head.

I drive aimlessly until I end up parked in the empty school parking lot near the football field. I kill the engine. The silence feels heavy, oppressive. My phone shows three texts from Ryan asking if I'm okay, and one from Coach about tomorrow's practice. I ignore them all, and step out into the cool night air.

The field is quiet. And dark. I hop the fence easily—a talent I've gained from years of sneaking into places I shouldn't. I tighten the laces of my sneakers and start stretching. Running has always helped clear my head, and right now my head is a mess.

The first lap is easy. The second is automatic. By the third, the ache starts creeping into my calves, and my lungs burn with every inhale. Good. It needs to hurt.

By the time I hit my tenth lap, my body is screaming at me to stop, but I don't. I can't. Pain is good. It's better than thinking. Better than remembering. Better than the twisted satisfaction I felt when Zack flinched at my words.

I push myself faster, harder, until the edges of my vision blur and my heartbeat drowns out everything else. Until there's nothing left but the rhythm of my feet. Physical pain is one of the only things that can chase me out of my head when it starts to spiral backwards. The sharpness of it shaves off the hard, brittle edges of memories I wish weren't mine—my mother arms covered in bruises, my father's lessons in being a "real man".

Zack reminds me too much of all the things I want to forget.

Collapsing on the fifty-yard line, I stare up at the stars. The same stars I've seen from a dozen different cities, each time wondering if this place would be different. If this time we'd be able to stay. My phone buzzes—mom checking in. I text back that I'm fine, knowing she'll worry otherwise. She's always worrying about me.

She'd never admit it, but I know she thinks about how much like my father I am. She's always watching me, hoping she didn't stay too long—that he didn't rub off on me and that I'll turn out different than what he wanted and expected.

The truth is, I worry about that part of me too. It's always there. I can feel it sitting right under my skin. The anger that surged through me at Mario's— that was *his* anger. The desire to hurt Zack, to make him pay for being all the things I hate the most? Those feelings are tapped straight from my father's side of my family tree. He'd destroy someone like Zack just to prove he could and never think twice about it. The difference between me and my father is that I can make myself walk away. I'll never allow myself to become him.

Standing up, I dust off my pants and head back to my truck. Tomorrow I'll have to face them all again—Zack, the team, the expectations. But, for tonight, I'm done.

As I drive home, I take the long way, past Sunny's house. Her light's still on. We're a lot more alike than she knows. Maybe that's why I can't seem to stay away from her, despite her warnings. Kindred spirits or some bullshit.

I pull into my driveway, finally feeling level enough to think about sleep. I'm still pissed. That never goes away completely. But, it's under control again. For now.

Chapter Nine

Sunny

Standing on the sidewalk at the edge of the school parking lot, I'm trying to talk myself into believing that it's not the real, actual gates of hell I'm trying to work up the guts to go through.

My heart is pounding out of my chest, I can't breathe, and I can feel a headache starting at the back of my skull. Class started almost thirty minutes ago. I showed up late on purpose, trying to postpone the awfulness, and now I'm frozen in place, panicking, and struggling to keep myself from getting sick.

I know I look like a complete idiot standing here. I know I'm only putting off the inevitable and making it harder on myself—confirming my already solid status as a freak in everyone's mind. I thought I'd be more ready for today. But I'm not. Definitely not.

One more year. Just one more year, and I'm out of this place. Once I'm gone, I'm gone for good. I'm never coming back.

It should be exciting to think about. It should give me plenty of motivation to get in there and get after it—mark another day off the calendar. But, all I can think about right now is how much I hate walking through those doors. The thought of facing everyone again makes my skin crawl. All the dirty looks and nasty comments. Judging me, acting like they know me, know my life.

I pull my sweatshirt tight around me, imagining it has the power to make me invisible. That it can somehow protect me against what I know is coming. But, even if it could shield me from the outside judgements there's nothing that can stop the little voice inside my head. No way to get it to stop playing the same old recording it's been stuck on since I woke up this morning. *A girl like you doesn't belong with them, Sunny. You know it. They know it. You'll never belong anywhere and everyone knows why.*

I should be beyond caring by now. I should've developed some sort of immunity to all of it, but, the truth is, I haven't. Every whisper, every stare, every disgusting little giggle and laugh when I walk by, is a cut. By the time that last bell rings and I'm starting the walk home it feels like I've been bled dry. Over the past five years I've learned to fake my way through pretty much anything, but, I don't think I have it in me today. I should just turn around and forget it. Try again tomorrow. Give myself another day to scrape the bottom of the barrel and pull together enough courage to make it inside.

My stomach twists again, tightening into a knot, and I make my decision. I can't do it. Not today. With a heavy sigh, I whirl around, ready to make my escape and start the long walk home, but, instead, I slam into something painfully solid. I bounce off, stumble backwards and struggle to stay on my feet.

A small yelp escapes as my backpack slides off my shoulder and falls to the ground with a heavy thud. A steady stream of curses falls from my mouth as I look up, wide-eyed, to see who or what I'd crashed into. My cheeks flush with embarrassment as I find myself staring into a familiar set of brilliant green eyes.

"I, uh..." I stumble over the words as they leave my mouth and shift uncomfortably.

Levi looks down at me, his expression unreadable. "You okay, Angel?" he asks, concern heavy in his voice.

I nod quickly, frowning at the ridiculous name, as I drop down on one knee to grab my backpack. "Yeah. I didn't see you there. Sorry." My voice comes out quieter than I'd like and I have to work to keep it from shaking.

He crouches down to help, but I snatch up the bag before he can reach it. "Don't. I can get it," I mutter, as I sling the bag over one shoulder and stand.

Levi straightens up, watching me shift my weight. "You skipping class or something?"

"No," I reply, a little too defensively. "Just running late." I feel my cheeks heating up again, and I look down at my feet, concentrating on the sidewalk crack under my toe. "What about you? Hanging out in parking lots, sneaking up on people being all creepy?"

A small smirk tugs at the corner of his mouth. "Sun-ny. And here I thought you were starting to like me."

My eyes snap up to his.

I wasn't expecting to hear him say my name. Not my real one. He's called me Angel for weeks now and I've never bothered to correct him. Every Saturday afternoon I get a note slid under the door inviting me to a party he knows I won't show up to. Every Saturday night about midnight I'm sitting on the stairs in my backyard watching what normal looks like from a distance.

Levi always shows up. He sneaks away and comes to sit with me. We don't really talk about anything important. Mostly we just sit there, *being.* It should feel weird, but somehow it's not. It's the exact opposite of that. I like it and if I were honest with myself, which I'm not ready to be yet, I would say that I've started looking forward to it. A little. Until this moment I couldn't imagine him calling me anything else.

But now, hearing him say my name...

My heart stutters at the way he stretches out each syllable, like he's tasting each letter as it leaves his mouth.

"I told you I'd find out what your name was." His voice is playful, teasing. "So. Are we ready to go in?"

I search his face for anything, any hint of cruelty that would warn me to turn around as fast as I can and walk away, but there's none. Not a trace. I adjust the pack on my shoulder and narrow my eyes. "Wait a minute. We? There is no *we.* There's me and there's you. That's it."

"That's exactly what I said. Me. You. We." He chuckles but stays standing there perfectly still and calm.

"You know what I meant. Why are you doing this to me?" The words slip out before I can stop them, and I immediately regret it.

"Doing what? I'm not doing anything *to* you. I got here late, saw you standing out here and figured you could maybe show me around a little. New guy, remember?" He shrugs, as if standing here with me is the most natural thing in the world, when I know it's not. "But, if you're not gonna stick around, you could probably talk me into that too."

His words hang in the air between us, and for a moment, I don't know how to respond. His confidence amazes me. I can't believe how easily he seems to twist and bend things to fit what he wants.

I mean he *is* the new guy. That much is true. He's also the new guy who obviously has no plans to leave me alone even in broad daylight when it's in his best interest. It's only because he's got no idea what it'll cost him to be seen with me. If he did there's no way he'd be standing here trying to get me to agree to... whatever it is he wants.

After what happened with Garrett he thinks he knows every-thing—has seen the worst. But he hasn't. It's hard to believe Ryan or Zack or one of the other assholes on the team hasn't spilled every bit of awfulness about me they can.

Of course, maybe they did tell him. Maybe he thinks I'm an easy target. Maybe he's a crazy psycho with some sort of bizarre savior kink. Or worse, maybe he feels sorry for me and he's only being nice out of pity. Whatever the reason, we both know he's lying right now. We both know he'd have no shortage of volunteers who'd love nothing more than to show him around.

"I'm perfectly capable of making it through my day by myself, you know. I don't need a babysitter." My words come out sharper than I intended. I know I'm being a bitch, but I'd rather get the humiliation and disappointment of whatever this moment is over and done with. Today's already hard enough. "I'm not some charity case."

"That's not what I think about you," he says simply, in a low, even tone. "I've no doubt you can take care of yourself. But I'm here. And you're here. So..."

I hesitate, glancing back at the school. The thought of walking through those doors with him by my side, is horrifying. I've spent the past five years doing everything I can in my power not to be noticed. To make sure I fly under the radar. There is not one good thing that could possibly come from us walking through those doors together.

But, somehow it doesn't feel as wrong as it should.

It feels like maybe there's a chance that the whispers and stares won't sting as much with someone by my side. That it wouldn't be only me—they'd be talking about someone else too and that might make it better.

I give it one more try.

"I think you should go inside by yourself. There are plenty of girls who'd be willing to show you around. Really. The last thing you want is to walk in there with me. Trust me," I say, half-heartedly. He deserves one last chance to change his mind.

He tilts his head slightly and softens his voice as he speaks. "I do trust you, but, what I want, Sunny, is for you to pick a direction for us to head in. That's it. My fate is in your hands."

I bite my lip, still unsure about what I should do. A part of me screams that I should turn around, keep doing what I've always done, stick to the things that have kept me mostly safe and gotten me this far. Pretend the last few minutes never happened.

There's another part of me—a quiet, dangerous part—that whispers maybe things could be different. That voice is reckless though. It's a voice that always gets me hurt. A voice that's been wrong before.

But as Levi waits, patient and unshaken, something in me gives way just a little. Just enough. I take a deep breath, release it slowly.

"Okay, fine. Let's go."

As we walk, side by side, following the sidewalk as it twists and turns its way to the front doors, I realize for the first time in a long time that I'm not holding my breath. The dread I was feeling just a few minutes ago is still there but it's not quite as suffocating.

I glance up at Levi and for one tiny moment I feel something I haven't felt in a long time. Gratitude. Maybe I was wrong. Maybe I *can* actually make it through today.

Chapter Ten

Levi

Sunny comes to an abrupt halt right outside the double doors that lead inside. She closes her eyes, holds her face up to the sky, takes in a deep breath and holds it. She's a nervous wreck. There can't possibly be anything on the other side of these doors that's *that* bad. I have her back. She'll see that soon enough. Exhaling loudly, with a hint of resignation, she says, "Let me see your schedule. I'll help you figure out where you're going."

I take the folded-up piece of paper out of my pocket and before I can hand it to her, she snatches it out of my hand and begins studying it. She's shaking.

She was right. Partially. I don't really need her help figuring out anything. Practices have been going on for over a month now and there isn't an inch of this entire place I haven't checked out. I know it like the back of my hand.

Her face scrunches with the same look of concentration she gets when she's reading. It's adorable and I can't help but smile. When she lifts her gaze to mine *she* is definitely not smiling. Her face is clouded with what looks like disappointment.

"We both already missed our first class, but your second one is the same as mine."

"Great! I—"

Sunny's expression turns even more sour, and the sarcasm is thick in her voice. "Yeah. Great."

Her eyes are shiny and her cheeks are flushed, and if I didn't know better I'd say she's about to start crying.

"You know, maybe we should just go in separately. It might be easier that way. For you. You don't need *me* to show you around. Again, I'm sure you'll have plenty of volunteers once you get in there. You should go. Seriously."

What could be so awful on the other side of those doors? I mean, it can't all be me. I know I make her uncomfortable, but there's nothing to be done about that right now. Time is the only cure for that. Time and patience, both of which I have plenty of. But, I'm not going anywhere today without her. She needs to know she can't get rid of me that easily.

"Sunny. You're starting to make me think you're embarrassed to be seen with me. I'm not going anywhere without you. You said you'd show me around and I'm holding you to it. Now, come on. Let's get inside," I say as I grab the handle of the door and pull it open.

She pauses and stares at me blankly for a moment before she speaks. "Fine. But, this is a bad idea. Don't say I didn't warn you," she says in a serious tone as she steps inside.

Making our way up the stairs, we start down the hall just as the bell rings and people start pouring out of the classrooms. It's the expected, typical first day of school chaos, but, as we ease our way into and begin navigating through the traffic in the hallway, it becomes obvious that something isn't right.

The hallway is packed, but people are giving us way too much room. They can't seem to get out of our way fast enough. It's impossible to ignore the steady stream of whispers and snickers that seem to erupt and follow us as we pass. As if those things weren't unsettling enough, I'm starting to feel like a monkey in a cage with all of the gawking and staring that's going on. It's unnerving.

Almost every single one of these faces has been at *my* house, drinking up *my* beer, enjoying themselves on *my* time, but there isn't one of these fuckers that'll look me in the eyes right now. If I didn't know better, I'd swear we crossed an invisible border and landed smack in the middle of enemy territory. I say *we,* but I know it's not me who's attracting all of this attention. It's Sunny. Sunny's the one wearing the target.

I understand now why it took her so long to decide if she wanted to do this or not. Why she was dreading walking through those doors. I gotta hand it to her. She's tougher than me. If I were in her shoes, I don't think I would've done it. Not if I knew this is what I had to look forward to. There's no way I'd put myself through this willingly.

But, she did. She knew what was waiting for her and, here she is. Next to me. And as awful as it is right now, I wouldn't have it any other way. I don't know if my being next to her is making it any easier or better for her though. I can hear my name in at least half of the whispers as we pass. But at least she's not alone.

God, I hate these assholes.

To her credit, Sunny's staying close to me as we walk. She's keeping her head held high and matching my stride like she doesn't have a care in the world. To most people it'd look like none of this was bothering her. But, most people probably wouldn't notice the way her fingers are wrapped so tight around the strap of her backpack that her knuckles are white. Or the way she's chewing non-stop at the inside of her cheek.

I'm impressed. Not everyone could stand up to all this bullshit, but, she's not giving them anything. Nothing.

I give her a silent *'Atta girl'* as we keep moving down the hall. I, on the other hand, am not nearly half as cool as her. I can feel my face twist in disgust, and my body tense as anger starts to settle in. I make a mental note of each and every sneer, stare, and comment, imagining how good it's going to feel to put each one of these fuckers in their place.

All in good time.

I hear Zack coming even before he turns the corner ahead of us. His voice carries over every other sound in the packed hallway and ricochets off the metal lockers lining the hall.

It's like nails on a chalkboard.

He's not someone I would ever choose to have anything to do with. Apparently though, he likes pretending we're best friends. Emphasis on the pretend part. What's that saying about keeping friends close, but enemies closer? I think that's his angle. My jaw tenses and I grind my teeth.

"Hey! Levi!" Zack's voice carries over the steady drone and buzz of conversation and bursts of laughter. I can easily see him over the heads of people trying to make it to their next class. I watch as he begins pushing and shoving his way down the hall towards me and Sunny.

"What's up, my man?" he says with a wide toothy smile as he offers me his knuckles. He seems completely unbothered that he's caused traffic on one side of the hallway to come a complete stop. I doubt he even notices.

It takes only a moment for his eyes to travel from me and land on Sunny. His smile dissolves into a cruel smirk as he looks her up and down. "Huh. I didn't know you two knew each other." His tone is cold as his eyes move from Sunny to me and back again. "Sorry man, I should've told you sooner. Warned you to stay as far away as you can from this... this... thing."

He curls his lip in a sneer. Pausing, his eyes narrow, focusing in on her with laser precision. For the first time, I see a crack in my girl's armor. She shrinks from the sound of Zack's voice and takes a step back.

"I know, I know. She's fucking hot, right? I'm pretty sure she didn't tell you that she's taken though, did she? Taken with a capital T. Property of—"

"Zack. Please don't. Leave it alone for once. Please," Sunny interrupts. Her voice is a desperate, pleading whisper. "Please."

Zack doesn't take his eyes off her. It's obvious with the way he's looking at her, gauging her reaction to his words, that whatever this is isn't new to either of them.

My jaw clenches as I struggle to keep my mouth shut. If I open it now, there'll be no way for me to stop what comes out of it, and *that* is a slippery slope I'm not willing to go down. Yet.

I do know, with absolute certainty, there's no way Sunny should be begging this guy for anything. Especially not for mercy. She's too good for this. Too good for him. My fingers curl into a fist.

"Awww, Sunny. What's wrong? Don't you think our new friend here deserves to know the truth?" Zack says loudly as he takes a step closer to her.

Sunny flinches as if each of his words strikes a physical blow, and it takes everything I have to maintain control. My nails bite into the skin of my palms as my fists tighten. It feels like someone lit a fuse in my skull—my entire body tenses waiting for the explosion. There's nothing I would love more than to destroy the guy standing in front of me. I remind myself that this isn't the time or the place.

When I look at Sunny, I can see she's struggling too. She's still holding her head up, but her gaze is unfocused and far away. She's not blinking, she's not moving, she's just staring straight ahead. She's checked out. There's a small group of people clustered around us now and the hallway sounds have become softer, more muffled.

"Now, as I was saying." Zack clears his throat dramatically and puffs out his chest like he's getting ready to give the speech of his life. His eyes move over the crowd gathered around the three of us before settling on me. "I'm just looking out for you, man. Being that you're new and all. A pig can never be anything but a pig, no matter how pretty it is on the outside."

A small chorus of chuckles erupts around us. Zack's smirk turns into a broad, smug smile. My teeth feel like they're going to crack and my knuckles twitch and ache to hit something.

"See, Sunny likes her guys a little bit older, a little rougher. Don't you Sunny? You're into some real twisted shit, aren't you sweetie?" He pauses, his eyes flicking between Sunny and I. "Her mom's boyfriend owns her ass. Literally. Has she shown you the tattoo yet?"

As soon as the words leave his mouth, and his eyes settle on mine, he realizes he's miscalculated this entire situation. The smile slides off his face and he takes a step back. He's not the only one. I don't say a word—apparently, my thoughts are coming through my expression loud and clear.

In my mind, Zack's already a dead man. I can see every step of how it's going to happen, what I'm going to do to him. I can practically feel the satisfying crunch of bone under my fist, watch as he begs for mercy. A low growl works it way out of my throat but before I can take a step forward, a soft brush of warm, smooth skin across my knuckles stops me in my tracks. My breath catches in my throat and I swallow hard, unsure if I really felt it.

I close my eyes and take a deep breath in as I feel it again. Sunny glides her finger over each knuckle, tracing tiny circles, forward and back, forward and back, again and again. It's a delicate touch, almost too light to feel, but it's there. She's there. When I open my eyes, she's looking up at me with a small, sad smile on her face.

"I'm okay. It's okay. Don't do this. Not here."

"Fuck." The world stops for a moment, and I breathe the word out as an exhale. What she's asking me for is physically painful. But she's right. Not here.

This was a mistake. A huge mistake. *My mistake.* I can see now that I should've listened to her from the beginning. Without a word, I relax my hand and shake out my fingers, resenting the loss of her touch. It's one more thing Zack will pay for when the time is right. Some of the tension drains from her shoulders and face as I start to relax.

Before she can object, I reach out and weave my fingers through hers, turn on my heel and begin pulling her back the way we came. I don't have to look behind me to know that Zack along with everyone else is watching us make our retreat. I'm sure he thinks he's won. This isn't over though. Not by a long shot. Sunny stepping in did nothing but delay the inevitable. Zack's over as far as I'm concerned.

Chapter Eleven

Sunny

We're halfway through the parking lot before I realize it.

He's still holding my hand. Not the quick grab kind of hold that happens out of necessity. No, this is different. His fingers are laced tight and secure between mine. It's intentional. It should make me panic.

But it doesn't. Or at least it hasn't yet. Maybe because everything happened so fast, or maybe it's because I'm too busy trying to keep up with him. Whatever the reason now that I'm aware of it, I can't think about anything else.

We stop in front of a sleek and shiny black truck that stands out like a sore thumb in the middle of all the beat-up sedans and rusty second-hand trucks. Levi's hand drops to his side, and for a second, neither of us seem sure of what to do next. Awkwardness settles into the space between us, thick and uncomfortable. It stays until he clears his throat, breaking the tension.

"So, uh, do you need a ride?"

I hesitate, looking first at Levi, then back towards the school as if I might actually be considering going back. I wouldn't of course, not now, but the idea of getting into a car with Levi, of being that close to him is... unsettling to say the least.

"No. I can walk." It's disappointing how weak the words sound.

"Sunny, I was only asking to be nice. We both know I'm not about to let you walk away from here by yourself. Not after what just happened." He pauses and raises an eyebrow. "Get in."

I open my mouth to argue but judging by the tone of his voice and set of his jaw, he's serious. I don't think I'd win the argument, regardless of how good a case I made for myself if it came down to it. And honestly? I don't have the heart to try right now.

I let out a slow breath and nod as he reaches for the door handle and pulls. I climb up into the passenger seat, and he shuts the door. I stare out the window focusing on keeping my breath under control even as my brain screams at me in protest for willingly allowing myself to get trapped.

Levi gets in on the driver's side, and for a moment, we just sit there, neither of us saying a word. The silence is heavy. And awkward. Finally, he starts the engine, the low hum filling the cab of his truck. "So… where to? Where were you gonna go if you hadn't gone to class today?"

"Nowhere." I pause and shrug. My voice comes out shaky. "A-anywhere. I probably would've spent the day walking. I didn't have a plan or anything."

Levi nods, his eyes focused out the window. "I can work with that." He starts the car, puts it into gear, and starts backing out. "Anywhere but here sounds perfect right now."

And then, a little softer, a little quieter. "You can relax. I told you I'm not going to hurt you."

We drive in silence for awhile. The rhythm of the tires on the pavement fills the quiet space and before long I do, much to my surprise, begin to relax. The streets blur together, getting further and further apart, as we drive into parts of the city it's been years since I've seen. One more sharp turn and Easton Creek begins to fade into the distance. Levi turns on the radio and I roll down the window. Classic rock blasts out of the speakers and a cool breeze washes through the cab of the truck. There's nothing but open road in front of us, and for the first time in a long time, I'm not thinking about school. Or Zack. Or Garrett. Just the hum of the tires on the road and the way the wind rushes through the window.

And then, I recognize the turn ahead. I sit up straighter, my heart picking up speed. "Hey. I know a place. Somewhere we can go. Turn up here."

When Levi turns on to the dirt road, all the memories come flooding back at once. Most of the only good ones I have were made at the end of this road.

I lean over, holding my head out the window, smiling when the wind catches my hair, swirling and whipping it around my face and leaving me breathless. I haven't been out here in over five years, but it's exactly the way I remember it.

"It's right up here, keep following the road."

When I pull my head back in, I replace it with my hand, letting my fingers surf the wind. Levi glances over at me and laughs. It's a low, warm, comforting sound, not the sharp, hard-edge laughter I'm so used to hearing. I close my eyes, and smile, letting myself sink into the pure pleasure of the moment. It's been a long time since I've felt this light.

When we round the last corner, the smell of warm earth and cool water fills my nose. I toss my head back and laugh—a deep, full-throated laugh that shakes my whole body. I don't care how I look right now or what Levi might think—for the first time in years, I can remember the person I used to be. The wind, the sun, the smells. They all remind me that there was a time when things were different. When *I* was different.

Another half mile and the lake comes into full view. It's even more beautiful than I remember. The carpet of soft summer-green grass leading to the edge of the lake is lush and untouched by fall yet. Bright patches of color—sunflowers, ironweed, yarrow and asters—dot the rolling hills surrounding the water. The air is alive with the sound of frogs and birds resting in the cattails growing out of the muddy bank. Tall trees—a mixture of oaks, cottonwoods and willows—cast deep shadows over the water that the mid-morning sun has turned into liquid gold. It's breathtaking.

Levi pulls the truck up to the spot where dusty gravel meets grass and turns it off. He's staring out the window and I hear him mutter, "Holy hell, Angel. This is amazing."

I barely wait for the truck to stop completely before I'm out and running towards the dock. It stretches out over the glowing surface of the lake. The faded wood creaks and groans under my weight. Each step takes me further out into the water with a satisfying hollow thud and a subtle shifting under my feet. When I get to the end, I sit down and rush to take off my shoes, stuffing my socks inside. I scoot to the edge, roll up my pants and let my feet dangle in the cool, clear water. My entire body lets out a sigh. It doesn't take long before the dock sways and rocks letting me know Levi is coming.

"I don't think I've ever seen you smile like this. You should do it more often. It looks good on you," he says wearing a very self-satisfied smirk as he settles down next to me.

"Yeah. Um, so you've told me," I say playfully.

I'm rewarded with a deep, embarrassed sounding laugh. When I look up Levi's cheeks are flushed pink and his eyes are focused on some distant point across lake. "That was pretty awful, wasn't it."

"A little."

"I'm sorry. I didn't mean it. I was an idiot." He shuffles his feet. "So, how did you know this place was here?"

I kick my feet in the water enjoying the sound of splashing and the cold water on my toes. "My dad and I used to come here a lot. He loved it here. We'd spend the entire day swimming and fishing. This is where I learned to skip rocks." I swallow down the lump forming in my throat. "We'd always have the whole place to ourselves. I don't think a lot of people know it's here. The last time we came out here was right before..." My voice fades and I tilt my face up to the sun. "It's been a long time."

"I'm sorry Sunny," Levi says. I turn to look at him and his face is serious, concerned.

"It's okay. It shouldn't bother me as much as it does still. I miss him though. A lot."

"Tell me about him."

I don't know what to say or where to start. It's been years since anyone's asked about my dad. He was gone an entire week without checking in before my mom started to worry. It was another week before she reported him missing. Within a week or two after that Garrett had moved in and it was like he'd never existed. Not to anyone but me.

I wasn't allowed to talk about him anymore. All of the pictures with him in them were taken off the walls. The scrapbooks and photo albums were picked clean. It was scary how easily he was erased. I still don't understand what happened or why.

"There's not a lot to say. He was a good guy. Smart. Funny. Kind. You know. All the things people say about someone once they're gone." I wiggle my toes and close my eyes.

I can feel Levi watching me. Waiting. "He was my favorite person. But obviously, I didn't really know him. He was gone a lot for work."

I sigh deeply. It feels strange to be talking to someone like this. "He wasn't who I thought he was. I mean, I'm sure you've heard the stories. About the kind of people he worked for. So, I guess when it comes down to it, he was either the horrible person everyone says he was and deserved whatever happened, or he was the horrible person who walked away from his family and didn't look back. Either way, it doesn't say much about him."

Levi's voice is quiet when he speaks. "No one's perfect Sunny. Most people are more than one thing. He could've been the person you remember, but maybe he was a few of the other things too."

I open my eyes slowly and look out over the lake. Levi's words are a lot for me to take in. He makes a good point, raises some good questions, but none I'm ready to answer. I swallow hard over the lump in my throat.

"So, tell me all about him. Everything you remember."

He asked, and so I do. At first, it's uncomfortable. Giving voice to something that's been so completely buried. I don't usually like to remember how things were before. It hurts too much—even after all this time But, somehow, he makes it easy.

Finally, breathless from laughing so hard, I run out of stories and turn the conversation to him.

"What about you? How did you end up in Easton Creek."

The question seems like an easy one, but he lets it hang between us unanswered. I'm almost ready to ask again, thinking maybe he didn't hear me, when he finally speaks.

"I'm here with my mom. Things with my dad are, um, complicated." Levi rubs the back of his neck, glancing out across the lake before looking at me again. "He's one of those people I was talking about before. He's a lot of different things. My mom couldn't do it anymore. She said she wanted more for me. A better life. So, we left. And this place...well, it's about as far away from where we used to live as you can get."

"I figured." I look behind us to his black truck shining in the sun. "You don't exactly blend."

He laughs deep and loud from the center of his chest, and I'd be lying if I said I wasn't starting to enjoy the sound of it. And the way his whole face lights up when it happens. And the way he runs his hands through his hair like he can't stop until he shakes it off. And...

When the laughter dies, and it's quiet between us again, his face turns serious. "Hey," he pauses, and takes a deep breath before continuing, "can I ask you something? Serious? You don't have to answer if you don't want."

"Shoot."

"What happened this morning, is it always like that?"

"Way to kill the vibe," I say with a small huff of disappointment. My mind races, running through the hundred different ways I can answer, from sugar-coated lies to brutal honesty. If it were anyone else, I'd settle somewhere in the middle, but it doesn't feel right to be less than honest with Levi. Not now.

"Usually. Sometimes it's worse though."

I turn to face him expecting to see him looking at me with pity, but all I see are questions. Ones there are no answers to. That day in the backyard with Garrett I'm sure he thought he'd figured everything out—that when I'd gone inside and he'd left, he knew what kind of life I had, what kind of girl I was. There was no way for him to know how bad it really is.

Zack wasn't lying when he said the things he said. No matter what I do or how much I try to hide it, the ink that Garrett put on my skin tells the world what I am, who I am. It doesn't matter how it happened. It doesn't matter that I hadn't wanted it, or that I'd kicked and screamed and fought until I was exhausted. All that matters is that I'm marked.

I tried so hard to hide it, but all it took was one towel slip in the locker room after gym class, and everyone knew. Everyone, including him now.

I force myself to look at him. I need to be looking at his face, into his eyes, when I say what I have to say next. "I need to tell you something, Levi." My voice splinters as I try to get the words out. "Everything Zack said about me is true. I wish it wasn't, but it is. I wasn't lying when I said I've got nothing you'd want."

"Sunny, I—"

I interrupt as soon as I hear him say my name. My face burns and my heart races. I don't want to hear what he has to say. The thought of him turning on me now, is too much. I'm not ready for this—whatever this is—to end. My next words are apologetic. Weak. Desperate.

"Wait. Look. I'm sorry. You don't have to say anything. It's probably better if you don't. I thought you needed to hear that though. Hear the truth. From me. And it's okay. I'll understand if you don't want anything else to do with me."

Levi's expression doesn't change. His eyes stayed fixed on mine and he stays quiet and still.

I want to look away, hide my face from what I know is coming, but I can't. I need to hear the words. See the hate and disgust take over as what I said sinks in.

I only hope it hurts bad enough to destroy me when it happens. So I know it's real. I need the pain to stomp out every last bit of hope I've let myself feel since I've met him. I need to be reminded that some things aren't for me. That some things will never be for me, no matter how badly I want them.

Finally, unable to bear the silence anymore, I start to stand. "We can go now. Can you at least give me a ride to the edge of town? You can drop me off and I can walk from there."

Before I can get my feet underneath me, Levi reaches out and grabs my hand, pulling me back to sit beside him again. "Sunny. Whoa. Hey. Slow down."

He stares at me for a long moment, and I can tell he's thinking of what he wants to say, or do, next. Finally, he turns his body towards mine. Reaching out, he cups my face in his hands. When my eyes lock onto his, my breath catches in my throat, and I freeze. I've seen that look in someone's eyes before. It's a hungry look sitting under a thin layer of concern. It's dangerous and scares the hell out of me.

My heart pounds wildly in my chest. I flinch back as a deep shudder works it's way through my entire body. I thrash and try to pull away, try to get away. But Levi holds me tight. "Look at me Angel. You're okay. It's me. I'm here. It's okay." His voice is steady as he repeats the words over and over, not letting me go, not letting me look away from him.

Eventually, his words cut through the haze and the fear begins to unravel. My heart rate slows and my breath becomes even again. He softens his hold and strokes my cheek with his thumb. "I will never hurt you Angel. Never. You have to believe that."

He leans in close, pressing his forehead to mine. "I'm not letting go of you and I won't let anyone hurt you ever again." His voice is rough, but tender, and his breath is warm against my skin. It makes my chest ache.

For a second, I think he's going to let go of me and settle back into his own space.

But he doesn't.

"Can I kiss you, Sunny?"

The question catches me off guard.

No one's ever asked me that before. They've always taken.

The word 'yes' sticks in my throat, too foreign to feel like mine, and my heart hammers against my ribs.

But somehow, I manage a small nod. And then—he kisses me.

Not rough. Not demanding. Just soft, warm, and impossibly gentle.

The world doesn't just fade—it vanishes. My body hums with electricity, and for the first time in my life, the voices in my head go silent.

This is what it's supposed to feel like. This is what it was meant to be. And God help me, I don't ever want it to stop.

I lean into him fully. All of the fears and doubts I'd been feeling dissolve away into nothing when his hand slides up to the back of my neck.

Tangling my hair in his fingers, he deepens the kiss and I can't help the soft gasp that escapes my lips. This is everything my first kiss should've been. It's everything that it wasn't. There's no taste of blood, no smell of whiskey, no pain. It doesn't feel dirty and I don't feel broken.

I feel safe. Cared for.

I press closer, my hands trembling as they find their way to his chest, feeling the steady, reassuring beat of his heart under my fingertips. The kiss is slow and intense, and I don't want it to end.

In this moment, I believe him—every word of what he said. He's already proven to me, twice now, that he's willing to do whatever it takes to keep me safe.

When we finally pull apart, he rests his forehead against mine. Our shallow, ragged breaths mingling in the impossibly small space between us.

"You okay?" he murmurs, his voice low and rough.

I nod, a small, self-conscious smile tugging at my lips. "Yeah. I'm okay." More than okay. The words feel strange on my tongue, but they're true.

Chapter Twelve

Levi

Every time I see Zack, I'm *this* close to losing it.

We've been back at school for weeks now, and the guy still hasn't learned his place. He's always there—walking right up to the line. He never crosses it, but damn if he doesn't come close. He's waiting for me to make the first move. He's smart like that—good at making it look like I'm the one who can't keep it together. That's what he's banking on.

He'd like nothing more than to get rid of me. But I'm not going to make it easy for him.

For the longest time I couldn't figure out what his deal was. I mean, I understand his problem with me—I took his spot, and all the stupid, little perks that came with it. But, with Sunny, it's obvious it goes way deeper.

Even after I was sure I'd heard all of the stories, all of the reasons, I couldn't seem to figure out where *that* much hate could possibly be coming from. But then I started noticing the way he looks at her when he thinks no one can see him.

It seems that her big, unforgivable sin is being the one thing he wants and can't have. What he's been punishing her for all these years is the fact that he didn't have what it took to stand up for her when it counted. He's a coward who's not worthy of her and everyone knows it. And for that, he's making sure she pays the price.

I glance over at Sunny sitting in the passenger seat. She's humming along to the radio, scrolling through the new phone I got her, completely unaware of the chaos in my head this morning.

She has no clue that she's the reason, the only reason, Zack still has all his teeth. No idea that *she's* the only thing holding me together when everything in me is screaming to settle things with him once and for all.

I meant it when I said I wouldn't do anything to hurt her. And that means, not doing anything that will pull me away from her.

She looks at me and offers up a soft, sweet smile. It's everything to me. She sees something in me no one else does. She's sees who I *can* be. She thinks I can be better, do better. And, she's got me thinking that maybe, with her, it's possible.

But is it really?

That thought claws at the back of my mind. She makes it so easy to believe that it can be different. That *I* can be different. But what if this is it—as good as it gets? As good as *I* get.

Sometimes, it feels like there are two versions of me, and they're constantly fighting. There's the one Sunny sees—the one she makes me want to be. That side is softer, better, more in control. But the other version, the one my father raised, is never very far away.

Sunny doesn't know that person, doesn't know that side of me exists and I don't want her to. Even that day in her backyard with Garrett, as bad as it was, wasn't as bad as it can get. But Zack... he keeps trying to drag that other me to the surface.

At least Zack hasn't gone near Sunny since that day in the parking lot. The memory of it still makes my blood boil, but I think he got the message finally. Words I can forgive, but touch my girl...

I was late getting out of practice—stuck in a pointless meeting with Coach. Should've known something was off when Zack bolted early.

He's always the last out of the locker room. He loves having a captive audience.

The reason became crystal clear as soon as I stepped outside. Zack had Sunny trapped against the door of my truck, his body caging her in. When he grabbed her wrist and yanked her closer, everything inside of me went deadly quiet. He leaned down, whispered something in her ear that made her face go pale, and I saw that look—the same terrified expression she had on her face that day when she heard that screen door open.

My vision tunneled. Nothing existed except the thrum of blood rushing in my ears and the sight of Sunny's fear.

The bastard knew exactly what he was doing. Knew I'd be coming out soon. He wanted me to see this—wanted to test how far I'd let him push me before I snapped.

I was on him in seconds. The sharp yelp when I wrapped my arm around his neck and dragged him away from Sunny had been deeply satisfying.

When I started to squeeze and he struggled against me, the adrenaline kicked in, and I was gone. Feeling his pulse pound against my skin, knowing he was completely at my mercy felt good. So fucking good. By the time he started to nod off, I was riding a serious high and didn't want it to stop.

Sunny's hand on my arm snapped me out of it. Her touch was soft, and my reaction was *unexpected*. She pulled me back from the edge and straight back into reality. If she hadn't been there, I might've—no, I *would've* ended it. Zack will probably never realize how close he came to losing more than that stupid, cocky grin he gets, or that Sunny was the one who saved him.

I glance over at the girl beside me and have to smile. She's relaxed and happy and I can't imagine wanting anything more than what I have right here in this moment.

"Hey," I say, nudging her leg with my elbow. "Your birthday's coming up, right? Next weekend? You have something you want to do?"

She looks over to me, eyes bright and wide with surprise. "Oh. I, uh... I don't know," she pauses, biting her lower lip thoughtfully. "Maybe we could grab some take-out then go back to your place. Watch some movies?"

A smile tugs at my lips. Takeout and a movie. It sounds so perfec tly... perfect. I can't believe what a difference a few weeks have made. For both of us. "That's it? Don't you want something a little more... special?"

She shrugs, scrolling through her phone again. "I don't need much. Just you."

The words are simple and she tosses them out carelessly, but they hit me square in the chest. *"Just you."* She has no idea what she's saying, or how much those words mean to me. She deserves a lot more than takeout and a movie, and so much more than me. I'm going to make sure that this is the best birthday she's ever had. One she'll never forget.

"You know, I think we can do a little bit better than that. It's your eighteenth, Angel. It's a big one. Let me make it special?"

"I don't know," she says as she stares down at the blank screen sitting in her lap. "It's really not a big deal. You don't have to—"

I don't wait for her to finish. I turn in my seat and fix her with a serious look. "Sunny." I reach out, sliding a finger under chin and tilting her face up to mine. "I don't *have* to do anything. I want to. It's important to me. *You're* important to me."

I can see her struggling with my words. We've come a long way together, but there are still spaces between us that feel wide and unmanageable. A no man's land that neither of us is willing to cross. Yet.

Eventually though, she rewards me with a smile that spreads across her face slowly.

"Okay then, since you put it that way."

"You won't regret it. I promise."

Her smile beams. Sliding out of the truck I walk around to open her door, my eyes sweeping the parking lot. Old habits die hard. The whispers have quieted down for the most part, but there's always someone watching. I feel like they're just waiting for me to slip up and leave an opening. Zack's good at playing people off each other. He managed to turn half the team against me by the end of the first week of classes. He's got fewer followers now, but the ones he has left are loyal.

Sunny hops out of the truck, slipping her hand into mine. Our fingers lace together effortlessly. A perfect fit. As we start toward the school, I lean down to kiss the top of her head, breathing her in. She smells like warm sunshine and vanilla. The tension in my shoulders eases slightly.

We're halfway down the hall, when I see him. Zack's leaning against the lockers, laughing with a couple of his buddies from the team. His eyes flick to Sunny, sliding over her like she's his, and my calm dissolves in an instant. He doesn't even have to say anything. The look on his face is enough.

Not yet. But soon.

I feel Sunny stiffen beside me, but she keeps walking, head high, shoulders back. She's so much stronger than she gives herself credit for. I wish she could see what I see when I look at her. I let go of her hand and wrap my arm around her instead, pulling her to my side.

It's for her, I tell myself. A reminder that I have her and won't let anything bad happen to her. But the truth is, it's selfish. It's all for me. To keep myself in check. To keep from going over to Zack and ripping the smug grin off his face, right here in front of everyone.

I pause, locking eyes with him just long enough to make sure he knows I see him. His smile falters, but only for a second.

He still thinks he's untouchable. He still thinks I won't do any-thing.

I keep walking with Sunny's warmth pressed into my side.

Zack's time will come. And when it does, it's nothing he'll see coming.

CHAPTER THIRTEEN

Sunny

Levi's arm is heavy and warm across my shoulders as we walk across the parking lot. I let myself lean into him, savoring the solid feel of him against my side. It's still new, this whole wanting to be touched thing. The casual way he holds me close makes my heart flutter. For once, I feel like I can breathe.

The thought barely registers before Zack's latest threat slithers through my mind: *"You still owe me for that date, Sunny. I never got what I wanted. But don't worry, I'll collect. Levi can't be with you all the time..."*

I shudder. The memory is still too fresh, too real. Even though it's been weeks, his words still have power. If Levi hadn't shown up when he did...

Stop.

I'm not letting my brain go there, not today. Levi *did* show up. He handled things with Zack. He took care of things. Took care of *me.*

"Okay," Levi says suddenly, breaking into my thoughts. "What's going on in that head of yours?" He nudges me gently, his voice teasing but I hear the concern underneath.

"Nothing," I lie, shaking my head, even though I can't help but smile.

He raises an eyebrow. "Oh, please. I know you better than that. I know that look."

"What look?" I laugh, pulling away from him just enough to give him a playful shove. "What are you even talking about?"

"That look where you kind of stare off into space, like you're putting together some sort of master plan," he says, squinting at me, chuckling. "Do I need to worry? You planning on taking me out? Getting rid of me?"

"Get rid of you? Take you out?" I roll my eyes but keep smiling. "Yeah, I'm definitely plotting how to take out the guy who could *literally* snap me in half."

The laughter dies in his throat, and he stops. His expression snapping to serious.

"You don't really see me that way, do you?" He turns to face me. His eyes are dark and worried. "I'd never hurt you, Sunny. You know that, right?"

The way he says it, so direct, so concerned— it makes my heart do a somersault in my chest. I swallow hard and nod.

Yeah, I do know that. I think.

Levi's never laid a hand on me in any way that I didn't want. He's gentle, reassuring, always promising that he could never hurt me. But I've caught a glimpse of the other side of him—the dark part that lives right under the surface, waiting for someone to push too hard.

It should scare me. God knows I've learned what happens when that kind of intensity gets turned on you. I've got the scars to prove it. But, the messed-up part? That dangerous side of him? That's exactly what makes me feel the safest. When he gets so fierce and protective, and looks at me like I'm his to defend... it should send me running as far away as I can get.

Instead, it makes me feel like nothing can touch me.

I know how stupid it probably is to think like that. I mean, how fucked up does it make me that the thing that should terrify me is the thing I trust and love about him the most? I can't make it make sense, no matter how I look at it or how hard I try. I don't know if I'll ever figure out how to be okay with it completely. But I'm trying.

"I know," I say softly, moving back under his arm. "I do."

It takes a minute before I feel him relax. "Good," he says, tugging me closer. "Because you're stuck with me now. I'm not going anywhere."

"I *guess* I can handle that," I tease, even though my heart beats a little faster at the thought. *Stuck with him.* I like the way that sounds.

We start walking again, falling into our easy rhythm. The whispers and stares that follow us don't dig under my skin like they used to. It's harder for them to reach me when I'm with Levi.

But there's still that cautious voice in the back of my mind, reminding me that it's only been a couple of months. People like Zack and Garrett don't just disappear. They don't forget.

I push the thought away. For the first time in years, I feel like I might have more than just survival to look forward to.

"I can't wait for your birthday," Levi says, his voice casual but clearly trying to change the subject. "You better be ready for it. I'm going to come up with something you'll love."

I laugh. "I told you already, it's not that big of a deal."

He stops walking again. "Too late. I'm determined to show you what a big deal it is. I mean, eighteen Sunny. It's huge. You can like... vote and whatever."

"Voting. Right. Civic duty and all that," I say, starting to walk without him. It's amusing how serious he looks. "I don't need a birthday to tell me I can... 'and whatever'. Birthdays haven't really worked out that well for me in the past."

"Well, that was before," he argues, grinning, "I'm here now, and I'm going to change all that. You deserve it. Just wait. You'll see."

You deserve it.

Something in my chest tightens. Those words sound so different not being spit at me in anger. I'm not ready to hear them like this, not ready to accept all of the good things they *can* mean. Levi makes everything sound so simple. And maybe it is for him. Like he can magically take things and change them through sheer force of will and desire.

Levi is *consuming.* He's contagious. When I'm with him it's so easy for me to see everything through his eyes, his point of view. What he sees when he looks at me seems so different than how I feel. He doesn't see me as some broken thing that's trying to put itself back together for the hundredth time. Sometimes I think it would be easier if he did see me that way though. At least I'd know what to do with it then.

I bite my lip, suddenly unsure of what to say. I want to believe him. I *want* to let myself just relax into this, into *him.* And part of me has. Part of me has quit fighting and arguing about every good feeling I have these days. But there's still that tiny part of me that's scared. Scared that once I let myself believe everything is good, it'll break into a million unfixable pieces.

"I don't need anything fancy," I say finally, trying to keep my voice light. "I'm serious. Just something simple. Something normal."

The word "normal" sticks in my throat. Nothing about turning eighteen is normal for me. Not like it is for other people. Other people get to celebrate freedom and independence. They get to be excited about becoming an adult. I get to wake up knowing that every single second I stay in my house is a choice I'm making as an adult.

It doesn't matter that Garrett never let me have a job, or any money of my own. It doesn't matter that I don't have the first clue about what it would take to make it by myself. What does matter is that to everyone on the outside looking in, it will seem that I *want* to stay. That if I really hated it, I could and would just leave. Like it's that simple.

I shiver, and Levi pulls me closer, probably thinking I'm cold. If he knew what I was really thinking about... but how can I explain how scared I am of my birthday? How it feels less like freedom and more like a noose tightening around my neck?

Mom's been talking about it too. About how I'll be an adult, responsible for my own choices. The way she says it makes it clear—if I leave, I'll be abandoning her. Leaving her alone to deal with *him* by herself.

"Normal, huh?" Levi's grin softens into something sweeter, and I feel his hand slide down my arm until his fingers are laced with mine again.

I could get used to this so easily.

"Do you ever think about it?" I ask, surprising myself with the question. "What it would be like if we didn't have to worry about all this other stuff? If it could be all be normal and was just... you and me."

He's quiet for a second, his face going serious. "All the time."

"Wait." Levi stops walking and his face lights up. "I've got the best idea for your birthday."

I groan. "I thought we settled this. Simple, remember?"

"Yeah, but, this is perfect." He glances at the school building, then back at me. His green eyes sparkle with mischief. "What do you say we skip today?"

"Skip?" My stomach does a nervous flip. "I don't know..."

"Come on, Angel." He bumps my shoulder with his. "Live a little."

I bite my lip, considering. Third period is waiting—the class I share with Zack.

Usually, I can handle it, the way he stares at me, how he whispers things barely loud enough for me to hear. But after what happened in the parking lot...

"You're thinking too hard again," Levi says as he reaches up and smooths the wrinkle between my eyebrows with his thumb. "I can practically hear the gears turning."

"I have a test in English," I lie weakly.

"No, you don't." He grins. "You had that test yesterday. You told me about it."

"Right." I forgot I'd mentioned that.

"Look." His voice gets serious. "If you really want to go to class, we'll go. But I saw how you tensed up when Zack walked past earlier. And honestly?" He runs a hand through his dark hair. "We could both use a day away from here."

He's right. It would be nice to get out of here for a day. "Okay," I say before I can talk myself out of it.

"Okay?" His eyebrows shoot up like he can't believe I agreed so easily.

"Yeah." I shrug, trying to seem more casual than I feel. "But if we get caught—"

"We won't." He's already pulling me toward his truck, practically bouncing with excitement. "Trust me. I got this."

"That's what worries me," I mutter, but I'm smiling as I say it.

"I heard that." He opens the passenger door for me, and I climb in. "And I'll have you know I'm extremely trustworthy."

I slide into the seat, breathing in the familiar leather smell of his truck. "Says the guy kidnapping me."

"Kidnapping?" He clutches his chest in mock offense as he gets in the driver's side. "I prefer to think of it as a strategic extraction for birthday planning purposes."

"You're ridiculous." But I'm laughing now, really laughing, and it feels good.

He starts the engine, and the truck rumbles to life. "Maybe. But you like it."

I can't deny it. Instead, I watch as he navigates out of the parking lot, taking the back exit where fewer teachers park. His profile is sharp against the morning light—strong jaw, impossibly long eyelashes, an adorable dimple in his cheek when he smiles.

"You're staring," he says without looking at me.

"Am not." I turn to look out the window, feeling my cheeks heat up.

"Are too." His hand finds mine across the center console. "It's okay though. I like it."

"Where are we going anyway?" I ask, desperate to change the subject.

"That would ruin the surprise." He squeezes my hand. "But I promise you'll enjoy it."

We drive in comfortable silence for a while, leaving the school and its drama behind us. I should feel guilty about skipping, but I don't. Instead, I feel light. Free.

"You know what else I was thinking?" Levi breaks the silence, his thumb tracing circles on the back of my hand.

"Hmm?"

"About what you said earlier. About things being normal." He glances at me quickly before focusing back on the road. "Maybe normal is overrated for us. Maybe we should decide what normal looks like for us."

"What do you mean?"

"I mean..." He pauses, choosing his words carefully. "Everyone else's version of normal kind of sucks, right? For us anyway. So maybe we make our own rules. Our own way of doing things."

I think about that. About how nothing in my life has ever fit anyone else's definition of normal. About how hard I've tried to pretend it does.

"Our own normal," I repeat softly.

"Yeah." His voice is gentle but sure. "And it starts with your birthday. No pressure, no expectations. Just... us. Doing things our way."

The way he says 'us' takes away my breath. Like there's never been a time it was any different. Like there was never any question that we'd end up here, together, skipping school on a random Thursday morning.

"You're doing it again," he says.

"What?"

"That thing where you think so hard you forget to breathe." He lifts our joined hands and kisses my knuckles. "Stop worrying about what's supposed to happen or what other people think should happen. Just... be here. With me."

And somehow, when he says it like that, it sounds so simple. So possible.

"I am," I whisper, and I actually mean it.

CHAPTER FOURTEEN

SUNNY

MY HEART SINKS INTO my stomach as Levi pulls into the massive parking lot of Riverside Mall. The gleaming glass and steel structure towers over us, stretching for what seems like forever in both directions.

"You brought me to a mall?" My voice comes out higher than intended.

"Not just any mall." Levi parks near one of the main entrances, turning to face me with that grin that usually makes my knees weak. Right now, it's not helping the anxiety bubbling in my chest. "This place has everything."

I press back against the seat, memories of my last visit flooding back. Dad had brought me for my thirteenth birthday. We'd spent hours exploring every store, sharing a giant pretzel. It was the last birthday we spent together.

"I haven't been here since—" The words stick in my throat.

"Hey." Levi's hand finds mine, his thumb brushing over my knuckles. "We can go somewhere else. Just say the word."

I stare at the entrance, watching people stream in and out. The sheer number of people makes my teeth itch. In Easton Creek, I know who to avoid, where the safe spaces are. Here, every face is a stranger.

"There's just so many people," I say under my breath.

"And not one of them knows us." Levi shifts closer, his voice low and steady. "We're just two normal teenagers at the mall."

The thought hits differently than I expected. He's right—no one here knows about Garrett, or my mom, or any of the rumors that follow me through the halls at school.

"Two *normal* teenagers?" I ask, hating how small my voice sounds.

"Remember what we said about making our own normal?" His fingers thread through mine. "This can be part of that. If you want."

I look down at our joined hands, then back at the mall. A group of girls about our age walks past, arms linked, giggling about something on one of their phones. They don't even glance our way.

"I haven't been shopping in forever," I admit. "I usually just order basics online when I absolutely need something."

"Well then, we definitely need to fix that." Levi's enthusiasm is infectious, but anxiety is still gnawing at my stomach.

"I don't have any money," I start, but he cuts me off.

"This is part of your birthday. Like the phone. My treat."

"Levi, no—"

"Yes." He squeezes my hand. "Let me do this for you. Please?"

The sincerity in his eyes makes my chest ache. I want to argue, to tell him I can't accept something like this. But I also, equally as much, want to pretend that I'm a girl, spending the day at the mall, shopping with her... Levi.

"Okay," I say finally. "But nothing crazy."

His whole face lights up. "Define crazy."

"Levi..."

"I'm kidding." He leans over and kisses my forehead. "Mostly."

I roll my eyes but can't help smiling. "You're impossible."

"That's not a no."

Taking a deep breath, I look back at the mall entrance. The glass doors reflect the morning sun, making them look almost welcoming. "I might need a minute. Before we go in."

"We've got all day." Levi settles back in his seat, still holding my hand. "Take all the minutes you need."

I watch another group of people enter—a mom with two kids, an elderly couple walking arm in arm, a guy a little older than us carrying what looks like a guitar case. None of them look threatening. None of them look at our truck or seem to care that we're just sitting here.

"The last time I was here..." I start, then stop, unsure if I want to share this memory.

"Tell me." Levi's voice is soft, patient.

"It was my thirteenth birthday. Dad took me." The words come easier than I expected. "We spent the whole day here. He let me try on ridiculous outfits at every store, even though we didn't get any of them. We shared this massive pretzel from the food court—it was bigger than my head."

Levi stays quiet, his thumb still tracing gentle patterns on my hand.

"He bought me books. So many books." I smile at the memory. "Said a girl could never have too many stories to escape into. I still have them all, hidden under my bed where..." I trail off, not wanting to mention Garrett.

"We don't have to go in," Levi says after a moment. "We can drive somewhere else, do something different."

I look at him then, really look at him. At the way his eyes hold nothing but understanding, the way he's completely still beside me, letting me work through this at my own pace. No pressure, no expectations. No disappointment

"No," I say, surprising myself with how firm my voice sounds. "I want to go in. I want..." I pause, trying to find the right words. "I want to make new memories here. Better ones."

"Yeah?" His smile is soft, and gentle—the one I've noticed he saves just for me.

"Yeah." I squeeze his hand. "But you have to promise me something."

"Anything."

"If I start to freak out, or if it gets too much..."

"We leave. No questions asked." He raises our joined hands and places them on his chest. "On my heart."

I take another deep breath, looking at the mall. It still looks intimidating, but less so now.

"Okay," I say. "Let's do this."

THE BOUTIQUE LEVI LEADS me into is nothing like any of the stores I've ever shopped at. Sparkling glass chandeliers cast warm light over racks of flowing dresses and delicate tops. Even the air smells expensive, like an expensive floral perfume.

"I don't know about this." I tug at the sleeve of my oversized hoodie. Everything here looks too pristine, too untouchable.

"Just look around." Levi's hand settles on my lower back. "No pressure."

The saleswoman is nice—genuine nice, not fake nice. She doesn't even seem to notice my ratty clothes or hesitate to hand me expensive dresses to try on. When she says I have a lovely figure, I almost believe her.

The first dress is blue. The fabric feels impossibly soft, and when I look in the fitting room mirror, I barely recognize myself. It hugs the curves I usually try to hide, and the color makes my skin glow.

"How's it going in there?" The saleswoman's voice is gentle through the door.

"I..." My voice cracks. "It's different."

When I step out, Levi's eyes go wide. He stands from the waiting area chair, his lips parting slightly. The way he's looking at me makes my skin tingle.

Each dress after that first one gets a little easier. The saleswoman keeps bringing options, and I find myself relaxing and starting to enjoy the process. With every new dress, I stand a little straighter, look in the mirror a little longer. The burgundy one shows off my shoulders. The green makes my eyes look brighter. Each reflection shows me something new about myself, something I've been hiding under baggy hoodies and slumped shoulders.

But it's the black dress that changes everything. Simple, elegant—it fits perfectly, and shows just enough skin to feel daring without making me uncomfortable. When I step out this time, Levi actually stands up straighter.

"That's the one," he says immediately.

I study my reflection, barely recognizing the girl staring back at me. She looks confident, beautiful even. Like someone who could walk into a room and turn heads for all the right reasons. For the first time, I'm looking at my reflection and don't feel like I want to disappear.

"What do you think?" Levi asks softly.

I bite my lip, considering. I can't imagine what it would feel like wearing something like this out somewhere. But, I think I'd like to find out.

"I love it," I admit quietly.

"Then it's yours." Levi's hand finds mine, squeezing gently.

"Levi, no—it's too expensive." I start to protest, but he shakes his head.

"Birthday gift, remember?" His smile is warm. "Plus, the look on your face right now? Worth every penny."

The saleswoman claps again. "Shall I wrap it up for you?"

I look at myself one more time in the mirror, at the way the dress makes me stand taller, shoulders back instead of hunched forward. At the way Levi can't seem to take his eyes off me.

"We should find you shoes to go with it," the saleswoman suggests as she carefully folds the dress.

"Oh, I don't—" I start to protest, but Levi's already nodding.

"She's right. Can't have you wearing those beat-up Converse with it." He gestures to my worn sneakers with a teasing grin.

The shoe section is just as intimidating as the clothing, rows of heels in every height and color imaginable. The saleswoman brings over several options, and I find myself drawn to a simple pair.

"Not too high," I warn, wobbling slightly as I try them on.

"These are perfect." Levi watches as I take a few tentative steps. "You can actually walk in them."

I catch my reflection again—the shoes make my legs look even longer. "They're pretty."

"One more thing." Levi disappears toward the jewelry counter, returning with a delicate silver necklace. A small solid heart pendant dangles from the chain, catching the light. "This too."

"Levi..." My throat tightens as he holds it up.

"Turn around," he says softly.

I do, and his fingers brush my neck as he fastens the clasp. The heart settles just below my collarbone, and when I touch it, it's warm from his hands.

"Beautiful," he murmurs.

The saleswoman rings everything up, and I deliberately don't look at the total. Levi takes a large wad of cash out of his pocket without hesitation, and soon we're walking out with several bags.

"I can't believe you just did that," I say as we head toward the food court.

"Believe it." He takes my hand, swinging our joined hands between us. "Now, I believe you mentioned something about a giant pretzel?"

The food court is busy but not packed. We find a table in a corner after loading up our trays—a massive pretzel to share, Chinese food for me, pizza for Levi.

"This is so weird," I laugh, looking down at my ratty jeans and oversized hoodie, then at the boutique shopping bags. "I feel like I'm living someone else's life."

"Why?" Levi steals a piece of my orange chicken.

"Because normal girls go shopping with their boyfriends all the time. They try on pretty dresses and eat mall food and..." I trail off, realizing what I just said.

"Boyfriends?" His eyebrow raises, but he's smiling.

Heat floods my cheeks. "I didn't mean—I just—"

"I like it." He reaches across the table, taking my hand. "Boyfriend has a nice ring to it."

"Yeah?" I can't help smiling back.

"Yeah." He tears off a piece of pretzel. "Though I have to warn you, as your official boyfriend, there will be more shopping trips in your future."

I throw a fortune cookie at him. "You're ridiculous."

"And once again I say, you love it."

"Maybe I do," I admit quietly.

His thumb traces patterns on my palm. "Good."

Chapter Fifteen

Sunny

I stand in front of the bathroom mirror, hands braced on the cool, porcelain edge of the sink, trying to breathe through the jittery, anxious feeling crawling up my spine. *It's like any other night,* I remind myself for the hundredth time.

C'mon girl. You're turning this into a nightmare. It's supposed to be fun. Breathe. You got this.

My reflection isn't buying it. Not one single word. In fact, the girl in the mirror looks ready to crawl out of her skin.

I'm a hot mess. My hair's only half curled—the hot iron's lying abandoned in the sink. It's in the same place I dropped it when I burned my ear. For the second time. My makeup looks cakey and streaked thanks to the fine beads of nervous sweat dotting my skin.

The dress Levi bought for me to wear tonight is hanging on the back of my bedroom door, where it's been since I brought it home. I keep peeking out of the bathroom to look at it. It's beautiful, and not something I would've ever had the guts to try on by myself. He'd made such a big deal about taking me shopping. I'd felt so special. And the way he looked at me when I came out of the dressing room...

No one's ever looked at me like that before, and I can't imagine ever wanting anyone else to. I'd walked out of that store feeling on top of the world, untouchable, like the most beautiful girl alive. It's the most expensive thing I've ever owned. But, now, looking at it hanging there, waiting for me, I swear the soft, black, silky material and plunging neckline are laughing at me. Reminding me that I don't really deserve to feel those things. Shouldn't get my hopes up because I know how it ends. How it always ends.

I tug on the belt of my comfy cotton robe and tell myself to relax. For the millionth time.

Levi wouldn't do anything to hurt you. You're safe. It's okay.

The mantra does little to stop the flutter of nerves that won't settle down. It's not that I don't trust Levi, because I do. As much as I can trust anyone anyway. But surprises? Surprises freak me the hell out. They always have. There's something about not knowing what's coming that makes my brain go all jumpy and haywire. I've worked so hard to be okay with this though. With *him.*

Levi's different. He's safe. He's good for me.

But that's the problem, isn't it? The sticking point. The big thing I can't seem to get past. Him being good for me.

It would be different if he treated me like everyone else. If he was mean. And rude. And demanding. If he took and never gave. I would know what to do with that. But I'm in unfamiliar territory with him. Lost. I don't know what to do with sweet kisses and kind words, patience and smiles.

I squeeze my eyes shut and grip the sink harder, fighting off the wave of nausea that hits me out of nowhere. I'm trying to focus on Levi, on *tonight*—how much he's done for me, how good he's been to me, and how excited I am to see what he has planned. But my mind keeps wandering back to where I was and what my life *was* like. Before him.

I want this. I want this one night of being special, of knowing that I matter to someone. Please, just give me this one night.

The sharp sizzle of a water drop hitting the hot curling iron snaps me out of my thoughts. I blink rapidly, trying to shake off these feelings, trying to ground myself back in the *now*, in this moment. But anxiety keeps pressing in. It's relentless tonight. My heart's racing, my palms are sweaty, and my hands tremble as I pick up my phone and check the screen.

No messages. No missed calls. I bite my lip and consider calling Levi, just to hear his voice. Something to calm myself down a little.

I bring up my contact list, tap his name and listen to the phone ring. Once. Twice. Three times. *Then, straight to voicemail.* I hang up quickly.

I stare at the screen, gnawing at my bottom lip, trying not to let even more panic and worry creep in. He *always* answers my calls.

He's busy. That's all, I tell myself. He's probably in the shower. Or putting the final touches on whatever he has planned.

God, I hate surprises. I'd trade it all away right now if I could hear his voice.

I tap his name again, let the phone ring, but this time I leave a message. "Hey Handsome. I'm almost finished getting ready and I, uh, I wanted you to know I'm thinking about you. I can't wait to see you tonight. I've got a surprise for you too. I'll see you in a few." I pause and take a deep breath before adding, "And hey... hurry up and get here already. I miss you."

I'm trying so hard to be okay.

I was telling the truth when I said I'd made plans of my own this past week. I decided that it was time. Time to let myself be okay with wanting what I want. And what I want is *him.*

All of him.

Unplugging the curling iron, I brush through my hair. My hands tremble as I give myself a quick once-over in the mirror. I'm still a wreck—makeup uneven, my heart racing—but it'll have to do. This is as good as it's going to get tonight.

"Okay, Sunny. Get it together," I whisper to myself, pushing off the bathroom counter with shaky hands. I drag my feet down the hall to the bedroom—that damn dress staring at me the whole way.

I stop at the doorway, my eyes focused on the bed, where I've laid out the lacy black lingerie I'd bought special for tonight. I'd *borrowed* some of the money my mom accidentally left out on the kitchen counter. She won't miss it. She probably doesn't even remember having it. I lied to Levi about not feeling good a couple days ago, so I could sneak off downtown and go shopping by myself. It was only a small little lie. I'm sure he'll understand. Later. After.

I can't believe I'm even considering wearing something like this. It's so delicate and *obvious*. It'd taken a whole afternoon to find something perfect and the guts to buy it. Something sexy, but with enough material to cover the tattoo I'm not ready for him to see. Which will be never. I'll never be ready for him to see it.

My stomach tightens, and I can't believe I'm actually going through with this tonight. These nerves aren't really about the lingerie and I know it. It's about *him*. Levi's been patient. He's never pushed — he's never asked for more than I'm ready to give, but tonight… tonight I want to offer it all to him. I want him to know how much I trust him, how much I want him.

I also want, no, *need,* to prove to myself that I'm not broken beyond repair. That no matter what came before, I can be normal, have normal things, good things, in my life. That I'm more than damaged goods. But staring at the lingerie, I can't help the wave of doubt that wants to sink me.

Can I really do this?

You deserve this, I remind myself, swallowing hard as I slip out of my robe. The soft black silk and delicate lace glide over my skin as I pull them on. How good the lingerie feels sliding over my skin is a stark contrast to how I feel inside. I'm shaking, and still nervous as hell, but I'm starting to smile too. Levi cares about me. I've never done this before—willingly offered myself to someone. And definitely not someone like Levi, not someone I care about.

I'm halfway through stepping into the dress when I hear it.

The front door. Opening and shutting. The heavy thud of boots crossing the wooden floor.

My pulse jumps, and for a second, relief floods me. *Levi.* He must've gotten my message and come over early. My nerves ease slightly and I hurry to finish pulling up the straps of the dress and rush out of my room and down the hall, my bare feet slapping against the hardwood as I call out, "Levi? You're early! Guess you couldn't wait, huh? I'll be right down!"

Silence.

I pause at the top of the stairs, frowning. "Levi?"

Then I hear it. A deep, voice that vibrates through my whole body. It stops my heart and sucks the air out of my lungs.

I shake my head confused. *That's not Levi's voice. It's not Levi.*

It takes me a moment to recognize the voice filtering up the stairwell to me.

It's Garrett's voice. Garrett's here. A pit settles into my stomach.

"Well hello Princess. Happy birthday." Garrett's standing at the bottom of the stairs looking up at me. His dark brown eyes are glassy and glazed over. He lets out a low whistle as he takes me in. "You're right. I couldn't wait anymore."

He winks and says, "Damn baby, you look so much better than I remember. You didn't have to go getting all dressed up for me. Kind of a waste really."

My entire body goes cold, and numb. Icy fingers of dread creep up my spine, freezing me in place. My heart starts to pound in my chest, too loud, too fast. I can't move. I *can't* breathe. He shouldn't be here. He *can't* be here. Not now. Not tonight.

But he is.

"Aww, you're making me think maybe all this isn't for me. Where's that little friend of yours, huh? I was kinda hopin' he'd be here by now." Garrett's voice is low, hostile. "You should've known I'd be back. You're mine Sunny."

I can't think. I can't think.

My breath shudders out of me, too fast, too uneven. My fingers dig into the banister so hard I swear my nails are going to start to pull off. I can't move. My feet feel like they've been cemented to the floor. My throat won't work. I need to scream. I need to—

He takes another step up.

A whimper claws its way out of my chest before I can stop it.

Chapter Sixteen

Levi

This is it.

I've set things in motion tonight that can't be undone. Sometime tonight Zack will understand the true definition of *totally fucked*. It's taken me weeks of planning and waiting for just the right opportunity to get here. It took forever to find people I could trust, people who know how to keep their mouths shut to help me. Zack has no idea what's coming for him, but by the time it's over and the shock of it wears off, he'll know he messed with the wrong person. Good luck putting the blame where it belongs though. As far as anyone knows I'm with Sunny tonight—have been and will be all night.

Normally, I'd never do anything that would involve Sunny, even as an alibi, in something like this. But it just happened to be unavoidably convenient this one time. And it benefits her too. A little something extra to make her night even better. It's a gift she'd never ask for, but I know she'll like. She might not ever know that I was the one responsible for getting Zack out of her life, and that's okay. At least she won't have to worry about the asshole bothering her anymore.

He thinks he's won. I've made a point of letting him think that. Hell, I've let everyone think it. Not my fault he's stupid enough to underestimate me.

Even after what happened in the parking lot that day, it was so easy for him to believe I was afraid of him. It made this plan so much easier. It made him confident. So confident that he quit locking his car doors. So confident he actually started falling for his own bullshit and believing he's untouchable. He doesn't think anyone would dare do anything to fuck with him. What an idiot.

The drugs were easy to get and even easier to stash. I planted them in his car earlier. Tucked them down into the shitty, smelly gym bag he tosses into his backseat after every practice. It was only a few pills, some weed, a bundle of small baggies and a small digital scale. Not enough to get him any big boy time, but more than enough to make sure everything he cares about is taken away from him. *If* someone were to find it.

And they will.

I called earlier and left a message with the cop who was kind enough to give me his card that afternoon at Sunny's. Tipped him off about the party at Ryan's tonight. Told him that I was really worried about Zack, and how deep into drugs he was getting lately. Took less than a five minute phone call, and some fake concern to make sure Zack's car gets searched. It'll be a controlled bust. Zack won't have a clue who set him up. He'll just know that his future's gone to hell. Those football scholarships he's been banking on? Gone. His reputation? Destroyed.

I glance at my phone. 7:00 p.m. Everything's in place, and I've got just enough time to get home, clean up, and pick up Sunny. She doesn't know it yet, but I've planned something special tonight. We're getting out of this town, for the whole night. I'm taking her over to Riverside for dinner. I've got a hotel room, and flowers, and it's going to be perfect. Her birthday, her night. She has no clue.

The phone buzzes in my pocket. I pull it out and look at the screen. *Sunny*.

I stare at her name for a second and I can't help but smile. I should answer, but I'm too wired, too amped up. I'm still riding the high from everything I've done tonight—from knowing Zack's about to get what's coming to him. I'll call her back in a little while. Right now, I need a few minutes to myself to enjoy this. It feels good to let this side of myself out to play for a change.

I watch the phone buzz until it stops. *One missed call.* I slide it back into my pocket, shaking off the small pang of guilt that creeps in. It's not like I'm ignoring her on purpose, and she didn't leave a message or anything. I need a minute to myself to cool down is all. This night's about her, and I want to be all-in when I see her. No distractions.

The truck engine roars to life as I pull away from Zack's neighborhood, and the adrenaline still pours through me. The streets are quiet, the world moving slower than my mind. Everything feels like it's falling perfectly into place. Zack is going to wake up tomorrow with his life in ruins, and I'll be with Sunny, showing her she's the only thing that matters to me.

The phone buzzes again. *Sunny.* Again.

I glance at the screen, my hand hovering over it. My thumb twitches toward the button, and something shifts in the back of my mind. Maybe I should answer. *No.* I need to settle down. I'm still too caught up in the rush of what's coming. I'll call her back when I get home, once I've had a chance to cool off a bit. She deserves more from me. I don't want her to hear the edge in my voice. I don't want to drag any of this into our night.

The phone stops buzzing again, and I turn up the radio, drowning out the nagging feeling that's starting to creep in. I ignore the *ping* from my pocket that tells me I have a voicemail waiting. It's nothing. I crank the radio, drowning out that small voice in the back of my head telling me I'm making a mistake. *She's fine.* She's fine. And soon, everything's going to be perfect.

I turn onto my street twenty minutes later, pulling into the driveway. The house is dark. Which is weird. The porch light's on a timer. Mom insisted on it. Said it made her feel safer. I kill the engine and grab my phone, finally feeling calm enough to call Sunny back, but something stops me. It's too quiet. Too still.

Something's wrong.

The hair on the back of my neck prickles as I step out of the truck. My boots crunch on the gravel, but the sounds seems too loud, too sharp tonight. This all feels... wrong. By the time I reach the door, my heart is pounding and every muscle in my body is tense. I push open the door, and step inside. The darkness swallows me as I stand there, listening.

"Mom?"

Nothing. No noise but the hollow echo of my voice on the tile.

I step further inside, the door clicking shut behind me. My hand slides over the light switch, but when I flick it on, nothing happens. The power's out. My stomach twists and a thin sheen of sweat coats my skin. I close my eyes and open them slowly allowing them to adjust to the darkness.

"Mom?"

I call out again, louder this time, but there's still no answer. Only a heavy, oppressive silence.

There's the smell of something familiar hanging in the air. Familiar but out of place. Metallic. Sharp. Wrong.

I take a step towards the hallway that leads to her room. Maybe she went to bed early. Maybe she's lying in bed, headphones on, listening to music, or reading. Maybe. My hands start to shake, and my pulse drums in my ears. Maybe, but not likely.

My foot slides through something slick, sticky, and wet sounding. When I look down the small amount of light coming in through the windows in the living room reveals dark streaks crossing the tile in the entry way. Realization slams into me.

No!

I move faster, my body on autopilot. I rush down the hall, the smell getting stronger the closer to my mom's room I get. It's cold, and coppery and out of place. It's overwhelming.

The door to her room is closed. And there are more red-tinged dark streaks—blood—smeared on the floor, splashed across the carpet and covering the doorknob.

No, no, no, no. My mind screams it over and over and a pit settles in my stomach.

I push the door open, cringing at the creak of the hinges. My feet move on their own, my mind racing to catch up even as it refuses to believe what I'm seeing.

My mom.

Lying in a pool of blood on soaked, stained sheets, motionless, her eyes staring blankly at the ceiling. My mind struggles to process what I'm looking at. It refuses to believe it's real. This. Is. Not. Possible.

I can't breathe. My heart thunders in my ears. The bitter taste and burn of bile rises in my throat and coats my tongue.

My mind goes blank. I can't *think*. Can't see past the blood—past the *emptiness* that wraps around me. My feet move forward even though I want them to stop.

When I get to the edge of the bed, I reach out, my hands shaking, my vision blurring. I have to check. I have to make sure.

A deep shudder runs through me as I place two fingers against the curve of her neck..

She's cold. So fucking cold.

I know it's too late. *I'm* too late. But it doesn't keep me from begging. From pleading and screaming into the silent room to feel just one tiny thump under my fingers.

But there's nothing. There's nothing there. Only more *absence of.*

Tears flood my vision, stinging my eyes and heating my skin as they track down my cheeks. My legs give out from under me and I collapse to my knees beside the bed. The weight of this moment settles on my shoulders, and crushes down on me. It's too much.

Everything else falls away. The only thing I register, the only thing I feel, are cold fingers of dread seeping into my bones.

My father.

Did he find us? Was this him? Did he finally get tired of waiting for us to come back? I've known since we left that he's had eyes on us. I knew he'd never let either of us walk away clean, but this…

Leaving her here like this, for me to find, doesn't seem like something he'd do. This seems too brutal, too vicious. Even for him.

I slide my eyes heavenward, forcing them to the ceiling as I work to pull more air into my lungs. I'm desperate for an answer. A reason. Anything. I run through a hundred scenarios, and then a hundred more. None of it makes sense. I take a deep breath and fumble for my phone trying to brace myself for the call I know I have to make and everything that comes next.

The noise and the cops and the questions and…

I just want a few more minutes. A few more minutes alone with her. A few more minutes to say goodbye. To start trying to imagine a world for myself that she isn't in. I take her hand in mine, squeeze it gently and offer a whispered apology.

It's not until I drag my eyes down from the spot where they've been fixed on the ceiling that I see it.

A message.

It's scrawled on the wall above her bed. Jagged, uneven letters smeared in blood.

'Not yours. Mine'

The words blur together, twisting in my mind until I can't see straight. My throat tightens, my chest heaves as realization sinks in.

It wasn't my father.

It wasn't Zack. It was never Zack I had to worry about.

This was Garrett.

He's back.

I stare at the words staining the wall, my breath coming in short, ragged gasps as the reality of it slams into me. The calls I ignored from Sunny, the message I didn't check—she needed me. And I ignored her.

My phone slips from my hand and hits the floor with a loud crack, that I barely hear. All I can hear is the roaring in my ears, the sound of my own heartbeat echoing in the silence.

My mom is dead.

Sunny's in trouble.

And it's all because of *me*. I did this.

Chapter Seventeen

Sunny

My body screams at me to take a breath, to find a way to fill my lungs. My head is swimming, and my heart is pounding painfully in my chest.

This can't be happening. Not again. Not this. Anything but this.

The weight of Garrett's body pins me down, crushing me into the carpet. He stinks of sweat and cigarettes, and his breath is hot and rancid against my skin. The panic sinks its claws deep into my chest and I remember. My body remembers. I've been here before. I've *survived* this before. I plead with myself to believe it. To hold on to that one thought even as his hand over my mouth grinds my lips into my teeth. I taste blood and every shallow breath I manage to suck in between his fingers feels like it's scraping my lungs raw.

"That's my girl." His voice slithers into my ear as I thrash beneath him, desperate to get him off me. "Keep fighting. Show me how tough you are. You know how I like it, baby."

I *am* fighting. With everything I have, I fight. My hands rake at his arms, my legs piston out trying to get leverage, but it's useless. Nothing works. He's too strong, too heavy. I can't move. I can't get him off. My chest burns from the strain, my arms shake from the effort, but he doesn't budge.

I'm trapped.

Garrett shifts, jamming his knee into my stomach as he moves to straddle me. It drives the little bit of air I have out of my lungs, and my body jerks against him. I gasp into his palm. He grins. The light from the lamp he knocked over casts deep shadows across his face turning him into a monster.

My monster.

My worst nightmare.

I can't believe this is happening. Not again. Not with *him*.

"I told you I'd come back for you, Sunny." He murmurs, his voice low and sickeningly calm. It makes my skin crawl. "You're mine. I own you. Remember?"

I twist violently, trying to roll to the side, but he's everywhere. His thighs squeeze me, holding me tight, his free hand pins my wrists above my head. His weight presses the panic deeper into my chest, dumping terror into my veins.

I scream, but it's a pathetic, weak, muffled sound. I gnash my teeth and bite, hard enough to taste his skin. Hard enough to draw blood. He loosens his grip on my face only for a second. I fill my lungs with sweet, cool air. It wasn't enough though. His hand clamps down even harder over my mouth.

More flashes of memory rip through my mind—sharp fragments that cut into me. Garrett's hands, his mouth, his weight. I hear the echo of my screams, feel the bruises bloom on my skin under the burn of his hands, feel myself break as I'm shattered from the inside out. It all comes rushing back to me. Every sickening moment I've lived through with him before bleeds into the now. The line is getting fuzzy. Confusing.

I've lived through this before. All of it. But this time? This time, I'm not sure I will. I don't know if I can do it again.

I don't know if I want to.

Garrett presses his forehead against mine, grinning. "No one's coming to save you Sunny. I made sure that psycho little boyfriend of yours will be busy for a while. You're on your own kiddo."

My stomach churns as his words sink in. *Levi.* Where is he? What did Garrett do?

My mind reels, grasping for answers. Is that why he didn't answer when I called? My breath comes in short, shallow gasps as his words find their home.

He's right. Deep down, I knew he'd be back. I wanted so desperately to believe things could be different—that I could have someone like Levi in my life, that I could feel safe, and be normal—I let it blind me. I knew it couldn't possibly last. Not for someone like me.

Whatever Garrett did to Levi, it's my fault. I knew better, but I was selfish. I overstepped. All of this—*this*—is my fault. I knew there'd be a price to pay, eventually. Tears fill my eyes, but I blink them back. I won't cry. No matter what he does to me, or what happens tonight, he won't get what he really wants. I'll never give him the satisfaction of watching me crumble.

Garrett's hand moves down, pawing at the front of the dress Levi bought for me, the dress I'd so carefully put on and felt so beautiful wearing. There's a sharp tear of fabric as he rips it away. The soft expensive fabric never stood a chance. The dress is ruined, the night is ruined—*I'm* ruined.

I choke on my next labored breath, and squeeze my eyes closed. My body shakes as his fingers slide down my exposed skin. I can't stop him. I can't—

"You know the rules," Garrett growls, "open your eyes and look at me."

I turn my head to the side, refusing, squeezing my eyes shut as tight as I can. *Please, let this be over soon. Please.*

"Don't fuck with me Sunny. I said. Look. At. Me." His voice is hard, angry as he spits the words at me.

I start to turn my head, but as I do I catch a glint of something shiny. Something resting just under the corner of my bed. I blink my eyes, trying to bring what I'm seeing into clearer focus. It's scissors. The handle of a pair of scissors. They must've fallen when I cut the tags off my dress. If I can just...

My heart races, adrenaline flooding my veins. I stop struggling. My body goes limp. And I hold my breath. I have one shot at this. Only one. He *needs* to believe I passed out. Give me just a few more inches of reach.

Garrett adjusts his position, settling back on to my hips as I go still. I close my eyes forcing myself to relax. He lets go of my wrists, and lifts himself up on one arm. I can feel him staring down at me.

"Sunny." His voice is irritated. "You're only making things worse for yourself."

He shifts again, and I feel him push himself up further. "Fine. Have it your way."

I'm not ready for the slap when it comes. It's fast and hard and lights the side of my face on fire. I scream from shock as much as pain. The second one is worse. It lands harder, making my head thrum and ache. There's a loud crack with the third one—the sound of metal hitting bone as his ring smashes into my cheek. This time there's blood. I don't how much, but I can see it on his fingers, feel the warm trickle down my cheek. I can't do anything but groan deep in my throat.

Garrett moves his fingertips over my wounded cheek. His touch is gentle, soft. He moves his thumb in tiny circles across the tender, burning skin. Leaning over me he presses his lip to my skin and laps at the sticky wetness.

"Why do you always make it so hard? So difficult? Huh? I don't *want* to hurt you." He murmurs the words over and over against my cheek, against my lips, against my neck. His hips grind into me. "Why do you make me hurt you?"

I slide my hand down, stretching it out, slowly reaching for the metal I can see out of the corner of my eye. My fingers brush the handle. Almost there. Almost—

Garrett shifts again and before I can grab the scissors another slap comes out of nowhere. My head snaps to the side and I can feel the delicate skin of my lower lip split.

"Look at me!" Garrett growls. His voice is a mix of rage and satisfaction. He grips my throat, squeezing, cutting off my air. "I think someone needs to be reminded how this goes."

I'm gasping, my lungs are burning, and my body's thrashing under him. The scissors...*the scissors*...

They're my only chance. I stretch my arm as far as I can, wiggling my fingers, desperate to get a hold. Finally, my fingers hook one of the loops and I pull it towards me. I slide my fingers into the handles, tightening my grip, securing my hold.

I don't think. I *can't* think. I just *do it.*

I swing my arm up, slamming the blades into Garrett's side with everything I have. He jerks back, shouting in pain, his eyes going wide with disbelief. Blood spills from the wound, seeping between his fingers as he stares down at it, his face twisting in shock. For a second, hope flares in my chest.

But it's not enough. I can see it in his eyes. It wasn't nearly enough.

"Fucking bitch!" he roars as he rips the scissors from his side. His hand curls into a fist, and before I can brace myself, he slams it into my face. My vision tunnels and I feel sick. The coppery taste of blood fills my mouth as pain explodes across my jaw. The room spins and I blink, trying to stay conscious, but everything is tilting away from me.

Garrett's hands shake as he looks down at the blood, like he's trying to convince himself it's real. That what just happened, happened. His face twists into something impossibly more terrifying. Something darker, more vicious than I've seen from him before. Slowly, he lifts the scissors, snipping at the air in front of my face. His smile is wide, and his voice is eerily calm.

"So, you wanna play big girl games, huh? Think you're ready, *Princess?*"

I make a grab for them, desperate for one more chance, but he's too fast. His hand snakes out, grabs my wrist and twists. Lightning bolts of searing white-hot pain shoot up my arm, and I scream—the sound ripped from my throat as I feel my bones snap beneath his fingers.

"Oh, I'm sorry," Garrett sneers, his voice low and mocking. "My bad. Did you want these?" He closes the scissors and offers them to me. "Here. You can have 'em. Take 'em. They're yours. Let's see what ya' got."

There's a dull ache coming from deep in my skull and my thoughts keep getting lost, drifting away from me and not making sense. I raise my hand, the one that still works, and get ready to take my shot. Garrett's words stop me cold.

"Are you sure you wanna do that? You know, that one'll snap just as easy as the other one did. Then what will you do."

I don't respond. I can't. My mouth is swollen and my tongue is thick and dry. My teeth throb and ache. The pain is too much. My arm falls back to the floor. I stare up at Garrett, watching, helpless, as he opens the scissors again.

His eyes flick from the blades, to me, and back again several times. Like he's considering what his next move should be. Trying to decide my punishment.

Silently, he opens the scissors and presses one of the blades to my skin. In one long, slow stroke he drags it across my chest. There's a moment of sharp, stinging pain and then slick warmth running down my side. He pauses, sliding the cold metal between my breasts. With one smooth motion, he cuts away the delicate, lacy fabric I'd been so nervous to put on. So scared to have Levi see me in.

He glides the scissors back up, gently dragging the sharp point along my skin. Stopping at my collarbone, he closes the scissors before he digs the tips of both blades into my skin again forcing a low groan from my throat. The scissors tear and rip a path in my skin, down my chest and over my ribs. It's agony—my skin's on fire. Leaning back, he looks down at me and smiles.

"Beautiful." He whispers the word as the scissors clatter to the floor beside him—just out of my reach.

His breath comes in ragged gasps as he bends over me and grabs my wrist again. His fingers curl around my broken bones, squeezing with deliberate precision. "Oh sweetie. This is going to hurt. But I think you kinda asked for it, didn't you?" The words leave his mouth the same instant he slams my hand down on to the floor above my head. His fingers lace between mine, and he squeezes, forcing them to bend. When the small bones of my fingers give, cracking and slipping out of place, the pain is blinding, breathtaking. I open my mouth to scream but there's no sound. There's nothing.

"Stupid games, stupid prizes," he says, his voice flat, bored, as if this—as if *I*—were nothing more than a major inconvenience. He presses his palm down harder, grinding my crooked fingers and tortured wrist into the floor. It drives the pain deeper until that's all that there is for me, nothing else exists. "We don't want that hand of yours causing any more trouble, do we?"

His other hand finds my throat, and squeezes tight, cutting off my air. I kick out, desperate to get him off me, to get free, to take a breath, but I don't think he feels it. His eyes are wild and his face is flushed.

"Did you really think a little cut would stop me Sunny?" he snarls, his voice thick and angry. "C'mon you know me better than that."

I can't breathe. I can't *breathe*.

I try to grab at his hands, tear them away from my throat, but every move sends waves of pain through my entire body. It's excruciating. I think I'm going to be sick. The edges of my vision blur—dark fuzzy spots creep in, dancing at the edges. I try again to scream, but, again, no sound comes out—only a silent gasp.

My skin is caked with blood. His, mine—too much to tell whose it is. I can feel it, thick like honey dripping down my side and pooling next to me. But again, he's right. I should've known it wouldn't have been enough to stop him.

"You know what I think?" He tenderly brushes a strand of hair out of my face. "I think you forgot the most important rule of our little game. How many times have I told you. You're either mine or you're dead. And look at you now baby. You're gonna be both."

Garrett's breath is hot and sour against my skin. "I hate to tell you this, but you really haven't left me much choice. You're gonna die here tonight, Sunny," he whispers, his voice low and venomous. "Right here. And everyone will know it was me but it won't matter because I'll be long gone. And you know what else? No one's gonna care. It's not going to make even one tiny bit of difference to anyone. Not to your bitch of a mother. Not to that little boyfriend of yours. Especially not him. He'll be balls deep in some cheerleader before your even in the ground. *You are nothing.* You'll be forgotten in less than a week. Just like your old man." He presses his forehead to mine again, waiting patiently for his words to sink in.

"Although, I gotta tell ya'... I didn't enjoy getting rid of him as much as I will you."

My chest heaves as his words slam into me.

It was him. He killed my father. He. Killed. My. Father.

My lungs are on fire, desperate for air. My body trembles. I can feel the need to fight slipping away from me, draining out with every second that goes by. I'm starting to feel so heavy. I can't... I can't fight anymore.

He's going to kill me.

This is it. I'm going to die.

The thought is crystal clear and deafening, even as the world around me turns to static and starts to fade. I should be terrified, should be fighting harder, but I can't. There's a cold, hollow emptiness spreading through me, swallowing me whole. It's all slipping away from me.

A universe of bright pinpoint stars explodes across the dark sky of my closed eyelids and I'm floating. Suspended in an icy pool of darkness with seashell waves crashing in my ears. The black nothingness is comforting. Calming. It's a relief.

Deep down, I knew this was how it would end. How I would end. There was never any other option, not really. No matter how much I wanted there to be.

Please don't let Levi be the one to find me. Please don't let him see me like this.

Garrett's voice is ringing in my ears, but I can't make out the words. I can feel the weight of his hands on my body, feel him moving inside me. But it's all so far away now.

It doesn't matter. None of it matters anymore.

My heart pounds, the beats weak and uneven, pulling me deeper into the dark. There's a brief flicker of memories, not nearly enough—liquid sunlight on water, Levi's lips against mine, laughter in the distance, my father's voice— before my thoughts break apart and start to disappear. The pain is gone now, finally.

I struggle to open my eyes. Garrett is above me still, his face blurry and out of focus, but I can still make out his expression. It's hideous, inhuman. I regret that it's the last thing I'll ever see. I regret that he's the last thing I'll ever feel. Him. Not Levi. Him.

I'm so sorry Levi. So sorry.

Chapter Eighteen

Levi

I park my truck a few houses down from Sunny's and quietly slip out. I don't want to make any more noise than I have to. There's no telling what I'm about to walk into but I know I should be prepared for anything.

Leaving my mom was the hardest thing I've ever done. There was nothing I could do for her though. I was too late. I should've been there, and I wasn't and there's nothing I can do to fix or change that now.

But for Sunny? Maybe it's not too late. Maybe I still have time. I have to believe that. It's the only thing keeping me standing. I can't lose them both.

The neighborhood's quiet for this early on a Saturday night. There are only a few cars in the driveways up and down the street, and most of the houses are dark. I stop at the end of Sunny's driveway, scanning the house, the yard, for movement or sounds, or anything out of place. From here, I can see the front door to the house is wide open. The house is dark inside—pitch black except for a faint glow coming from a room on the second floor. Sunny's bedroom.

I make my way to the porch and stand, staring into the doorway. Every instinct I have is telling me to run inside and find her, but I'm frozen—locked in place with a heavy sense of dread unlike anything I've ever felt. Fear isn't something I'm used to, but right now? I'm terrified. My mind races through a million different scenarios, each one worse than the last.

I can feel it. The same stillness, the same weighted silence I felt at home right before I found my mom. My chest tightens and the blood in my veins turns to ice.

Please let her be okay.

I whisper the words over and over even though each passing second makes me more positive that this is the last moment anything will ever be okay. The certainty of it settles deep into my bones. I take another step forward, coming to stand just inside the door. I close my eyes and open them slowly, giving them time to adjust to the darkness.

I step deeper inside, listening. There's nothing but empty silence. If anything happened here it's over now. My breath hitches as the room comes into shadowy focus. The front room looks the same as always. I'm ready to breathe a sigh of relief, but then, I see it.

Dark streaks smeared across the door frame leading into the kitchen. Stains, like small drips of black ink making a trail on the carpet, leading up the stairs. The scuffed wooden floor at my feet is a maze of boot prints. *Bloody boot prints.*

My stomach twists, my hands clenching into fists so tight my knuckles crack. There's so much blood. Too much. I follow the trail up the stairs, even as my mind screams for me to turn around, to go back. But I can't. I have to know. I have to find her. Adrenaline pushes me forward.

The air at the top of the stairs is thick, suffocating. The hallway leading to her room is littered with evidence of a struggle. Broken picture frames lay in piles of shattered glass, books with broken spines and torn pages are stomped into the carpet. The door to Sunny's room is cracked open, casting dim yellow streaks of light along the walls. Every part of me is screaming in panic, but I can't stop now. Not when

I'm this close. I press a shaking hand to the door and push it open, slowly.

My eyes are filled with red—a hundred different shades of the color are splashed on the walls, the door, the edge of the bed. And in the center of it all is my Angel. Pale, as if she were carved out of marble. The stark white of her skin is a deep contrast to the sea of crimson that covers her skin, her dress, her tangled and matted hair, the floor around her. And she's… she's not moving.

Tears well in my eyes. The beautiful dress I bought her is ripped to shreds, the wet scraps clinging to her body. Her face is swollen, covered in the same deep purple and dark blue bruises that cover the rest of her. A series of deep slashes are carved into her chest from her collarbone to her ribs. There's so much blood. So much fucking blood that it's hard to imagine it's all hers.

My knees buckle before I even realize I've moved, and I fall to the floor next to her, my hands reaching out for her, aching to feel her warmth. But she's cold. So cold. And so still. I stare at her, willing her to move. But she doesn't. Her chest doesn't rise. Her lips don't part. Her eyes stay closed tight.

When I grab her wrist and lift it, her hand falls to the side, limp and twisted awkwardly, her fingers bent at impossible angles. Bile rises in my throat at the sickening feel of bone grinding against bone. I close my eyes for a second, swallowing hard. I lower her hand gently and reach for the other one.

My pulse thunders through my body so loud I can barely think. My hands won't stop shaking as I press unsteady fingers to the soft skin of her wrist. As I wait, I graze my lips over her fingers, kissing each one, tasting copper and the salt of the tears that are now streaming down my face.

"Sunny." Her name escapes as barely a whisper, my voice shaking. I close my eyes, my fingers still pressed to her wrist, waiting.

Please, just one beat. One thump. Let there be something… anything.

I sit motionless, straining for the faintest flutter, the slightest thrum. My hands are trembling, and the air feels heavy with static. My breath comes in ragged gasps, drowning out everything else.

There's nothing there.

My heart seizes and my eyes burn—I lower her hand and press my ear to her lips, hoping for a sound, a breath, anything to tell me I'm wrong.

The silence seems to grow louder, pressing into my ears, filling me until there's only her cold stillness and the endless echo of my own heartbeat.

She's gone.

A strangled sound escapes me, something between a sob and a scream, and my whole body shudders. I grab her, pulling her limp body into my arms, her blood soaking my clothes, smearing across my hands, my face, but I don't care. I don't fucking care.

I shake her, gently at first, then harder. A small stream of bright red blood trickles from the corner of her mouth. "Sunny. Please. Please… wake up."

Nothing.

The world crashes down around me, and all I can do is stare at her, my mind refusing to believe what's right in front of me. She can't be gone. She can't be *gone*. Not like this. Not because of *him*.

Garrett.

My body is numb, my mind barely able to process everything that's happened tonight, the overwhelming *hollowness* inside me. First my mom. Now Sunny. He's taken everything and everyone that matters away from me.

And I let it happen.

The guilt slams into me, hard and brutal, ripping through me and tearing me apart. I ignored her calls. She needed me, and *I wasn't there*. I promised her I'd be there for her. I said I'd keep her safe, no one would ever hurt again and *I wasn't fucking here for her*. Not when it mattered.

My chest heaves with a pain so deep I feel it in every muscle of my body. I tilt my head back and scream—a raw, animal howl that tears through the silence. It goes on and on until there's nothing left inside me. I clutch Sunny close to me, my hands slick with her blood. I want to stay like this. I'm not ready to let go of her. But, I know I have to.

I reach into my pocket, pulling out my phone. The thought of reporting this, of giving voice to what's happened tonight, making it real, turns my stomach. The thought of anyone—everyone—seeing the two women I love more than anything else in the world reduced to this… guts me. But I can't walk away now. I'm responsible for this. I need to make sure they're going to be taken care of. I failed them in every other way that mattered, I have to do this for them.

My fingers shake as I dial 911. I barely hear the operator's voice before the words start tumbling out.

"There's been…an attack." My voice breaks, and I squeeze my eyes shut, fighting to keep control. "Two addresses. One…" I give my address, barely recognizing the emotionless, detached tone of my own voice.

"And the other—" I choke, but I force the words out. "The other's here, at…." I recite Sunny's address, holding her tighter, my voice turning to ground glass in my throat with every word. "It's bad. They're gone. Both of them. I wasn't here. I should've been here, but I wasn't. It's all my fault. I did this—"

"Sir, please remain on the line. Units are on the way—"

I'm already moving, my voice a broken rasp as I cut her off. "Make sure they take care of them. They deserve that."

I end the call before she can say anything else, and the silence around me settles in again. My vision blurs as I look down at Sunny one last time. This is it. This is my last goodbye, and then there's nothing left for me. *Nothing left but him.*

Something glints in the dim light, catching my eye. The silver heart necklace I gave her lies broken on the floor, partially hidden under the bed, its chain snapped and smeared with blood. My hands shake as I pick it up, the metal cool and sticky against my palm.

I slip it into my pocket, unable to leave this piece of her behind. Unable to let him take everything.

I have things I need to take care of. Things I have to do. I have a new purpose.

I stand, shaking, Sunny's blood drying on my skin as the world blurs around me. There's only one thought that slices through the haze—one clear thought that leaves me breathless:

Garrett will pay for this.

The cops can fuck themselves. This piece of justice won't be theirs to decide. Not for Sunny. Not for my mom.

This is mine. He's mine.

The Aftermath

Chapter Nineteen

Levi

Seven Years Later

"Please," he whimpers, spitting out a tooth. "I told you everything I know."

"Everything you know is shit." I grab his hair, yanking his head back. "You sold me garbage intel, and now you're going to pay for wasting my time."

Behind me, I hear Zane shift his weight. He's getting antsy. They both are. I can feel Colt's eyes boring into my back too.

They think I'm losing it.

Maybe I am.

My knuckles are split wide, but I barely feel it anymore. Physical pain is nothing compared to the hollow ache that's lived in my chest for the past seven years. Seven fucking years of dead ends and false leads. Seven years of becoming everything I swore I'd never be.

"I swear," the man sobs, blood bubbling from his lips. "The guy in Newport said—"

"The guy in Newport?" I laugh, but there's no humor in it. Only ice. "The guy in Newport was playing you, just like you tried to play me."

His ribs cave under my fist with a sickening crunch, the vibration traveling up my knuckles. His scream echoes through the warehouse, bouncing off metal walls and concrete floors.

"Levi." Zane's voice is low, warning. "That's enough."

But it's not enough. It's never enough. The monster inside me craves more, needs more. Needs to make someone else hurt as much as I do.

"You know what happens to people who waste my time?" I grab the man's face, forcing him to look at me. His eyes are wild with terror. Good. "They disappear."

"Boss." This time it's Colt who speaks up. "We still need him alive if we want to trace things back to his source."

Logic. Always with the fucking logic. I know he's right, but the rational part of my brain is drowning in a sea of red. All I can see is Sunny's broken body, my mother's blood on the wall. All I can think about is Garrett, still out there somewhere, breathing free air while they're both cold in the ground.

I step back, wiping blood from my hands onto my ruined shirt. My father's ring catches the fluorescent light—the same ring I took off his corpse after putting three bullets in his head. The ultimate proof that I've become exactly what I was always afraid I would.

"You're right," I say, not turning around. I can't look at them right now, can't bear to see the concern in their eyes. They're the only family I have, and sometimes I wonder how long it'll be before they realize I'm too far gone to save.

The man tied to the forklift sags in his restraints, relief evident in his posture. Poor bastard thinks he's getting off easy.

"Take him to the basement and call Doc to check him out and make sure he lives through the night," I order, finally turning to face my friends. "We'll continue this conversation tomorrow."

Zane nods, his face unreadable. But I catch the look he exchanges with Colt— the one that is a combination of doubt and concern.

"And Levi?" Colt calls as I head for the door. "Maybe get some sleep? You've been at this for days."

I don't respond. Sleep is just another form of torture for me. A place where I'm forced to remember the way things were. Where Sunny's brown eyes stare at me with disappointment, where my mother's blood-stained fingers point accusingly.

Look what you've become, they whisper. *Look what you let happen to us.*

The worst part is, they're right. I've exceeded my father's expectation. I'm ruthless, feared, powerful. The empire I built from his ashes is twice what his ever was. But the cost...

I flex my bloody fingers, feeling the sting of split skin. These hands used to hold Sunny so gently, used to wipe away her tears. Now they only know how to hurt, how to break, how to destroy.

Every day, the darkness inside me spreads, swallowing the memory of what light even felt like. I'm starting to forget everything except the only mission that matters—find Garrett, make him suffer, make him pay.

Even if it kills whatever's left of my soul in the process.

I shove through the heavy metal door, the night air cool on my face. The loading dock's familiar rust and oil smell mingles with copper—blood. My blood. His blood. Does it even matter anymore?

My hands shake, as I pull out a cigarette, muscle memory taking over while my mind races. Behind me, I hear Zane's deep voice giving orders, the scrape of boots on concrete as the crew starts cleanup. Another night. Another dead end.

"Get him downstairs," Colt calls out. "And somebody mop up that mess before it stains."

I light the cigarette, inhaling deep enough to burn. The ember glows bright against the darkness, like the reflection in her eyes when we'd lay in the grass and look up at the stars. *Fuck.* Seven years and I still can't stop the comparisons, can't stop seeing her everywhere.

My phone weighs heavy in my pocket—another addiction I can't kick. I pull it out, fingers leaving smears of red on the screen as I navigate to the one folder I transfer to every single phone I carry. The one I swore I'd delete a thousand times. The one that's killing me slowly, surely, but I can't help but keep coming back to.

One message. One voicemail. Thirty drawn out seconds of exquisite torture locked inside a digital time capsule.

My thumb hovers over the play button. I should stop this. I should let her rest. I should try to forget her voice and the way I used to love hearing it wrap around me.

I press play.

"Hey Handsome..."

My eyes close, chest tightening as her voice fills the night air. Happy. Excited. *Alive.*

"I'm almost finished getting ready and I, uh, I wanted you to know I'm thinking about you. I can't wait to see you tonight."

The cigarette burns forgotten between my fingers. All I can see is her, probably standing in the middle of her room, looking so beautiful, so sweet, so fucking… perfect. I can hear her nervousness in that small hesitation. I would bet anything she'd been twirling her hair around her finger like she always did when she was feeling unsure.

"I've got a surprise for you too."

God, the way she said it—shy but determined. I never got to find out what that surprise was. Never got to see her in that black dress again except...

"I'll see you in a few. And hey... hurry up and get here already. I miss you."

The message ends. It always ends too soon. Thirty seconds that I play on repeat, reminding myself what I lost. What I caused.

If I hadn't been so focused on Zack, so determined to make him pay. If I'd answered just one of her calls instead of letting revenge consume me—

The door creaks open behind me. I quickly pocket the phone, but not before catching Zane's reflection in the loading dock's grimy window.

"You good?" he asks, though we both know I'm not. Haven't been for a long, long time.

"Fine." I take another drag, letting smoke fill the silence between us.

He doesn't know. Neither of them do—not really. They know Garrett killed her, know he murdered my mother. But they don't know about what happened the day I met Sunny—what I did to set all of it in motion. They don't know about the calls I ignored. Don't know I was too busy setting up Zack to notice that payment for everything I'd done had come due.

They think it was a matter of both the women I loved being in the wrong place at the wrong time. That Garrett had finally gone off the rails and went on a rampage. That I couldn't have prevented it. Their loyalty and sympathy is built on a foundation of half-truths and omissions that would crumble if they knew the whole story.

"We'll find him," Zane says, his certainty unchanged after all these years.

I nod, not trusting myself to speak. The guilt rises in my throat, choking me—for lying to them, for failing her, for becoming—this.

I turn to face Zane, flicking my cigarette out into the darkness. "I don't get it. How does a piece of shit small-town dealer just vanish into thin air? Seven years, Z. Seven fucking years of throwing everything we have at finding him. And nothing."

The frustration rakes at me. We've built an empire that makes my father's look like child's play. I have eyes and ears in every major city, connections that reach into most of the darkest corners of all of them. Yet Garrett might as well be a ghost.

"He's not smart enough for this." I run my hands through my hair, the dried blood on my knuckles flaking off. "A drunk who got his kicks abusing women and dealing cut-rate meth to teenagers. That's who he was. So how is he outmaneuvering us?"

Zane leans against the wall, his face half-hidden in shadow. "Maybe that's what we're missing. We're looking for who he was right then. Maybe we need to go backwards. Or forwards."

"What do you mean?"

"People change. You did." His words hit deep. "We haven't been able to find out a whole lot about his past. Maybe we should go back and start there."

I laugh, but it comes out hollow. "Men—monsters like that don't change. If there was something significant to find we'd have found it by now."

"Men "like that" don't change? We all did."

The words hang between us, heavy with implications. He's not wrong. We've become something else entirely over the years—deadlier, darker. The scared kids we were are long gone, replaced by men who deal in fear.

"I'm tired, Z." The admission costs me something to voice out loud. "Not of looking, I'll never stop looking. But I'm tired of being one step behind. Tired of following leads that go nowhere. Tired of failing her."

"You've never failed her." Zane's voice is firm. "Garrett did this. Not you."

If he only knew. The weight of my secrets presses down, threatening to suffocate me. How do I tell him that every dead end feels like losing her all over again? That each false lead is another reminder of how I chose revenge over protecting her that night?

"Something's not adding up." I pace the loading dock, mind racing. "We've checked every possible connection we could find. Offered money, favors. All for nothing. Nobody can disappear that completely."

"You think someone's protecting him?"

"I think..." I stop, the pieces slowly shifting in my head. "I think he's definitely had help along the way from someone who knows what they're doing."

Zane straightens—interest sparked.

"Think about it. He kills Sunny, kills my mother, leaves that message—and then just vanishes?"

The more I say it out loud, the more certain I become. "Someone had to have helped him. Someone with resources, connections. Someone who knew how to make people disappear."

"Someone like your father?" Zane's question is careful, measured.

The thought has crossed my mind before, but I've always dismissed it. "No. I think Garrett was exactly the kind of man that my father always avoided. I remember him saying *Some dogs never take to the leash, and those are the ones to stay away from. You'll never be able to trust them.*"

"Your father had a lot of friends. Powerful ones."

"And enemies." I lean against the railing, staring into the darkness. "What if... what if this was never about Garrett at all? What if he was just a weapon aimed at me?"

The possibility makes my blood run cold. All these years chasing a puppet while the puppeteer has watched from the shadows, laughing at my failure.

"If you're right," Zane says slowly, "we need to change our approach. Stop looking for Garrett and start looking for whoever's pulling his strings."

I nod, feeling the familiar darkness rising inside me. If someone orchestrated this, if someone used Garrett to take everything from me—

The rage builds, hot and familiar.

"We need to be smart about this though," Zane continues, reading my expression. "If someone powerful enough to hide Garrett for this long is behind this, we can't go in blind."

I watch Zane disappear back into the warehouse, his words echoing in my head. Seven years of dead ends, only to find out we may have been playing the wrong game entirely.

The night air carries the scent of coming rain. I roll my shoulders, feeling the familiar ache of tension. Every muscle screams for rest, but rest means dreams and dreams mean her.

The warehouse door creaks again. I know it's Colt without turning—his footsteps are lighter than Zane's, more precise. Everything about him is calculated, measured. It's what makes him so damn good at what he does.

"We're all set," he says, joining me at the railing. "Got him secured downstairs. Doc's checking him out now—making sure he'll be stable enough for round two tomorrow."

I grunt in acknowledgment, watching ash fall from my cigarette.

"You should see some of the intel we pulled from his phone already," Colt continues. "Looks like—"

"Tomorrow," I cut him off. I can't process anything else right now. My head is too full of possibilities.

Zane emerges again, wiping his hands on a cloth. "Everything's cleaned up. No trace left." He claps me on the shoulder, his grip firm. "Go home, brother. Get some rest. This'll all still be here in the morning."

They both head back inside, leaving me alone with my demons. The warehouse door closes with a metallic clang that echoes through the empty lot.

My fingers are already pulling out my phone before I consciously decide to do it. The screen glows blue in the darkness as I navigate to that folder, to that message. To her.

"Hey Handsome..."

I close my eyes, letting her voice wash over me again.

If someone helped Garrett disappear, if this was all some elaborate plot—that means that someone out there knows what happened that night when he left. Someone knows where he is. And when I find them—

"I'm almost finished getting ready..."

The rain falls harder now, but I barely notice.

"I miss you."

"I miss you too, Angel," I whisper out to the emptiness. "I miss you too."

CHAPTER TWENTY

Levi

I LEAN BACK IN my chair, rubbing my temples as I stare at the stack of invoices cluttering my desk. The sound of metal clicking against metal draws my attention to where Zane sits methodically cleaning his guns. His long dark hair is pulled back in a neat knot, his movements precise and focused.

"Man, those girls last night..." Colt's voice drifts over from the leather couch where he's sprawled out, still wearing his clothes from yesterday. "They were something else. You shoulda come with me, Z."

Zane doesn't look up from his work. "I don't want to hear about your conquests."

"Come on, man. When's the last time you actually went out and had some fun?" Colt props himself up on an elbow, his blonde hair sticking up in every direction. "You know what they say about all work and no play."

I catch the slight twitch at the corner of Zane's mouth as he tries to maintain his stoic expression. "Some of us have standards, Colt."

"Standards? Is that what we're calling it now?" Colt grins. "Because from where I'm sitting, that sounds an awful lot like a fancy way to say 'I've given up on all the things that make life worth living'."

"Unlike you, I don't need to chase everything in a skirt to validate my existence." Zane methodically reassembles the pistol in his hands.

I can't help but smirk. "He's got you there, Colt."

"Et tu, Levi?" Colt clutches his chest dramatically. "It's not exactly my existence I need validated, thank you very much. And, I'll have you know the ladies I spent last night were excellent conversationalists. Very mentally stimulating."

"Really?" Zane arches an eyebrow. "So you spent the entire night enjoying their… conversation, hm? What did you talk about? "

"Um, well." Colt pauses, his brows furrowing. "I don't remember. But to be fair, there were two of them and they just loved to… talk. And talk, and talk and talk. You know me. I'm easily distracted." Colt waggles his eyebrows.

"I'm sure," I deadpan, shuffling through more paperwork.

Colt rolls onto his back, staring at the ceiling. "Seriously though, Z. You need to get out more. I'm sure they'd be up for making it a double—"

"No." Zane's voice is firm but there's amusement in his eyes.

"Oh! A little too advanced for you huh? Well, let's see. I'm sure they have a friend that'd be more your speed. A Sunday school teacher maybe, or…"

I watch as Zane's composure finally cracks, a deep chuckle escaping as he shakes his head. "You're ridiculous."

"That's why you love me." Colt beams. "Come on, seriously though. When's the last time you actually went on a date?"

"Some of us actually work." Zane picks up another gun to clean. "You know that thing that keeps us all fed."

"Hey! Networking is a very valuable skill," Colt protests. "It takes practice."

I snort. "Anything for the business, huh?"

"You're both just jealous of my... skills." Colt stretches out on the couch. "It'd be wrong to keep all this charm to myself. I'm just sharing my gifts with the world."

"Such a generous guy you are." Zane mutters, but there's no heat in his words.

The banter continues as I try to focus on the numbers in front of me. It's comfortable, this dynamic between us. Even in my darkest moods, Colt manages to make me laugh. And Zane, for all his seriousness, has a dry wit that perfectly complements Colt's... whatever it is.

"Seriously though," Colt sits up, his expression suddenly earnest. "You should come out with me sometime, Z. Just... you know, live a little."

Zane pauses in his cleaning, looking at Colt with an unreadable expression. "I live plenty."

"Playing with your gun all day isn't living, it's existing." Colt's voice carries a note of concern beneath the teasing. "Even Levi gets outta here sometimes."

"For work," I interject, not looking up from my papers.

"Details." Colt waves his hand dismissively. "The point is, you're young, you're hot— in a terrifying is-he-a-serial-killer? sort of way—but still. You deserve some fun."

Zane sets down his cleaning cloth, his blue eyes intense. "I don't do that."

Colt stands up, stretching. "But you could."

Zane sighs heavily, but I can see him wavering. "If I say yes, will you shut the fuck up and let me finish this?"

"Absolutely not," Colt grins. "But I'll buy the first round."

I clear my throat, interrupting. "As entertaining as this is, we need to focus. We need to make a decision on Oak Valley. It's becoming an issue."

Colt's playful demeanor shifts instantly, his blue eyes sharpening behind his glasses. "What kind of issue?"

"The kind that requires our attention." I pull out a manila folder from my desk drawer. "Remember that safe house on Cherry Street?"

Zane sets down the gun he's cleaning. "Your father's old place?"

"That's the one." I spread out several photos across my desk. "It's been sitting empty since he died. But I think it's time we got it operational again."

"Operational for what exactly?" Colt moves closer, studying the pictures of the dilapidated but sprawling ranch style house.

"If we don't make some moves to re-establish our presence there, we're going to lose it. It's been neglected for a long time." I tap my finger on a photo showing broken windows and overgrown landscaping. "Oak Valley used to be central to everything when my father ran things. We've let it slip."

"And now you want it back." Zane's voice is neutral, but I catch the slight tension in his shoulders.

"We *need* it back," I correct him. "The competition's getting bold. They think because we've been focused elsewhere, they can move in on what was always ours. It's fine for now, but it'll hurt our business, especially the guns, in the long run. Makes us look careless, weak."

Colt picks up another one of the photos. "This place looks rough, man. How long are we talking to get it ready?"

"A week, maybe two." I lean back in my chair. "We need to install new security systems, reinforce entry points, the works. It needs to start looking lived in. Neighbors need to get used to having company again."

"Neighbors." Zane's lip curls slightly. "That was always the problem with that house. Too many eyes."

"Which is exactly why it's perfect for us." I stand up, pacing behind my desk. "It's quiet. Unexpected. My father understood that. It's why he chose it in the first place."

"Speaking of your father..." Colt hesitates, glancing at Zane before continuing. "You sure going back there is smart? There's a lot of history back there. He may be gone, but there's a lot of people who remember him and remember what happened."

"That history is exactly why we need to do this." My voice hardens. "People there need to be reminded that things changed. They need to remember who we are."

Zane sets aside his cleaning supplies completely, his full attention on me now. "Why now? Last time I checked, you wanted nothing to do with any part of the business that was your father's."

I keep my expression neutral, even though I'm irritated by the lack of vision I'm surrounded by. "I don't. But, I also don't want to take any hits on anything we've built for ourselves."

"You sure that's all it is?" Zane stands, his height making the office feel smaller. "Because from where I'm standing, it looks an awful lot like you're trying to prove something to people who don't matter anymore."

"Z..." Colt warns softly.

"No." I hold up my hand. "Let him speak."

"Going backwards like this is never a good idea," Zane continues, his blue eyes intense. "Who gives a fuck about Oak Valley. We've got plenty of other things to worry about besides stirring up all that old business."

"Concern noted." I say, my tone icy.

Colt moves between us, his usual lighthearted demeanor replaced with something more serious. "Maybe we should focus on the logistics first. Give me a day to get together with Wolf. We'll draw up some plans."

I force myself to take a deep breath, reining in the anger that threatens to spill over. "Fine. But I want preliminary designs by to-morrow. Z, I need you to make some calls and figure out what we're up against. Get all the details on who's who and what they're moving."

"And you?" Zane asks, still watching me carefully.

"I'm going to make some calls of my own." I sit back down at my desk. "There's a lot of bad blood there, but there are also a few people in Oak Valley who owe my family favors. Time to collect."

"Your father's old contacts?" Colt asks hesitantly.

"My contacts now." I pull out my phone. "Whether they like it or not."

Zane and Colt exchange a look I pretend not to notice. There's that worry again.

"Let's plan on two weeks. Three at most," I say to them. "I want that house ready to move some guys into. A full team. Whatever it takes."

"Whatever it takes," they echo, but I hear the reservation in their voices.

I understand their concerns. Oak Valley represents everything I've tried to leave behind about my father's legacy. It's where he got his start—working as a middle man, storing and moving goods—anything there's a market for—for the guys at the top. He clawed and scratched and fought his way up until he was *the* guy at the top. The last man standing. Until me. I know how risky a move like this is, but I won't take a chance on losing any more in this life than I already have.

"I want to get out of here first thing in the morning. So let's get everything finished up and secured," I order, already scrolling through my contacts.

They leave without another word, with Zane's disapproval hanging heavy in the air. Once they're gone, I allow myself a moment of weakness and pull out the phone that contains Sunny's last voicemail. I pause for only a moment before hitting play. I listen to it once and remind myself that the next couple weeks are all about making sure no one ever threatens what's mine again.

Chapter Twenty-One

Sunny

I grab the clothes I packed for the night out of my bag before tossing it into the old, dented locker. It hits the bottom with a heavy *thud,* and I slam the door a little harder than I'd wanted. The sharp metallic clang echoes off the walls of the empty dressing room, making me jump.

I rattle the latch to double-check that it's locked. I get along with most the girls here, but there are a few that'll take anything that isn't nailed down. Especially if it's mine. Jealous bitches.

I drag the fistful of clothes I'm holding over to one of the long counters and lay them out. What little there is of them. Benny's cool about letting us wear what we want, but like he says, *'less is more.'* He's right—the more skin you show, the more cash you earn. And when you start out with nothing but hospital discharge papers and a fake ID some guy made for you in his basement, you learn the wisdom of those words fast. I mean bills don't pay themselves.

The name I chose was obvious. Angel. The perfect reminder of exactly how much trusting someone can cost.

I catch my reflection in the mirror as I change. The girl looking back at me doesn't look anything like the one who stepped off that bus seven years ago. That girl was all bruises and bandages, held together with staples and sporting a dirty, wet cast. This one... well, this one at least *looks* like she has her shit together. Even if it is all smoke and mirrors.

My fingers trace the edge of my collarbone—the starting point of the tattoo that winds down my body. Jade helped me design it—a thick ribbon of night sky and stars behind a waterfall of wildflowers. Every single kind I could remember from the lake is there. It covers the full length and width of the scars that carve a trail from my shoulder to just below my ribs. It continues down over my hip where it buries the ink I got from Garrett and wraps around my thigh.

It's beautiful and only someone who knew the scars were there would ever be able to see them underneath. Cost me three months of tips, but it was worth it to stop having to spend a couple hours each night painting myself with body makeup.

Jade's good at finding solutions like that. I consider her my best friend. I'm as close to her as I can imagine being to anyone. She found me in the bus station bathroom, trying to change my bandages one-handed, out of money, and out of options.

She gave me a spot on her couch until I could get on my feet. She's the one who convinced Benny to give 'Angel' a shot at working behind the bar.

I pull out one of the hard molded plastic chairs, and collapse into it. I've got almost an hour before my shift starts, maybe half that before the dressing room starts filling up. I like to get here early, especially on the weekends. It still takes me time to work up the courage to get my ass out onto the floor. I'm good at what I do, but I've never really settled into it.

Given a choice, I'd rather be doing something else. But it all comes down to money. There's no way I could make what I make in a night here anywhere else. Not with my lack of education and experience. I mean, I don't even have a high school diploma.

The day I got released from the hospital I got home, packed a bag, grabbed all the money from the stash spots as well as the main jar in the kitchen and headed towards the bus station.

The cops had told me there'd been no sign of Garrett since the night he almost killed me. They assured me that he was probably long gone and wouldn't risk coming back. They didn't know him like I did. I caught the first bus leaving Easton Creek and I've never looked back.

I'm lucky I had someone like Jade willing to take me under her wing. I owe her so much. But, I'll admit, some nights it's easier than others to find enough gratitude to give away. Especially when the job is more about dodging hands on your ass then serving drinks.

Not that Benny messes around when it comes to safety. He won't hesitate to sic one of the bouncers on anyone who can't take no for an answer. It happens more often than it should—at least once a night on the weekends. Usually the dancers are the target, but no one, not even us bartenders are immune.

I pull my old, faded T-shirt over my head, and shimmy out of my cut-off jean shorts, letting both fall to the floor. My toes wiggle and dig into the worn denim at my feet as I get used to the cool air on my skin.

I gently massage the scars that run down my body before getting dressed. They may be hidden under layers of ink now, but I can always feel them. The skin feels like it healed too tight in places and it always seems to ache and itch. It gets worse when I get nervous. I swear sometimes I can still feel the sting and burn of those scissors digging in and dragging across my skin.

My doctor tells me there's nothing he can do to help if I won't go talk to someone. He doesn't think it's a physical problem. He's probably right. But I have a hard enough time getting through a day with the few ghosts who won't settle enough to ignore. I don't need to go digging up the whole damn graveyard. It's better to leave some things buried and silent.

I stare at my reflection another minute before slipping into the tiny scraps of fabric I laid out. Snow white lace—my signature look as Angel. Judging by the tips I take home on an average night, I've gotten fairly convincing at playing the good girl—big brown eyes under thick long lashes, long honey blonde curls wrapped up in silk ribbons, and an easy, innocent smile. Guys eat that shit up. They all seem to want a sweet girl they think they can ruin. They're a little late to the party, but what they don't know won't hurt them. They aren't paying for truth.

I'm tugging up the straps of my top when the door swings open and Jade breezes in, all long legs and confidence. She's just coming off her afternoon shift. Her short, shiny, black hair is teased up into spikes and her deep red lipstick is as perfect as always.

"Girl!" she says, tossing the black leather bag that matches her costume onto the counter next to me, "You're in for one helluva night. It's crazy out there. The regulars are already showing up for the night, and Benny said there's three different bachelor parties scheduled. He asked if I'd stay over, but I promised my sister another visit and help with her kids, ya' know?" She stops mid-step, scans me from head to toe, and smirks. "I still think it's such a waste. You should really think about getting up on that stage, Angel baby. Package like that, you'd rake it in. Seriously, they'd be eating out of your hand."

I give her my best playful smile, half-posing as I start to weave a length of white satin ribbon into my hair. "I can't dance. No rhythm," I say, winking at her in the mirror. "Besides, I'm not really a center-of-attention kind of girl. Never have been."

"Yeah right, sweetie. Like you have a choice." She laughs, running her fingers through her hair. "Suit yourself. But if I had your looks, I'd be retired by now."

"And here I am just focused on trying not to kill myself in these heels," I reply, blowing her a kiss.

Jade rolls her eyes but grins, as she turns and heads towards her locker.

She starts rambling about a customer from her last table—some high roller who left her a hundred-dollar tip for letting him buy her a shot. I half-listen, nodding and laughing in all the right places, focusing on adjusting the tiny straps of my top.

When she finally heads out, I check myself one last time in the mirror. I wish I could be her sometimes—sweet, charming, fun. Sexy. If only.

I bend to fasten the strap on the six-inch platforms I'm wearing, stand up straight, push my shoulders back, and throw a sultry look at my reflection. "Why hello again Angel," I murmur. "Go get 'em, girl."

The sound of bass throbs from the other side of the wall as I head out into the dim hallway. The familiar mix of stale beer, cheap cologne, and perfume thickens as I make my way over to my tables. It's busier than usual with men already clustered around tables or lining the four stages in the center of the club with drinks in hand. Pretty soon it'll be standing room only. Jade wasn't lying.

Flashing lights hit the four large stages where girls writhe and gyrate in time to the music. That's where the real money is made, but I wasn't lying. I'll do a lot of things to get by, but that's where I draw the line. I'm not my mother.

I catch sight of one of my favorite regulars at the end of the bar and walk over. His eyes stay glued to me the entire time. I give him a playful tap on the arm. "Back again, huh? Thought you'd have had enough of this place by now, Tony."

He grins, taking a sip of his beer. "Not a chance, sweetheart. Seeing you is the highlight of my week. You know that." He digs in his wallet and hands me a fifty for a drink he hasn't even ordered yet.

"Tony, you sure know how to treat a lady," I say, tucking the bill into the soft velvet bag around my waist with a wink. "Let me get you a drink, on the house this time."

"Hell, *you* start buying *me* drinks Angel baby and you'll never get rid of me," he jokes.

I laugh and give him a wink before turning around and heading towards the bar. I pause, long enough to blow a quick kiss to a table of guys who get loud when I walk by. I keep the perfectly rehearsed grin plastered on my face—wide enough to be friendly, but not so wide it looks fake. I toss a coy look over my shoulder at them as I step behind the bar and start making a whiskey sour. The guys at the table I passed can't take their eyes off of me. It's going to be a good night.

Tony gives me a soft smile when I drop his drink off. "Let me ask you something serious, Angel. You ever think of doing something else? Something better than this?"

His concern hits a little too close to home. For a second, I'm back at that bus station, barely eighteen and terrified, counting wrinkled bills and praying it would be enough to get me somewhere Garrett couldn't find me. Somewhere I could disappear.

I force Angel's smile back onto my face. "Aww, you're too sweet Tony. But better than this? This is as close to heaven as I'm ever going to get, baby."

It's not even a lie. Seven years ago, I was bleeding out on my bedroom floor thinking I was done for. Now I'm alive, independent, and nobody owns me. It might be a long way from heaven, but it's better than being fucking dead.

Chapter Twenty-Two

Sunny

A SHRILL RINGING DRAGS me out of the quicksand of sleep. I jolt awake, gasping, disoriented. For a split second, there is no present, only past. No Angel, only Sunny. I fight my way to the surface against the surge of memories trying to pull me under. The sting of antiseptic, the dull ache of broken bones, the sharp bite of metal in bruised skin. Hands on my throat.

My stomach lurches as my fingers move over my neck, my chest, searching for open wounds. There's nothing there. Only the raised scars under my fingertips.

The ringing doesn't stop. I blink and shake off the remnants of the nightmare, my pulse hammering in my ears until the room starts to make sense again—gray evening light spilling through the half-closed blinds, the dresser I got at the thrift store down the street, and my phone rattling across the nightstand.

The screen flashes with Benny's name. Great.

I sigh and rake my hand through my hair, trying to compose myself before I answer. I don't need him to hear how I feel right now—like I'm barely hanging on and exhausted from sleep that isn't really sleep.

I feel like I've gone more than a few rounds in the ring with a prize fighter.

Swiping the screen, I plaster a smile on my face before answering. "Hey, Benny, what's up?" I make my voice light, airy. Angel's voice. The one that says I'm fine, I'm whole, I'm whatever you need me to be.

"Angel, sweetheart, I know it's your day off," he begins, his voice already laying it on thick, "but I'm in a bind tonight, and you're my girl. I got a special request for the VIP room, and I've got no one to bartend back there. The client requested the best of the best and was willing to pay for it. I need you to come in."

My stomach twists itself into a knot. The VIP room. I hate getting stuck back there, and he knows it. It's too dark, and a little too private. Not to mention that most men who have enough money to book it for the night are entitled assholes. The kind that are used to getting exactly what they want and never being told no. They assume they're buying a whole lot more than some drinks and private dances.

"Benny, c'mon! It's my only night off this week. And you know how much I hate it back there."

"I know, I know, babe. But you're my best girl. You're reliable, classy, and I swear to God, the money follows you. I'll pay you double for the night, plus you keep all the tips and…," he pauses, his voice dropping a notch, "how about ten percent of whatever you sell in booze."

He's gotta be desperate. He'd never offer all that if he weren't. I close my eyes, exhaling slowly. It's hard for me to say no to Benny when he gets that pleading tone in his voice. He has done *a lot* for me. I don't know where I'd be without him. I feel like I owe him. He doesn't ask for favors often, and truthfully I could use the cash. It's only one shift, right?

"C'mon, Angel. Help me out? These guys could be good for business."

I force a light laugh. "Fine, Benny. But, I expect a drink waiting for me when I get there."

"That's my girl. You're a lifesaver, Angel, really. I owe you." He chuckles, clearly relieved. "Be here no later than eight."

After he hangs up, I sit for a moment, letting the silence close back in around me. It's uncomfortable. It's crazy to me how rattled a dream can still make me. Not to mention how hard it can be to shake it off.

I let out a long breath, forcing myself to pull it together, then push myself off the bed, and head into the bathroom for a quick shower. I wiggle my toes against the cool tile under my feet and stare into the mirror. I look awful. The lack of sleep is starting to catch up with me.

I've had seven years to practice keeping my shit together, and I do an okay job, mostly, but lately things are slipping through the cracks. Maybe it's the anniversary of that night coming up. Maybe it's something else. Either way, I can't afford to let it show. Not tonight. Not in the VIP room.

"You've got this," I whisper to myself as I step under the hot water. It's a well-worn lie wrapped up in a few shaky syllables. It's not the worst one I've told myself lately. Not by a long shot. I'm glad I don't have time to second-guess it tonight.

Twenty minutes later, I'm heading to the closet, grabbing my work clothes and shoes, and tossing them into my bag with my makeup. I grab my keys and toss my phone into my purse and force myself to stop and take a deep, calming breath before I open the door.

It's still hard. You'd think after all this time, I'd be more grounded in my life here. I'd be comfortable with who I am now and it wouldn't take so much effort to live it out every day. I mean it should *feel* like my life, but it never does. It still feels so unnatural. Walking out my front door as Angel and stepping into the carefully curated version of her life feels as strange to me now as it did the first time I did it.

FIGURES. I'M ON TIME, but the guys were early. I had just enough time to make a quick stop by the bar, knock back my drink, get the preference list and details from Benny, and get my ass over to the lounge. The two massive men standing outside the door, one on each side, instantly calm my nerves. They break into smiles as I approach, and I can't help but smile back.

They look tough—all hard edges and seriousness—I've seen them drag plenty of guys out the back, but to me, they've never been anything but sweet and kind. Jade used to scold me for tipping them out so well every night. I give them at least double what they get from the other girls. I can't help it. It never made sense to me to cheap out on the guys who've proved they'll be there to save your ass if you need it.

It took a awhile but she finally gave up trying to talk sense into me.

I admit I feel better about tonight knowing they're the ones watching out for me.

"Hey Jake. Hey Eddie," I nod, as I stop in front of the door and adjust the ribbons in my hair. "How's it looking for tonight?"

"Should be a pretty easy night. It's a small group. Benny sent Jade in to cover the bar for you until you got here, so it's the two of you. And the dancers, of course."

"Of course," I say the words, only slightly regretting the snark that comes with them. It's not that I have an issue with anyone here directly, it's more the issue they seem to have with me. It's like high school all over again most of the time. It's taken me years to learn to ignore it and let it go.

I grab the handle of the door, close my eyes and take a deep breath.

"You're good Angel. We got you," Jake leans over and whispers. "You're gonna kill it tonight."

Those words were the boost of confidence I seemed to need. I pull the handle, throw the door open wide and step into the dimly lit lounge. The door closes behind me and the relentless thump of bass and heavy beats flooding the floor of the main bar and stages, softens into something silkier, softer. Low, seductive rhythms pulse hypnotically, just loud enough to force conversation close in. It's a completely different world on this side of the doors.

Dark leather couches and armchairs line the space, arranged around small glass tables. There are a few small stages lining the far wall—all fixed with color changing LED lights and shiny chrome poles stretching up to the ceiling.

I count seven men scattered around the room. They're sitting comfortably with the kind of confidence that comes with serious money. And power. I stride over and come to stand beside one of the couches.

"Good evening, gentlemen," I say in my sweetest, flirty voice. "My name is Angel, and I'll be taking care of you tonight."

Seven sets of eyes land on me, almost in unison, all of them appraising me. I offer them my widest, brightest smile and give them plenty of time to drink in the view. This is probably the only time tonight that I'll have all of their attention to myself and attention equals money, so I do my best to make sure I leave a lasting impression.

"Angel, huh?" The man closest to me leans forward, his lips quirking into a lazy, lopsided grin. He's broad-shouldered and rugged looking with a deep voice that matches his rough exterior. "Fitting. I'm Zane. Call me Z."

He offers his hand, and I shake it lightly, keeping my smile firm. His eyes linger a second too long on mine before he sits back and drapes his arm over the back of the couch.

"And I'm Colt." The voice comes from a man planted in one of the overstuffed armchairs. He barely spares me a glance. Jade, who is supposed to be behind the bar, is sitting on the arm of his chair, leaning against the back instead. Her fingers rest on his shoulder.

Good thing it's a small group because the smirk on her face tells me she's found her home for the night. His hand absently trails up and down her thigh, clearly more interested in her than my introduction.

"That's Chase over there," Zane gestures lazily to a guy practically drooling over a redhead's routine. "Next to him is Jayce." Both men barely acknowledge the introduction, transfixed by the show.

"Ty's the quiet one," Colt adds, nodding toward a brooding figure in the corner who lifts his glass in silent greeting.

The last guy, sprawled on a leather chair, tears his eyes away from the dancers long enough to flash me a grin. "They call me Wolf," he says with an exaggerated wink, before being drawn back to the entertainment.

"Well, let me say I'm looking forward to serving you tonight." I turn and head towards the bar.

"Indeed."

I barely catch the word, but it makes me smile.

Chapter Twenty-Three

Sunny

T HE BASS-HEAVY THRUM OF music fills the lounge. I lean against the back counter of the bar, looking across the room and take a moment to let myself breathe. It's been hours and these guys don't show any signs of slowing down. It's going well. The girls are working their magic, the guys are having a great time and spending like crazy, and Jade couldn't be happier.

She's perched on the arm of Colt's chair, her fingers threading lazily through his hair as they talk. He's staring up at her like he's a starving man and she's his last meal.

A laugh slips out before I can stop it. Poor guy doesn't stand a chance. He has no idea what he's in for with her.

I wish all nights in the VIP were this easy.

I'll admit, when I first walked in and saw the perfect, tailored fit of these men's suits and the shine of their shoes, I expected arrogance. The usual rich-guy bullshit—ego trips and out of pocket demands. Instead, they're actually… fun. Friendly. But there's something else there too. Something right under the easy smiles and casual laughs. Something I recognized immediately. It's the potential for danger, for violence.

It's restrained and held tightly in check, but it's there. Sharp teeth and razor claws hidden just under the surface.

It *should* scare me. My instincts were honed by years of dealing with men who caused pain for no other reason than they could. But, these guys? They aren't tripping any of those wires for me.

The only exception is Zane.

He followed me from his spot on the couch when I went behind the bar and hasn't moved since. While the others are caught up in the action around them, Zane's been quiet, observant, keeping himself separate from it all. I don't think he's missed anything anyone's done or said all night. I know that's true for me. His attention to me has been deliberate, and focused. It's not creepy or leering or dangerous exactly—it's more thoughtful than anything—but, it's unnerving. And intense. And I don't think it's going to change anytime soon.

I grab a clean tray from under the bar and set it on the bar. I'm not here to analyze the customers. My job is to keep the drinks flowing and the room running smoothly and nothing more. And so far, I think I'm nailing it.

Even the times when I've made my way through the room, dropping off drinks and picking up glasses, I can feel Zane's eyes on me. It's like a cord tying us together, pulling tighter and tighter the more I try to ignore it.

"You do know there's a whole room full of sexy, topless women right behind you. You're missing out." I tease, my voice lilting as I glance at Zane and slide back behind the bar.

"I never miss anything," he replies, his tone low and even.

I chuckle, grabbing the bottle of tequila off the premium shelf and lining up glasses on the tray. "Hate to break it to you, but this is as exciting as it gets on my side of the room. I'm pretty sure you'd have more fun if you turned around."

"I don't think I would," he says, his ice blue eyes steady on mine.

The moment stretches out between us. He's definitely got my curiosity piqued. "So, tell me—what kind of guy spends the night in a private lounge full of beautiful women and decides to hang out with the bartender?"

"The kind of guy who can see that the bartender is easily the most incredible and beautiful woman in the room."

"Oooo. Love the confidence. A little on the cliché side though. I'll give it a solid C." I take one of the glasses off the tray and slide it across the bar to him with a chuckle.

"I'd bet though," I say as I lean in over the bar, "with those eyes and that smile, a line like that probably earns you an awful lot of A's."

"You wound me." He laughs as his hand flies to his chest, and lands over his heart. His fingers splay out, and there's a playful glint in his eyes. "It wasn't a line, only the truth. It did it's job though. I got you to smile, didn't I?"

"One," I say as I toss my hair and lift the tray of drinks. It settles on my arm and I let it balance before stepping out from behind the bar. "You got one."

As I move through the lounge, the tray balanced carefully, the room buzzes with life. Laughter rolls beneath the bassline, and the guys toast the dancers and each other with rowdy cheers.

I approach one of the tables, setting the tray down with a flourish.

"Alright, gentlemen. Who's ready for another round?"

The response is an instant mix of grins and laughter as they reach for the shots.

"Angel," one of the guys says, raising his glass to me. "You're the best baby."

I wink at him, flashing a playful grin. "You have no idea."

That earns me a solid round of catcalls.

"Alright, no excuses," I say. "Everyone drinks."

They all raise their glasses, toasting the dancers who reply with smirks and giggles, as they do a collective cheers and down the drinks.

I drag out the moment, letting myself enjoy it. Usually, my anxiety is through the roof when I have to work in here, and I end up staring at the clock waiting for my shift to be over. This is a nice change.

Once the tray is full again with all of the empties, I saunter back to the bar, my hips swaying in time to the music. When I set the tray down, Zane is waiting.

"You missed the cheers." I say as I set the tray down behind the bar and start cleaning up.

"I didn't miss it. I was waiting for you to join me."

His tone is confident and doesn't leave much room for me to refuse. It's not pushy, or demanding… just definite.

I laugh. "Thank you. I appreciate it. But, I'm on the clock. I've got a rule about drinking at work."

He arches his eyebrow and chuckles. "C'mon. It'll be our little secret. No one will ever know that Angel is really a rebel at heart. And you are. Deep down. I can see it."

It's irritating how charming he is. And that stupid, lopsided grin…

While it's not against the house rules, it's against *my* rules.

Without really understanding why, or letting myself give it too much thought, I grab a clean glass and pour. "Fine. I'll take one shot if you promise not to ask again or get any ideas. That's all you get. There are some rules I *never* break."

"Interesting." His smile is slow and smug. "I think that's a list I'd love to get a look at sometime though. Deal."

We lift the glasses, clink them together and swallow. The tequila burns its way down my throat and settles into my stomach. I slam the glass back down on the bar as the warmth of it starts spreading. I meet Zane's gaze head-on.

"You're good at this Angel," he says finally, his voice low and easy as he relaxed back. "Everyone's seems to be having the time of their lives."

I glance at him, my lips quirking. "That's the goal."

"So, tell me about the tattoo. It's beautiful."

The question catches me off guard. "It... I, uh."

I falter for half a second, barely a blink, but he catches it. It's not like no one ever asks. Usually I have an answer ready. This time it escapes me. My hand moves to rub gently at the place the ink starts, right above my collarbone.

"Must be one hell of a story," he says, leaning forward, resting his forearms on the bar.

"No, not really." I say, straightening and meeting his gaze with a tilt of my head. I can tell he's not going to leave it alone.

"It's pretty boring actually," I lie, before beginning the well-rehearsed story I've constructed out of half-truths. "There was this lake back where I grew up. It was the prettiest place you could imagine. There were always the most amazing wildflowers that bloomed in the fall…" My words drift off and I start to become lost in the memory.

"It's where I got my first real kiss." Now *that* wasn't a part of the story. Definitely not something I'd ever tell a complete stranger. *What the hell, Sunny?*

I suck in a deep breath and shake my head, chasing away the ghosts I woke up. "So, that's it. No real story. Boring actually."

Zane doesn't respond right away. He watches me like he's piecing something together, getting a peek under the surface, and for a moment, it leaves me feeling naked. It's uncomfortable and I don't like it.

"It *is* a good story," he says. "Not boring at all. I'm sorry it makes you sad. I shouldn't have asked."

I shift my weight, suddenly feeling self-conscious. "It doesn't—" I stop, reluctant to put another lie between us.

He adjusts in his seat and hands me his glass without a word, letting me off the hook.

I laugh despite myself, shaking my head as I gather the clean glasses from the back counter and get ready to pour another round of shots. "So, it's only fair. Tell me something about you."

Before he can respond, someone claps him on the shoulder—a solid thud that breaks whatever invisible thread was holding us together.

"Wolf," Zane mutters without looking, his jaw flexing.

"Damn, boss," Wolf says, sliding onto the stool next to him with an exaggerated sigh. "We spent a fortune to spend the night in a VIP lounge with all these gorgeous women, and you're over here brooding at the bar." He glances at me, his grin wide and teasing. "Not that I can blame you really."

I roll my eyes but can't help the small smirk tugging at my lips. "I told him the exact same thing."

Zane turns his head slowly, shooting Wolf a look that would send most people running. He just laughs, clapping him on the back again.

"Come on," Wolf says, jerking his head toward the group. "You've been sitting here all night. Time to stop being an unsociable dick and join the party."

Zane exhales a long, slow breath, his gaze flicking back to mine. For a moment, I think he's going to stay, to brush the guy off and keep this quiet, charged moment alive.

But then he stands, his movement slow and deliberate.

"Duty calls," he says quietly, his eyes still locked on mine. There's a flicker of something in his expression—reluctance, maybe—but he masks it quickly.

I shrug, keeping my tone light even as something inside me knots. "Don't let me keep you."

He holds my gaze for a heartbeat longer before turning and following Wolf to one of the tables with a stage where all the guys are sitting.

I should feel relieved. I should be glad for the interruption, glad for the space to breathe. Instead, I find my eyes drawn to him, tracking his every step across the room.

As he joins the group, he glances back once, catching me watching him.

I don't look away.
Neither does he.

Chapter Twenty-Four

Levi

THE MAPS SPREAD OUT in front of us tell a story of careful planning—property lines marked in blue, security checkpoints in red, potential weaknesses circled in yellow. Early morning sun filters through the office windows, highlighting the coffee cups that litter the polished, wooden desktop. None of these guys got more than a few hours of sleep after the club, but work doesn't wait.

Z looks as put together as he always does despite the late night, his black hair pulled back neatly, his T-shirt perfectly crisp and white. I'd swear the guy's part machine. Only the slight shadows under his eyes give away his fatigue.

"The security system needs a complete overhaul," Z says, tapping a spot on the blueprint. "Especially around the back entrance. Chase found three blind spots yesterday."

I lean over the desk, studying his precise handwriting in the margins. "Timeline?"

"Two weeks, maybe three. It depends on how fast we can get the equipment." He rolls his shoulders, a subtle tell of exhaustion. "The renovation crew starts on Monday in the east section of the house."

"Good." I straighten, catching the slight tremor in Z's hand as he reaches for his coffee. It's barely noticeable—anyone else would miss it. But I've known him too long. Something's off.

"So, you had Colt pull information on the club." It's not a question.

Z's expression doesn't change, but his pause before answering is a fraction too long. "Seemed worth looking into. The location alone makes it valuable."

"Since when do you care about territory?"

"Since you made this project a top priority." He meets my gaze steadily, but there's something new there, something I can't quite read. "It might be useful. At least worth checking out."

Before I can answer, Colt strides in, his designer sneakers silent on the hardwood floor, tablet in hand. He looks irritatingly fresh and even more put together than Z. You'd never know either of them had been up all night drinking. It's a little impressive.

"This better be important," Z says, scrubbing his face.

"Actually, yeah." Colt doesn't flinch. "Got that info on the club you asked for. Been there for over twenty years. Looks legit on the surface, but something wasn't adding up. So, I looked a little deeper. Tapped into their system and got a peek at their books. They're clean."

Z straightens, interest sparking in his eyes. "How clean?"

"Too clean." Colt swipes through several screens. "Perfect down to the penny for the past six years, and let me tell you, no business is that precise. Especially not a strip club dealing in cash and especially not in that part of town."

I watch Z's reaction more than the numbers. His brow is furrowed and I can see his mind working through what Colt is saying. Yep, something's definitely off. Z doesn't typically show this much interest in potential acquisitions. His focus is on the tactical, logistical side of our operation. He could care less about this side of things.

"Think the owner could be persuaded to sell?" I keep my tone casual.

Colt whistles low and soft. "It would cost. It's a solid business on the legit side. Place was packed last night. The guy's making a fortune."

"We should get eyes back in there." Z rolls his shoulders, a sign I've learned over the years means he's holding something back. "They're running some kind of side business through there."

"Could be worth a closer look," Colt adds, flopping down onto the leather couch and kicking his feet up. "We could always go back. Another night in the VIP might give us all the answers we need."

"Subtle, Colt." I arch an eyebrow at him. "That idea wouldn't have anything to do with that dancer I heard you couldn't take your hands off, right?"

His grin is shameless. "Jade? Man, she's something else." He sits up, suddenly animated. "It wasn't just me. Z, c'mon man. Back me up a little here. I know you'd love to go back and get another shot at that bartender."

I don't miss how Z's shoulders tense at the mention of the bartender, or how his eyes drop back to the blueprints without a lot of focus.

"I don't do strip clubs." The words come out harder than I intended. "If you think there's something worth investigating, take a team and go."

"Come on," Colt protests. "It's a nice place. You'd like it."

"I said no." The edge in my voice silences him. Only a slight over-reaction. I've never seen the point in strip clubs. Damn waste of money. Not that I'm above spending money for company. I've discovered over the years it's the easiest and best way to handle my needs. A simple transaction that doesn't mean anything.

Z sets down his coffee cup with deliberate care. "This isn't about the girls, Levi. If you're serious about getting us going here again, we need to start looking at already established operations we can get in to. It's easier and safer. You're looking at splitting up our team, cutting our man power in half until we can find more guys. It won't do us any good to fight for territory we can't defend. We need options like this."

Z's obviously given this more thought than I gave him credit for.

"That kind of accounting usually means someone's taking a lot of care to *not* raise any red flags. It could be a good opportunity for us. But, we need to know what we're dealing with."

"And you need me there because...?"

"Because you're the best at reading people," Colt jumps in. "And because you're starting to look like a hermit, man. When's the last time you went anywhere that wasn't work-related?"

"Fine." I straighten from where I'm leaning against Z's desk. "One night. We go in, you get your intel, and we're done."

"I'll let Wolf and his guys know." Colt's face splits into a grin. "We're going back in." His voice is a little too triumphant.

"And I'll make the arrangements." Z is already reaching for his phone, but I catch the slight uptick at the corner of his mouth. "Same private room as last night?"

"Whatever." I head for the door, already regretting this decision. "I just want to make it clear that this is business."

"Of course." Z's voice follows me out. "I'll request the same girls. For consistency."

Consistency. Right.

I pause in the doorway, glancing back at my two closest friends. Colt's practically bouncing as he texts, probably already making plans with Jade. And Z? His expression is guarded as he makes the call, but his fingers drum against the desk anxiously. In all the years I've known him, it's something I've never seen him do before.

Something's definitely up. With both of them.

CHAPTER Twenty-Five

Sunny

THE PHONE BUZZES, VIBRATING across the nightstand, and I groan, fumbling to answer it. Just seeing Benny's name on the screen is enough to set my nerves on edge. He of all people should know that there's no way I'd be up this early. Can't the man give me a break?

"Afternoon Benny," I say, mustering up a chipper tone, though my body is still craving sleep.

"Angel, darling, you're something else. You know that?" His voice is bright and enthusiastic, which is rare enough that it actually wakes me up a little. "You crushed it last night. I don't know what you did, but they loved you. *A lot.* They left you a real nice thank-you gift. Wanna guess?"

I yawn and stretch, not really in the mood to play games. I want to get back to sleep. "C'mon Benny, it's too early for games."

"Fine, fine, fine. You'd never guess anyway."

There's a brief pause, and I huff, irritated. "Ben-ny," I say, covering a yawn.

"Ten grand." When I don't say anything, Benny repeats himself. "Did you hear me, Angel. I said they left you ten grand. I mean they tipped everyone over the top, a lot more than average, but you..."

"What?" I blink, and sit up in bed, speechless. I mean, I know I'm good at my job, but seriously?

"You heard me right, doll. Ten. Thousand. Dollars. Cash." He's doing his best to sound casual, but there's no hiding the excitement in his voice. "And to top it off, I've got that guy Zane on the phone. They want to come back again tonight. Said the big boss wants to check out the club. He's practically begging me to make sure you'll be there. Doubled the fee for the room if I can make it happen."

His voice turns sheepish, cautious. "Now look, I know I said this morning when you were leaving that you could take the next couple days off, but I told them I'd see what I could do." He pauses only long enough to catch his breath. "So, you in? Same deal as last night."

A flicker of uncertainty crossing my mind. A VIP repeat with the same men as last night. Plus one. To be honest it wasn't *horrible*. But ten grand? I can't help but wonder what they're expecting in return—what *Zane* is expecting in return. That's some serious cash, especially if they tipped out everyone even half as well.

I'd be an idiot to turn it down. "Yeah," I say slowly, rubbing the back of my neck. "Alright, I'll do it. I'll be there." And then as an afterthought, "But I want Jake and Eddie at the door again."

"You got it!" Benny's voice booms with satisfaction. "Trust me, sweetheart, just go in there tonight and do whatever it was you did last night. I'll go over all the rules again with them and make sure they understand that the only thing you or any of the girls owe them is a full glass and a couple laughs. That's it."

I roll my eyes even though he can't see it. "Yeah, sure, Benny. I'll be there by seven. See you later."

Hanging up, I find myself with a strange twinge of anticipation under the thin layer of nerves. Last night with those guys was…

different. Zane, Z, kept it interesting. Maybe tonight will go just as smooth.

I wake up late and decide to get ready at home. This is the busiest time in the dressing room and I don't feel like fighting for a spot. After my shower I decide it might be fun to amp it up a little. I unzip a garment bag hanging in the closet and take out my newest dress—a virgin white satin number that's really nothing more than a couple scraps of material held together by a few delicate gold chains at the neck and sides. It was way more expensive than it should've been and it barely covers anything, but I love the way it shows off my tattoo.

Once I'm dressed, I throw on a baggy hoodie that comes almost down to my knees, grab my backpack and heels and head out, feeling a small buzz of excitement start. It's probably just the thought of that ridiculous tip, but still—it's been a minute since I've had anything to look forward to. By the time I walk in through the back entrance, the club is already ramping up for the night.

"Angel, honey!" Jade's voice rings out as soon as she sees me step into the dressing room. She makes her way over, a wide grin lighting up her face. "I'm so glad you decided to come in tonight! Last night was amazing! I heard about your nice little parting gift. I knew you were killing it."

I laugh, rolling my eyes. "Yeah, well, you had a lot to do with it. It wouldn't have gone half as well without you."

Jade smirks. "Maybe. I mean, I didn't do much really. I was kind of distracted. My tip was nothing to complain about, but girl, yours was on a whole other level." She nudges me, her green eyes sparkling. "It's you and me tonight again."

I can't help but laugh, the last bit of nerves melting away. "Thank God. We make a good team. I actually didn't mind last night though, it was kinda fun."

"Yeah? It looked like you were enjoying the company. Z, right? He seemed pretty into you, and it looked, from where I was sitting, that the feeling might've been a little mutual," Jade says with a wink. "Don't think I didn't see you take that shot."

I offer up a guilty shrug. She follows me over to my locker and takes a seat on the bench. I open the door and toss the bag in before pulling the hoodie over my head. I toss my head shaking out my hair and adjust my dress. "I know you—"

"Holy hell." Jade looks up at me, her eyes wide with appreciation. "That is some dress."

"You like?" I do a small twirl, laughing at the low whistle she gives me. "Here let me get that for you," I say bending down and pretending to wipe a little drool from the side of her mouth.

Jade watches as I finish slipping into my heels. "Girl, between the two of us, they won't know what hit 'em."

When we step out of the dressing room into the hallway, we stop in front of the mirror just outside the door. She nods approvingly at our reflection. Her dark spiky hair, black leather corset, fishnets and thigh high boots are a perfect contrast to my long blonde, ribbon-tied hair, white satin dress, and stilettos. We definitely make an impression.

Together, we take our time making our way across the club, enjoying the comments and looks of appreciation. Talk about a confidence booster. I don't know about Jade, but on nights like tonight when it all comes together and seems to work, I feel... powerful.

When we reach the VIP entrance, Jade takes a moment and adjusts the top of her boots. I adjust the ribbon in my hair, and smooth down the front of my dress. Jade glances at me, and we share a little nod, both of us pulling our shoulders back and lifting our chins slightly.

Jake and Eddie are standing outside the doors again, and I say a silent 'thank you' to Benny. They do a double take as we approach and Eddie pulls the door open for us. We walk through arm and arm, striding in with swagger and confidence. The lounge is already high energy. Each one of the guys from last night is lounging in one of the plush leather chairs or stretched out along one of the sleek couches.

They already have a drink in hand and there seem to be a couple more dancers in here than there was last night. It's the perfect start to the night,

Jade flashes her best million-watt smile. "Gentlemen," she drawls, her voice full of silk and honey, "hope you saved some energy for us."

All eyes turn to take us in. We both bask in the attention, enjoying the stunned expressions. I let go of Jade's arm, kiss her on the cheek and turn to go and take my place behind the bar. I'm not too surprised to see Zane already seated there, instead of sitting with his friends. He stands and watches me cross the room towards him.

"And here I thought there was no way you could ever look more beautiful than you did last night." Zane says once I'm in front of him.

I laugh, feeling a little of the tension drain away. "Even more charming the second time around, I see."

I step around the back of the bar, but I can feel his gaze follow me. "I'm glad you decided to come tonight, Angel. I was hoping you'd be here."

Moving around to the back of the bar, I start double checking to make sure everything is stocked the way it should be for the night. "Well, what can I say. You made me an offer I couldn't refuse." I chuckle as I reach for his glass. "That was, uh, quite the gift you left for me. Thank you."

"It was from all of us. But, there's no need to say thank you. Last night was exactly what we needed. Honestly, it was less than what you deserve."

A comfortable silence falls between us as we both watch the scene in the lounge. Everyone does seem to be enjoying themselves again tonight and it seems to be a bit more relaxed than it was last night. Most of the same girls are back, dancing and socializing. Jade is firmly planted on the edge of Colt's chair, and while I can't hear what she's whispering to him, I can see it's enough to make him need to adjust his position. More than once. I laugh out loud when she pats him on the head. It seems that Zane isn't the only one with a favorite.

I excuse myself, making my rounds around the room, collecting drink orders, ensuring everyone is comfortable and happy. Zane sticks to his spot at the bar though. His attention seems to be for me, and me alone. His eyes follow me, tracking my every movement. It should be disturbing, being watched like this, but I'm enjoying it. At least as much I did last night, if not more.

Satisfied I've got things handled, I circle back toward the bar. The connection between Zane and I is back, subtle but solid. I'm trying not to let it get to me. He's leaning on the bar, nursing the drink in front of him with that easy grin tugging at the corner of his mouth.

I reach for a clean glass and a bottle and Zane starts talking—telling me a story about the first time he ever got drunk, and it pulls me in immediately. He's quicker, funnier, and sharper than I gave him credit for. Before long, I'm laughing without even thinking about it.

I'm busy pulling glasses from under the bar when I hear Zane let out a deep chuckle behind me.

"Hey man! I'm glad you're finally here. We were all starting to think you changed your mind."

There's a pause and hearty laugh. "Yeah, you all look like you're missing me. Can't live without me." I hear the distinct sound of metal scraping on the floor as one of the barstools is pulled out. "So, where is she? Where is this girl? Anyone who can get that kind of reaction outta you is worth meeting."

I smile, feeling my face color slightly as I pretend I didn't hear what I just heard from under the counter.

Zane laughs. "Smooth, man. Real smooth. Thanks a lot. She, um, she's right behind you."

I stand and look up from what I'm doing to see Zane smiling at me sheepishly. The man he was talking to has his back to me, his focus directed towards the center of the room.

"Oh." There's a long pause, and a whispered, "Sorry man," as he turns around.

I look up, with my sweetest, brightest smile ready to greet him. When his eyes land on me, the rest of whatever he was going to say, dies in his throat, and the color drains from his face.

The seconds stretch out into a long, excruciating silence. My eyes stay locked on his. Perfect, endless pools of deep green that I've spent the past seven years trying to forget. Seven years of pretending I couldn't still see them every time I closed my eyes.

"Angel?" He chokes the two syllables out in a barely-there whisper.

His face is harder now, more mature, more angular. More beautiful. The scattered freckles across his nose have faded slightly. The small jagged white scar on his chin he got during his first football game when he was eight still stands out.

It's a face I still know by heart. I know exactly how his skin would feel under my fingertips if I were to reach out and touch him.

My breath is shallow, and I can feel the blood drain from my own face. I stumble back, dizzy, grabbing at the counter behind me for balance as my entire world spins off it's axis. Those gorgeous, brilliant eyes that used to look at me with fierce love and absolute devotion are now staring at me in stunned disbelief and shock. And horror. Mostly horror.

Levi.

I'm rooted to the spot I'm standing in, trapped like a bug—pinned by his gaze, and it's like the entire room has been stripped away—the music, the people, even the lights—all of it disappears, and it's just us. Me and him.

…That's what I said. You. Me. We….

My heart thunders painfully in my chest, like it's trying to claw its way out. My body feels too heavy to move. The air is thick and suffocating and I can't breathe.

Levi's hand falls away from Zane's shoulder and he takes a step back, knocking over the barstool next to him. His eyes stay locked on mine, unblinking.

"Sunny?" he breathes the name I haven't heard out loud for years. The name I never wanted to hear again. He says it the way I remember him always saying it, like he's reciting a prayer.

My throat closes up, and all I can do is nod, and stand there with tears blurring my vision as the reality of him standing here in front of me, crashes down and threatens to drown me. Everything I've tried so hard to forget for so long comes rushing back. I remember it all—the sweet words, the gentle kisses, the promises. The love. I take a shallow, shaky breath.

I start to tremble as his arm reaches out for me across the bar. There's a haunted look in his eyes that squeezes my heart. My hand lifts in response, reaching out for him the way it used to. The moment our fingers touch, a piece of something inside of me breaks wide open.

I'm crushed under the weight of remembering—overwhelmed by the memory of his leaving—every broken promise, every lie, every tear and every scar. It's too much. The pain is devastating as it barrels over me, and before he has a chance to say anything, I back away, yanking my hand out of reach.

"What the fuck?" Zane's voice is confused and concerned as he looks from me to Levi and back to me again. His voice cuts through the haze and pulls me back into the present. "Angel? What's wrong? Are you okay?"

I shake my head, but can't look up at him. I am definitely not okay. I have never been less okay. I want to scream it into his face, but I can't. The words are stuck in my throat. I'm frozen in place and I'm not even sure I'm breathing anymore. My fingers shake uncontrollably, and I lose my grip on the bottle I'm holding. It falls to the floor and shatters. The sound is deafening in the silence that's formed around us.

My body moves before my mind can catch up. I turn on my heel and break for the door. Each step I take vibrates through me and I feel as if I might shatter, but I can't stop. I have to get out of here—away from the heaviness of his stare. Away from the memories threatening to swallow me, destroy me.

The door is within reach when I glance back. Levi hasn't moved. He's standing frozen at the edge of the bar, his face a mask of unbearable pain and something impossibly worse. It makes my chest ache in ways I thought I'd never feel again.

Our eyes meet, and the air between us turns electric. My legs nearly buckle, but I force them to keep moving. I push through the door, stumbling out, my heart pounding in my ears. I need out.

I can't look back again. If I do, I know it will break me.

But before the door swings shut, I hear it—strangled words, broken and raw—ripped from somewhere deep inside of him.

"Sunny! Please!"

The sound follows me, as I run.

Chapter Twenty-Six

Levi

My world stops the moment I see her face.

Seven years of carefully constructed reality splinters in the space between heartbeats leaving me breathless. The bass from the speakers thuds against my skull, but I can't hear it over the roaring in my ears. Because she's standing right here. In front of me. Breathing. Whole. *Alive.*

My hands find the bar's edge, gripping it until my knuckles turn white. The polished wooden surface is the only solid thing left in a world that's suddenly liquid, unstable.

Angel. The nickname I gave her that day under the tree. The day everything started. The day I set us both on this path.

The room tilts dangerously as she bolts. "Sunny! Please!" The words tear from my throat, but she's already gone. It's too late.

Please come back. Please come back. The words echo through my head, a desperate prayer to a god I stopped believing in the night I found her broken body on her bedroom floor. Except she wasn't dead. She wasn't fucking dead.

The truth slams into me, burying me under its weight. Every kill I've ordered, every drop of blood I've spilled, every brick of the empire I've built – all of it was founded on her death. On justice. On vengeance.

My chest constricts, lungs forgetting how to pull in air. The core memory I've spent years trying to forget claws its way to the surface—her blood on my hands, the weight of her limp body in my arms, forcing myself to walk away. I left instead of checking one more time. One more fucking time.

The watching crowd blurs at the edges of my vision. My men's confused murmurs mix with the whispers of the dancers, creating a suffocating cocoon of sound. No one moves. They're all caught in this moment, watching me fall apart under the weight of a truth too heavy to bear.

I feel Zane's presence before I see him—his stare burning into me as he moves closer. Seven years of brotherhood built on a foundation of lies. His eyes dart between me and the door where Sunny disappeared.

"Levi." The way he says my name is careful, measured, like he's talking to an injured, cornered animal. "What the fuck just happened?"

A broken, strangled laugh escapes from my throat. "That was Sunny." Her name cuts like shards of glass after all this time. "My Sunny."

"Your Sunny?" Wolf's voice sounds distant, confused. "But she—"

"I thought she was dead." The words rip out of me. My grip on control keeps slipping, unleashing memories I've fought for years to keep buried. "This isn't possible."

The room falls dead quiet. Seven years of unquestioning loyalty hang in the balance as my men watch their leader come apart at the seams. I can feel their eyes on me but I can't look at them. Can't face the questions I know are forming.

"You need to explain." Colt's voice cuts through the silence. "Now."

But there aren't any explanations that will make this right. No words that can justify seven years of revenge built on half-truths.

My voice, when it finally comes, is cracked.

"I found her that night." Each word feels like confession and condemnation both.

"There was so much blood. She wasn't breathing. No pulse." The memory slams into me like a physical blow. "I checked. I fucking *checked*."

The edge of the bar is the only thing keeping me upright as the room spins out. Words I've never said to anyone but myself pour out of my mouth. "It was my fault. I should've been there to stop him—"

I cut myself off, but it's too late. The images flood in, impossible to stop. The black dress I bought her shredded and soaked with blood. Purple-black bruises mapping a world of violence across her skin. Deep slashes carved into her pale white flesh. I squeeze my eyes shut but the images stay.

"What do you mean, you were there?" Zane's voice could cut glass.

The coldness in his eyes tells me he's already piecing it together. There's no taking it back now, no way to stuff this truth back in the tidy little box I constructed for it. It's all starting to crumble like sand.

These men—my brothers—they've only ever heard the sanitized version of what happened. I fed them lies because I couldn't face the truth. It took me years to bury the worst of that night, transform it into something I could live with—a version that didn't make me want to put a bullet in my head every time I closed my eyes.

But now...

"I need to find her." My voice is heavy with grief. "Right fucking now."

The room closes in, air turning thick and heavy. Bile rises, burning my throat making me feel sick. One of the girls breaks for the door.

Her heels strike the floor like gunshots as she runs. Colt's right behind her, his worried voice calling after her.

"Jade, wait!"

The door slams behind them, and somehow their absence makes the weight of truth even heavier.

"You were there?" Zane grabs my arms, holding me in place. His voice cuts like a blade, his eyes boring into mine. "But you said... What else are you lying about?"

I meet his stare, feeling something vital crack in my chest. "Zane—"

My voice sounds foreign, distant over the ringing in my ears. "I owe you answers. All of you. But not here. Not now."

"Not here?" Zane advances, rage rolling off him in waves. "Not *now*? We've gone through hell with you. *For* you. Seven years, Levi. Seven fucking years we've bled for you, killed for you, bought into your bullshit. And now we find out it was all lies?" His voice splinters on the last word, betrayal bleeding through the anger.

His accusation hits me hard. I flinch, nails breaking skin as I clench my fists, fighting to maintain control. "I thought she was dead, Zane," I force out through gritted teeth.

"I thought—" The words die in my throat. "I can't do this right now."

"Yeah, you can." He steps closer, fury radiating off him. "You don't get to drop this on us and walk away."

"I'm not walking away," I snarl, my tone sharp enough to make him pause. "But I need to find her. Right *fucking* now, Z. *Please.*"

His jaw locks as he searches my face, looking for something—remorse maybe, or a reason not to swing. Whatever he finds makes him step back, but the rage doesn't leave his eyes. "Fine," he spits, ice in his voice. "But when you're done? Every last detail, Levi. No more lies."

The challenge hangs between us. Without another word, I push past him and through the door. The bouncers don't try to stop me as

I make my way through the club, following a couple dancers down a dark hallway. My heart hammers against my ribs as I spot what I'm looking for—a heavy metal door with a glowing exit sign.

The night air hits me like a slap in the face when I burst into the alley. Cold enough to drag me back from the edge I've been teetering on. I scan the shadows but there's nothing. Just the muffled thump of bass from inside.

I make it halfway across the parking lot before reality stops me cold.

Seven years. Seven years I've built an empire on vengeance, dedicated every breath to hunting down her killer. And not once—not *once*—did I go back to Easton Creek. Couldn't face visiting the graves of the two women I loved most. One visit would have shown me the truth. But I was too much of a fucking coward.

My fists clench until they shake. Has she spent all this time thinking I abandoned her? That I never showed up that night? Or worse—that I found her bleeding out and just walked away? She has no idea how much she meant to me. Still means to me.

I check every car, but I already know. She's gone. Again. I've lost her again. But this time—this time I can fix it. I have to.

I storm back into the club, tearing through hallways, throwing open doors until I reach the dressing room. Startled screams greet me as I burst in, only to find myself face-to-face with a wall of muscle blocking my path.

"*Enough.*"

The voice is calm but deadly serious. Benny—the club owner I spent some time talking to earlier. He seemed reasonable enough then, but now he's planted in front of me like a wall, flanked by the two VIP bouncers. His command hangs in the air, absolute and non-negotiable.

"She was here. Angel was here." I plead. "You have to tell me where she is."

Benny's eyes turn to steel. "I don't *have* to tell you shit. Even if I knew where she was, hell would freeze over before I'd tell you. You're done here." He doesn't flinch as he nods to the bouncers, who close ranks, cutting me off from the dressing room completely.

"You don't understand—" I start, but my words crash against his resolve like waves on concrete.

"Oh, I understand *plenty*." Benny's voice slices through mine.

"When I met Angel, she was a goddamned mess. Half-starved, scared of her own shadow, fresh out of the hospital." His lip curls in disgust. "Running from *someone* who'd beaten her half to death. Now you show up, ripping through my club like a fucking maniac. I don't know if you're the one who did that to her, and I don't care. You're not getting anywhere near her. If you come within twenty feet of her again, it won't be because anyone here helped you. We clear?"

"She's mine." The words escape before I can stop them, rough and primal. Despair claws its way up my throat, but Benny's expression doesn't waver.

"Maybe you think that's true. What I know is Angel's fought like hell to put whatever happened behind her. She doesn't need you showing up and dragging her back down into it. Don't come back here." His voice drops to deep in his throat. "Leave. Now."

The bouncers move in, and for the first time in years, I let someone else dictate my actions. They escort me out the back entrance, shoving me into the cool night air.

She's alive. She was here. And just like that, she's gone again.

And there's not a damn thing I can do about it right now.

Chapter Twenty-Seven

Levi

My hands won't stop shaking.

Sunny's alive. Up until an hour ago, I would've thought that was impossible.

There hasn't been even one second, in all these years, I've doubted what I saw or felt that night. I'd been so positive. So sure that she'd been taken away from me.

Everything I've built. Everything I've created. All of it was for her. An attempt to balance the scales. To make at least one part of it right somehow. And this whole time…

Angel. The fact that she's been using the nickname I gave her, a memory from the first day we met, to hide behind all this time makes me want to put my fist through something.

The drive back to the safehouse is endless, each mile dragging. Colt and Z are behind me in their own cars. They deserve answers. They deserve the whole truth. Even the parts I don't know if I'm ready to face again.

That truth feels destructive. Like it's waiting to tear apart everything we've built.

When we pull into the gravel drive, our crew takes one look at Z's face and vanishes. Smart.

I stalk into the dark house, my body humming with the need to break something, to hurt something. To make something on the outside match the chaos ripping through me. My fist clenches, aching to put it through the nearest wall, but I force myself to the bar instead. Seven years of trying to maintain control, of waiting, of planning—I won't let myself slip now. Not even for this.

The whiskey bottle is steady in my grip even though nothing else about me is. The first shot burns as it goes down, but it doesn't come close to matching the acid that's already burning a hole in my gut. The glass hits the wooden surface too hard when I set it down, the sharp crack echoing in the dark.

"Start talking."

Z's voice comes from the shadows. He doesn't move from where he's standing in the door frame, arms crossed, but there's violence in his stillness. Those ice-blue eyes of his cut through the darkness and lock onto mine.

I've seen that look on his face before, plenty of times. I never thought I'd see it aimed at me.

"That night was the worst night of my life. I found her covered in blood, Z." My voice comes out steady, rehearsed. "No pulse. I called 911 and—"

"And what?" Zane steps into the room and flips on the lights, his movement fluid, predatory. Colt follows behind him.

"You dialed the phone and walked away? Didn't you wait for the ambulance? For the cops? Please tell me you waited. Tell me you weren't that stupid."

"I couldn't stay!" The reasoning, the certainty that I've clung to for the past seven years starts to crack. "My mother was dead. Garrett killed her that same night. I had to—"

"Had to what?" Colt rises, his usual warmth gone.

"She was dead." But the words aren't true. I thought they were but they're not. They sound different now.

"No, she wasn't. You realize what that means right? That, you left her there to die. Alone." Z's voice is frigid. "The girl you supposedly loved."

"I did… I do love her! I was barely eighteen! Cut me some slack!" The defense sounds hollow, ridiculous even to me. "I'd just found my mother murdered, and Sunny—" Her name catches like barbed wire in my throat.

"You weren't there. You didn't see her, how still she was, all the blood—" I close my eyes against the memory.

"I couldn't protect either of them. I failed."

"To say the least." Colt's quiet agreement cuts deep. "And then you lied to us about it."

"The threat was real." I grip the bar's edge, anchoring myself to this one truth. "None of this changes that. Garrett killed my mother. He tried to murder Sunny."

"Tried." Z steps closer. "She survived what he did. Survived being left for dead. By you."

The truth of it hits even harder spoken out loud. "I know."

"Know what?" Colt presses. "That you're a coward?"

Something snaps. I'm in Colt's face before I realize I've moved. "You think I don't know exactly what I am? You think I don't live with it every fucking day?"

"Back off." Z's grip on my shoulder is iron, yanking me away from Colt.

I wrench free, my words a low hiss. "Don't touch me."

"Or what?" Z's eyes are cold, emotionless, daring me to give him a reason.

"Everything I've done since that night has been about finding Garrett," I snarl. "About making him pay for what he did. To my mother, to Sunny."

"Sunny's alive!" Colt shouts. "She's been alive this whole time, a few hundred miles away, right under your nose! While we've been running ops and cracking skulls, she's been right here!"

The reminder that she's been so close, living as Angel makes my head spin. "I didn't know."

"That's your excuse for everything, isn't it? That's not going to cut it." Zane's contempt is palpable. "What else don't we know, Levi?"

The question hangs in the air between us. Seven years of partnership, of brotherhood, threatening to break under the weight of these stupid lies.

"Tell us everything," Colt says. "No more bullshit. No more half-truths. Everything."

"Fine. No more lies." I pour another whiskey, not sure I can get through this without it. "That night... I was supposed to be with her. It was her birthday. Her 18th."

"But you weren't," Zane prompts when I pause.

"No." Shame competes with guilt as I continue. "There was this asshole. Zack. He'd made it his mission to make her life miserable. He'd been threatening her, stalking her, pissing me off. I came up with a plan to get rid of him. Teach him a lesson." I laugh bitterly.

"That's where I was. That's what I was doing when…" I hang my head. "I was running late. I was supposed to be back, but I wasn't. When I got there, Garrett had already been there and left."

The memory of finding her, broken and bleeding, threatens to drown me. I grip the glass harder. "It was too late when I got there. Or I thought it was. Z. Colt. You have to believe me. It was bad. You know we've seen a lot. Done a lot. I've never seen anything that even comes close to what he did to her."

I drain the whiskey, my hands shaking as I set down the glass. Colt's question hangs in the air between us, the one I've dreaded. The one I'd managed to push into the back of my mind and bury.

"Why would Garrett go after them in the first place?" Colt's voice is calm but insistent. "It sounds like he waited. Like it was personal, not random like you said. There's more to the story. There has to be. I can see it."

I can barely breathe through the heaviness of my guilt. "You're right."

"Then tell us." Zane's eyes bore into me. "All of it."

"The first day I met Sunny..." My voice cracks. I clear my throat and try again. "That first day… I found her crying in her backyard. She was beaten, bruised. Garrett had—" I clench my fists. "He'd hurt her. Badly. And when he came outside looking for her, drunk and talking about how she needed to come back inside with him... I lost it."

The memory of that day floods back, crystal clear. "I knocked him down the stairs. Broke his ribs, his leg. Could've killed him. Should've killed him."

"Jesus," Colt mutters.

"I thought I'd handled it. Thought I'd scared him enough to stay away." A disgusted laugh escapes me. "I was so fucking young and stupid. All I did was paint a target on our backs."

I start pacing, unable to stay still. "After that, all he had to do was wait for the perfect time to get even. He must've had eyes on us. Following her. Following me. I wouldn't have noticed, I was too wrapped up in her. I was so proud of myself for saving her and protecting her."

"There's no way you thought that would be it," Zane says. It's not a question.

"Yeah." The words are acid on my tongue. "I think a part of me knew that someone like Garrett wouldn't spook that easily. I knew, I just chose to pretend I didn't. I loved her so much."

"What about your mom?" Colt asks. "How'd she get involved?"

My throat closes. I have to force the words out. "Mom? She wasn't involved at all. She'd only met Sunny a few times and I'm pretty sure she'd never met Garrett. I think he used her as another way to get to me. To take something away from me and hurt me."

"Shit," Zane breathes.

"She spent her whole life telling me that I needed to pay attention. That I was too much like my father and that nothing good would ever come of it. But I wouldn't listen. Thought I knew better. Thought I could handle anything."

I grab the whiskey bottle, pouring another shot with trembling hands. "Every single thing that happened after that first day—it's all on me. *My* choices. *My* arrogance. Thinking I could do that kinda damage to someone like him and there wouldn't be consequences."

"So, that night..." Colt prompts.

"I left her alone." The words come out forced. "Left her vulnerable because I was off dealing with Zack. I told myself I was doing it for her, which is only partially true. I was doing it mostly for me. I couldn't stand what he was putting her through. And Garrett..." I down the whiskey, needing its burn. "He was smart. He went after my mom first. Made sure I'd find her. He went for Sunny while I was distracted."

The silence in the room is deafening. I can feel their eyes on me, processing the weight of my confession.

"All these years," I continue, my voice barely above a whisper, "I've told myself I was seeking justice. Revenge. But the truth is, everything that happened to them—to my mom, to Sunny – it all traces back to that first day. To me thinking I could fix everything. I didn't see the bigger picture until it was too late."

"Levi..." Colt starts. His voice is sympathetic, soothing.

"Don't." I hold up a hand. "Don't try to make this better. You wanted the truth? This is it. I got my mother killed. I left the girl I loved to die alone because I couldn't face the damage I'd caused. And then I dragged you both into my vendetta, built a whole life on lies because I couldn't admit the truth—that all of this, every bit of it, is my fault."

The silence in the room is heavy, oppressive. I watch Z's jaw clench and unclench, his hands flexing at his sides like he's fighting the urge to hit something. Hit me. Can't say I'd blame him if he did.

Colt sits back down on the couch, running his hands through his hair. His expression is softer than Z's, but no less troubled.

"Look," I say, my voice rough. "I know I fucked up. Not just that night, but every day since. Lying to you both, using your loyalty for my own agenda..."

"We trusted you." Z's voice is sharp. "I've been willing to follow you to hell and back. And the whole time—"

"The whole time I was too much of a coward to tell you the truth." I meet his burning gaze. "You're right. I betrayed that trust. With both of you."

Colt leans forward, elbows on his knees and lets out a deep sigh. "We were kids back then, man. All of us. Making shit decisions, thinking we were invincible—"

Z whirls on him. "Don't make excuses for him."

"I'm not." Colt holds up his hands. "But I get it. The panic, the guilt..."

"You're a coward," Z says through gritted teeth.

"You're right. I couldn't face any of it. Not what happened to my mom, not what I'd let happen to Sunny... It was easier to focus on revenge."

"And now?" Colt asks.

I laugh, but there's no humor in it. "Now? Now I have to live with knowing she survived. That while I was out here playing vigilante, she was trying to survive. Alone."

"Because you ran," Z corrects.

"Because I ran," I agree. "I know I don't deserve forgiveness. From either of you. From her. Hell, I don't even have the right to ask for it."

Z pushes off the wall, stalking toward the door. "No. You don't."

"Z..." Colt starts.

"Don't." Z turns back, his voice cold as he speaks. "You want to stick around, that's your choice. But I need to get out of here before I do something we'll all regret."

He storms out of the room. Slamming the door when he leaves with enough force to rattle the windows. I close my eyes, feeling like I'm watching one more important thing slip through my fingers.

"He'll come around," Colt offers.

"He shouldn't." I pour another drink with shaking hands. "Neither should you."

"Maybe. Maybe not." Colt stands, crossing to the bar. "But it's my choice."

I look at him, stunned. "After everything I've done? All the lies?"

"Yeah." He takes the bottle from my hand, pouring his own drink. "Because under all that bullshit, you're still my brother. That counts for something."

"It shouldn't." My voice is barely a whisper. "Not after this."

"Well, tough shit." Colt downs his whiskey. "Because it does. Z will figure that out too. He just needs to calm down."

I shake my head. "I don't think so Colt. I don't think this can be fixed."

He sets down his glass. "Time will tell, brother."

He's right. I've got nothing but time now.

Chapter Twenty-Eight

Sunny

My apartment is quiet and still, except for the muted sounds of evening traffic filtering through the thin walls and windows. It's comforting—that dull hum of life happening somewhere else, somewhere far away from me. I haven't left my bed in days, and honestly, I don't care if I ever do again.

My whole body feels like I got hit by a truck. I'd sooner die than let anyone know just how wrecked I am though. I spent so damn long building up this badass image, convincing myself and everyone around me that I'm untouchable. But seeing Levi again? Yeah, that did it. Apparently, I'm not as unbreakable as I've been pretending to be.

I press a hand to my chest covering the spot where the ache has been constant. It feels permanent. The part of me that was wrenched backwards, straight into the past can't seem to find its way back. I'm lost there. Images of Levi, standing there with his hand on Zane's shoulder like it was the most natural thing in the world, are there constantly. His eyes—the ones that I spent so much time trying to forget—looked like he'd seen a ghost when he saw me.

His expression had been shock at first. But that hadn't lasted. He'd been horrified when he realized it was me. It was written all over his face. It was clear that I was the last person he expected to see, and, more importantly, the last person he *wanted* to see. Seeing that expression on his face was almost worse than being left by him in the first place. It's all I can do to remember to breathe and let the minutes crawl by without drowning in them.

He's been trying to find me. I know because Benny told me he's had to kick him out of the club almost every night. Sometimes more than once. My phone buzzes for what's probably the hundredth time today, but I ignore it. It has to be Jade, or Benny. No one else knows my number.

Jade stopped by once. A few days ago, I think. She banged and kicked on the door until I finally answered—more to avoid someone calling the cops than because I wanted to see her. She'd barely gotten a glimpse inside my apartment before I shoved her out, promising her I'd eat, that I was fine, and that I just needed a little more sleep. Not one of those things was true and she knew it as well as I did. I simply wanted her gone. I need to be alone.

With a shuddering sigh, I turn over, burying my face into the pillow. Maybe if I close my eyes tight enough, I can block out everything and if I do that maybe, eventually, it'll all go away. The memories, the worry in Jade's voice, even the buzzing phone. Everything.

But I can't seem to get my mind on board with the plan. Every time I close my eyes I go back to that night with Garrett—the soft material of the dress on my skin when I put it on, the scrape of heavy boots on the floor, the sharp crack of bones breaking, and the feel of cold metal. I wake up shivering and sweaty, clenching my teeth around a scream. I flail, reaching out and expecting to feel the sticky, wet, heat of blood covering my skin. But there's nothing. Nothing but scars.

I wish that the memories of Garrett are the worst. I wish those were as bad as it gets. But they aren't what stick around and drag all of the things I feel up to the surface and into the light. They aren't the ones that threaten to break me apart and erase who I am. Nothing Garrett did to me was worse than being left on that floor by Levi—worse than knowing I didn't matter enough to try and save.

It's late afternoon, and I'm exhausted, drifting in a warm, soft place somewhere between sleep and waking. A loud, insistent, sudden knock on the door, forces me to drag myself up from the bed, my limbs heavy, my thoughts cloudy. It's probably Jade again—worried enough to come over and yell at me, which honestly, I deserve.

I shuffle toward the door, not bothering to check the peephole, already preparing for the scolding I know is coming. I swing the door open wide, irritation at the ready.

"Alright, Jade, I swear if you—"

But it's not Jade.

It's Zane, leaning casually against the doorframe, hands tucked into his jacket pockets. The easy grin I've seen on his face is dimmed, his gaze soft, but serious. He doesn't bother to hide the way he looks me over, taking in everything. I know I'm a disaster—I'm sure it's obvious in my face, and in my knotted, greasy hair and the clothes I haven't had the energy to change in… days, I think.

"So, sleeping in, huh?" he murmurs, his voice low and somehow gentler than I'm expecting. There's a beat where I think I could just slam the door shut, pretend he never showed up here in the first place. But I can't seem to summon the energy to care enough to even try. I sag against the edge of the door instead, fingers curled around it.

"How did you find me?" I ask. I go still.

"Jade. She came to visit Colt at the house. She's worried about you, you know." He gives a small, almost shy shrug, scratching the back of his head.

"Jade told you where I live?" I can't hide the suspicious look on my face, the panic rising in my voice.

"I don't think she would've if you'd answered your phone the dozens of times she's tried calling. She said you'd have a harder time throwing me out than you did her. So, here I am." His voice is calm.

I stare at him, waiting for him to tell me this all some kind of set-up. That it's a trick.

"It's okay. No one else is with me. I'm here by myself. Why don't you call her?"

"Fine." I slam the door and lock it. My heart's beating out of my chest as I head into the bedroom to grab my phone. Sprawling on the bed, I dial.

The phone rings once.

"Angel!" Jade sounds breathless—like she *knew* I'd call and has been waiting for this exact moment.

"So he wasn't lying," I bite. "You really gave him my address."

"I needed to know you were okay," she says, too fast. "You haven't answered *anything*. No texts, no calls—nothing."

"That doesn't mean you get to decide who shows up at my door." My voice rises. "You know some of what I've been through. You *know* what it means for someone to just—appear."

She exhales hard. "I know. I *know*, Angel. And I'm sorry. I didn't do it to hurt you. I did it because I'm scared for you. Because I didn't know how else to reach you and get you to talk to me."

"So you send Zane?" I'm pacing now, barefoot, heart pounding. "Some guy I just met and don't even know. You know I just threw open the door. He could've been *anyone*, Jade."

"If it helps, I trust him," she says quietly. "I've gotten to know him over the past few days. And I thought… I don't know, I thought maybe you could use someone *you* could trust right now. Someone who knows more about what you're going through."

I close my eyes, fingers trembling around the phone. "You blind-sided me."

"I know. I'll make it up to you. I promise. No one else knows anything. He's just there to make sure you're okay, for me. Will you just let him do that. Please?"

"Fine," I grumble and hang up the phone.

When I open the door again, Zane is still there. Still waiting.

Something tightens in my chest, a flicker of resistance, but it's so faint it hardly registers. Mostly what I feel is resignation. A deep sense of I-don't-give-a-damn blended with a hollow kind of acceptance. Thanks to Jade he's here, and she's not going to be satisfied unless he can tell her I'm fine. She needs to hear it from someone who isn't me.

"It's just you?"

"It's just me." His tone is warm, his expression open. "No one even saw me leave the house. Except Jade."

I continue to stare at him and the longer I look, the less energy I have to argue. This has all been too much.

I step back and open the door, gesturing him in. He steps inside, his gaze moving over my tiny, cluttered apartment. It's trashed, but there doesn't seem to be any hint of judgement on his face as he takes it all in.

He doesn't seem bothered by the mess that's built up over the past week or so, or the lack of light from having the blinds drawn shut. There's a faint smirk on his lips, but his eyes stay soft, careful, like he's trying to take in as much as he can and still be respectful.

"So this is where the infamous Angel hides out," he says, giving a small nod. "Nice place."

I let out a weak laugh, though it sounds foreign to me. "You don't have to be polite. I know it's a mess."

He shrugs, not taking his eyes off me. "I never say anything just to be polite. There's nothing wrong with messy. Messes are... inevitable." He leans down and moves a pile of papers over before settling down on the couch. He looks up at me like he's waiting for me to join him. "We don't have to talk. Not right now if you don't want to," he says after a moment. "I just thought... maybe you could use some company."

I weigh the meaning of his words. If he's being honest, he's offering me kindness. It's not something I would ever ask for or expect. I don't know how to accept it and don't have the patience to try to figure it out.

"Actually, I want to be left alone," I huff as I sink down into the chair across from him, a little unsteady on my feet. We sit there in silence, a quiet tension filling the space. It's not awkward or uncomfortable, not really. He doesn't press me for information, doesn't ask what's wrong, doesn't try to make any of this seem better than it is. He just sits—arms stretched out over the back of the couch, watching me. Like he belongs here. The corners of his mouth twitch like he wants to say something, but he remains quiet.

We sit like this for a long while. Him looking at me while I look anywhere but at him. Finally, he clears his throat. "I meant what I said Angel. No one knows I'm here. Levi's been tearing this city up looking for you, but I'm not planning on saying a word," he pauses and sighs, "Unless you want me to, of course."

His tone is reassuring, sincere. My shoulders drop a fraction as some of the tension I've been holding since I answered the door drains away. Some small part of me seems willing to believe him.

"That would be a hard no." I say, tilting my head, voice flat. "I'm not sure I understand why you're here. You don't know me."

He shrugs and clears his throat, looking slightly ruffled. "I was worried about you. The way you left the club was..." He pauses, choosing his next words carefully. "Dramatic."

"Oh. Let me guess... you're gentlemanly instincts kicked in and you felt the need to make sure the hysterical chick you spent two nights hitting on wasn't sitting in a corner, crying, ready to slit her wrists."

Zane smirks, leaning forward slightly, his forearms resting on his knees. "I didn't say hysterical, I said dramatic. And, something like

that. I mean, you're not sitting in a corner right now, so that's a win."
His eyes flicker over me, gentle but assessing. "And crying? You don't strike me as the type."

"Well, that only leaves the wrist slitting." I arch a brow, my lips curving into an acidic smile. "But, as I'm sure you've heard… I've got some experience with sharp, pointy things. It gave me a phobia of watching myself bleed to death. Again. So, no worries there."

His smile fades, and anger flashes across his face. It's gone quickly, mellowing into something more tempered, almost tender. "I'll take your word for it."

His voice dips lower. "I needed to see for myself that you're doing okay."

I snort softly, sinking further into the chair. "Yeah. I'm just peachy. Can't you tell?"

He laughs, and the sound is low and warm as it cuts through some of the fog in my head.

"Sure. You've really nailed the aesthetic."

"Thanks," I mutter, but there's no heat in it. I glance toward the window, my chest tightening against the ache that's been lodged there since I ran out of the club. "So tell me why you're really here, Z? I'm not buying the good Samaritan crap."

He leans back, letting the silence settle before he answers. "I think you underestimate me. I *did* come to check on you. I know what it's like to have something from your past catch up with you—I've felt the ground drop out from underneath me a few times. It can be nice to have someone around who gets it."

Of all the things I thought he'd say, that wasn't anything close. I don't quite know how to respond to that. He doesn't elaborate, simply leaves it sitting between us, waiting for me to pick it up if I want.

He glances toward the kitchen, and without a word stands, brushes his hands on his jeans, and strides towards it with purpose.

I blink, sitting up slightly. "What the hell are you doing?"

"Fixing you some food," he calls over his shoulder, as he starts opening cabinets like he's on a scavenger hunt. "You look like you haven't eaten in days."

I narrow my eyes, but there's no real bite behind it. He's right. I've lost track of time and can't remember the last time I ate something. For all I know it could've been days. "So, you're just making yourself at home now?"

"Yep," he says, popping the P. He pulls out a pan, then rifles through my fridge with a low whistle. "Damn, Angel. Prison meal trays have more options."

I can't help the faint tug of a smile at the corner of my mouth as I stand and wander into the kitchen. I lean against the doorframe, observing. "Why on earth am I not surprised you'd know what comes on a prison meal tray?" I cross my arms over my chest watching him open cabinets that are mostly empty.

"I know it's sad. I don't cook much. I usually eat out or get something delivered."

"Tsk, tsk, tsk. Well, not today. Prepare to be amazed." He glances back, grinning as he holds up a carton of eggs and a sad-looking block of cheese. "Scrambled?"

"Fine," I mutter. My stomach growls loudly at the prospect, and Zane raises a brow at me with a knowing smirk.

"Uh-huh. Thought so."

He moves around the kitchen with surprising efficiency, his motions practiced and deliberate. The smell of melting butter and coffee begins to fill the room. It's wonderful. I could almost forget to notice the pain in my chest. Zane turns and leans against the counter looking me up and down.

"No offense Angel, but you need a shower," he says. His voice is calm but matter-of-fact. "It'll help get your head straight. Breakfast will be ready when you get out."

I tense at the suggestion, my stomach knotting. The idea of stepping away, leaving him alone in my space, feels too vulnerable. Too dangerous. Zane must sense it because he doesn't move, doesn't press. He just sits there, leaning back against the counter with his hands loose on his thighs.

"You're safe with me, Angel," he says softly.

I snort and roll my eyes. "I keep hearing that, but I don't think it means what people think it does."

I regret saying it as soon as the words leave my mouth. He looks genuinely wounded. And honestly, I haven't picked up any insincerity or outright dishonesty behind his words. I don't feel like he's trying to convince me of anything.

"I'll be right here. I'll stay in the kitchen. Take your time and lock the bathroom door. I won't touch anything, and I promise I won't try anything. Food will be ready when you're done."

I scoff. "So, a shower is magically going to fix everything?"

"Nope." He grins, but it's gentler than before, his usual cocky edge tempered by something softer. "But, I think it *will* make you feel a little better, and that's a start."

I exhale slowly, the knot in my stomach loosening a fraction. "You're just going to… wait here?"

"Scout's honor," he says, holding up three fingers in a mock salute.

I hesitate, searching his face for a crack, any sign that this is some kind of trick. But there's nothing but steady patience.

Finally, I stand, my legs shaky beneath me. "Okay, I'm going. Be warned though. I'm taking my phone with me. If I hear so much as a single creak of the floor, I'll call the cops."

"Fair enough," he says, his grin widening. "Now go. I've got breakfast to make."

I roll my eyes but don't argue. I make a production of grabbing my phone off the counter before marching down the hall and into the bathroom.

Chapter Twenty-Nine

Sunny

I WOULD NEVER, EVER admit it to Zane, but the shower did help. A tiny bit. I feel better than I have since before that night at the club. He was right, but I'll take that information to my grave. He's one man I'm thinking doesn't need an ego boost.

It takes me some time to dig through the clothes in my drawers and find something clean to put on. By the time I make my way out to the living room and collapse on to the couch, Zane is waiting with a warm heaping plate of food and hot cup of coffee. He drops several packets of restaurant sugars and powdered creamer on to the coffetable.

I don't argue, I just take the plate from his hands and dig in. It's simple—eggs, cheese, a little salt and pepper—but it tastes better than anything I can remember having. It's delicious. Zane sits down on the opposite end of the couch, watching with an amused expression as I dump ten packets of sugar and two creamers into the coffee.

I shovel fork after fork of the amazing breakfast into my mouth trying to ignore that easy, crooked grin of his.

"So," he says, leaning back. "I won't push, and I'll only ask you this one time, but I do have to ask. I'd like to hear your side of things. About what happened between you and Levi?"

I freeze, my fork halfway to my mouth. The mention of Levi sends a fresh wave of anger and hurt ripping through me, and for a second, I can't even look at Zane.

"I don't want to talk about it," I say finally, letting my fork fall to my plate before setting it down on the coffee table. "I'm sure he told you everything."

Zane doesn't back down, just nods slowly and keeps his eyes steady on mine. "Fair enough. Like I said, I won't push. He did tell me—and Colt—what happened. He was full of information. He gave us a version. His version. But, I'm not sure whether I should believe any of it. He lied to us, Angel. For years. And I don't know what exactly that means or what to do with it now."

As an afterthought he adds, "For what it's worth… he seems almost as wrecked as you are."

I laugh bitterly, shaking my head. "Yeah? Well, good. He deserves at least that."

Zane tilts his head, watching me. "You want to tell me why?"

My appetite's gone and my stomach is queasy. The words bubble up and I don't even try to stop them. "Because he left me," I say, the bitterness in my voice cutting through each word. "He walked away from me, Zane. He said he loved me, told me I was his whole world, and then ditched me."

Zane's jaw tightens slightly, but he stays silent, letting me fill the space in my own time.

"I was in the hospital for almost two weeks. I waited for him to show up. To call. To visit. And, nothing. He disconnected his phone, and the one he'd given me. He disappeared." I don't even bother trying to hide the sadness.

"And that's not even the worst part of it." I feel my voice gather strength as words pour out. "It's *how* he left me that I can't get over. I was lying there on the floor, barely alive, sliced open and bleeding, and... " The words trail off as I pull my feet up underneath me and wiggle my toes into the cushion under me.

All of it comes flooding back, and for a moment I'm there again. Lying on the floor, the cold seeping into my bones. The metallic tang of blood filling my nose, my mouth, my lungs. The devastating sharp pain of broken bones and bruised skin. My hand moves unconsciously to my chest and traces the hidden scar. Zane's eyes catch the motion, and he grimaces.

"I don't know how much he told you, but he was there that night with me. After... after Garrett left. I heard him come up the stairs calling my name. My eyes were closed but I could hear him, feel him." My voice feels separate, distant.

"He lifted me off the floor and held me. I was so cold and he was so warm, and I was so thankful he was there. I knew he'd make it all okay again." My vision blurs as my eyes fill with tears. I blink them back and clear my throat to steady my voice.

"I couldn't say anything, I couldn't move. I knew I was dying. He laid me back down on the floor, and I heard him call the police. I was so thankful I wasn't alone anymore. But then, he left. Stepped over me and walked out the door.

I kept waiting for him to come back. But he never did. He never came back. I never heard from him again."

"Angel." Zane's voice is filled with emotion and comes out as little more than a whisper, even as his fists are clenched against his thighs. "I'm so sorry."

Something in me tightens at the name, and before I can think twice, I'm correcting him. "Sunny," I say, my voice catching. "My name is Sunny."

His eyes flicker caught off guard for a split second, but he doesn't make a big deal of it. He simply nods. "Alright, Sunny," he says, weighing out my name like he's testing the shape of it on his tongue.

For a moment, I let myself sit with everything I've just said. I've never told anyone about that night, or what happened after. I let myself feel the strange, soft warmth of having someone here—someone who's neither asking anything of me nor forcing anything on me. It's unexpected and feels both foreign and necessary. Minutes tick by in silence.

"Eat up," he says finally, gesturing to the plate I set down.

I roll my eyes. "Bossy."

"When I need to be."

"Look, I'm sorry," I mutter, as I pick up the plate and force myself to take another bite. "Didn't mean to dump all that on you. You're the first person I've ever told that to."

Zane shakes his head. "No apologies. You didn't dump anything. I asked. Remember?" He pauses, looking down at his hands.

There's a raw honesty in his tone that hits me hard. I'm used to people wanting something from me. But here he is, looking at me with nothing but quiet sincerity. I want to shrug it off, make some sarcastic comment and throw up my shield again, but I can't quite bring myself to do it. I don't know if it's because I'm tired, or simply don't care anymore.

"Thanks, Z," I say finally.

He nods and leans back again, giving me space enough to let what I've told him settle. I've never said any of it out loud before. I've never had anyone I *could* tell before. Even Jade has only ever heard half. I glance at his plate, realizing he's only taken a few small bites of his food since I started talking.

"What about you?" I ask, surprising myself. "How'd you end up with… him?"

He lets out a low sound that's half a sigh. "You want the long answer or the short one?"

"How about short, with the option for more," I say, smirking a little.

He takes a bite of food, chews and swallows before he answers. "I grew up around a lot of chaos, with people for parents who didn't care much about right or wrong. They only cared about power, control and making money any way they could. So, I had a choice— let myself get swallowed up in all of that, or try to find something different. I made some bad choices, got involved in some, uh, questionable things, but Levi gave me an out. An option that didn't involve selling my soul or spending the next thirty years in jail."

I nod, listening. It feels like I'm seeing him in layers, each one a little clearer, a little more real. "So, Levi's...what? Your boss?"

He hesitates, his expression darkening slightly, and nods. "Yeah. Sort of. But it's more than that. We're brothers. Family, you know?" His gaze drops to the table for a moment, and when he looks up, something genuine, something deep flickers there.

It's been years since I thought about family—what it's supposed to mean and feel like. I shrug. "I guess. I don't think I've ever had anything like that."

I take the few last bites of food and set the plate down again.

"Glad to see you've got your appetite back."

Zane chuckles softly, standing up to clear the plates, and I watch him, wondering what it was about him that made him so easy to talk to and confide in.

After doing the dishes, Zane pulls a scrap of paper and a pen from his jacket pocket. He jots down a number and hands it to me where I'm lying stretched out on the couch. The food made me sleepy and I'm struggling to keep my eyes open.

I look down at it, raising an eyebrow. "You know I'm not really big on calling people," I say, my tone skeptical. *Especially not people close to Levi.*

"I figured as much, but this way you'll have it if you need it." He grins, just a hint of that easygoing confidence breaking through. "I won't say a word about you or that I was here to anyone. Well, except Jade. She's a little scary, and I don't know what she'd do to me if I don't report back." His smile is genuine. "We've got a little bit of business left here to finish up, but we should be clearing out in a few days."

My fingers linger over the number. I don't respond, but something in me softens, just a little.

"If you want to talk," he adds, his voice low, "or if you need anything—anything at all—just call."

I nod slowly, managing a small smile.

"Thank you," I mutter.

He gives me one last, reassuring look and heads to the door. "Get some rest, Sunny. Take care of yourself."

Once he reaches the door, he turns and gives me an intense, serious look. "I hope you realize that you're stronger than you think you are."

And then, he's gone, closing the door softly behind him. The silence that settles in his wake isn't as heavy as it has been. I stare at the slip of paper, a mix of relief and doubt twisting in my chest. Part of me still doesn't know what to make of Zane, but somehow, tonight, even if it was just for a couple hours, things felt a little more bearable with him here with me.

For the first time in a week, when I curl up on the couch and pull the blanket down over me, sleep comes easily.

CHAPTER THIRTY

SUNNY

I STARE AT MY phone, biting my lip, my finger hovering over Zane's number. I don't remember putting it in my phone and saving it, but here it is, and here I am. I've been sitting in this exact position for close to half an hour trying to work up the nerve to press the button.

It's been three days since he was here, and I haven't stopped thinking about him—or, Levi. Every time I close my eyes, I see Levi's face, hear him say my name. The raw emotion it brings rattles around in my mind, refusing to settle.

But this isn't about that or them. I need to start getting my life back.

I take a deep breath and tap the screen, pressing the phone to my ear before I can talk myself out of it. The ringing feels endless, each second stretching longer than the last.

"Sunny." His voice is warm and low, like he's genuinely happy to hear from me, and something in my chest loosens at the sound. My fingers grip the phone harder and I swallow hard.

"Hey," I manage, my voice barely more than a whisper. "I, um… I wanted to check. Did you guys—did Levi leave town?"

The silence stretches so long I almost hang up. Finally, Zane speaks. "Yeah, Levi's gone. Left two nights ago with Colt and a few of the guys. I stayed back with everyone else."

Relief floods through me so fast it makes me dizzy. I exhale loudly and sink deeper into the couch, my body heavy. "Good. That's... good."

"Which part?" Zane's voice has a faint edge of something I can't quite read.

"Oh. Um, all of it. Maybe," I admit. The honesty in my answer surprises me. "I don't know. It's been a rough week."

"Yeah," he agrees quietly. "It *has* been that."

My free hand finds the edge of my blanket, twisting it between my fingers. "I thought... I mean, I assumed you'd all leave together."

"No." His voice is careful, measured. "Things came up here that someone needed to stay back and handle."

"Things?" The word comes out sharper than I intend, old fears and insecurities rising to the surface.

"Business," he says, but there's something in his tone that gives me pause.

"In Oak Valley?" I ask, trying to keep my voice steady. "I can't imagine there's a whole lot here to stick around for."

There's a heavy pause. "I disagree."

My heart stutters a bit at his words. "Z, I just... I didn't expect you to still be here."

"I could leave," he says quietly. "If that's what you want."

"What do you mean?"

"What I said Sunny. One word from you, and I'm gone." His voice is steady, matter of fact. "Or say nothing and I'll stay."

"That's not really my call," I say with a nervous laugh. "Why would you do that?"

"Because I refuse to do anything that would hurt you or make things any harder for you." The simplicity in his answer catches me off guard

The silence stretches between us, heavy with things unsaid.

"Sunny?"

"I have to go," I manage to choke out, clutching the phone like it might slip from my grasp.

"Okay," he says, his voice is rock solid and calm despite the abruptness of my words. "I'm here if you need me."

I hang up and set the phone down slowly. My apartment feels too quiet, too small now. The space that had felt like a refuge for the past week and a half suddenly feels like a trap, holding me hostage to my own thoughts.

The thought sends me to the kitchen, desperate for a distraction. I grab a glass and pour myself a drink—soda, nothing stronger. The last thing I need right now is a fuzzy head. I sip it slowly, leaning against the counter and staring out the small window above the sink before heading back to the living room.

I sit cross-legged on the floor. Zane's voice lingers in my head as my gaze drifts out the window.

The sunlight streaming in feels good. Bright, warm, alive—everything I haven't been since I locked myself inside this apartment.

I press my fingers to my temples, trying to quiet the thoughts warring in my head. *It's not just about going back to work,* I tell myself. *It's about getting back to some semblance of a life.*

My hand drifts to the scars at my collarbone, brushing over them lightly. A memory surfaces unbidden—Zane's steady eyes locking with mine, his voice soft but firm as he said, "You're stronger than you think."

I roll my eyes at the memory, but a faint smile tugs at my lips. *That man could sell ice water in a blizzard.*

Standing up, I smooth my hands over my thighs and look around the apartment. The mess I've let pile up stares back at me—a reflection of the chaos I've been letting consume me.

"No more," I whisper.

I lean back and find Benny's number. Hesitation bubbles up in my chest making me pause.

What if it's too soon? What if it's a mistake?

But then I hear Zane's voice in my head again. *You're stronger than you think.*

I press the button before I can second-guess myself anymore.

Zane

I STARE AT MY phone, thumb hovering over Sunny's number. It's been almost a week since she called to see if Levi was still around.

My phone buzzes with another text from Colt: "You can't avoid him forever, Z."

I toss the phone onto the bed without answering. He's right, but I'm not ready to deal with Levi yet. I need the space from him as much as he probably needs it from me. Our last conversation replays in my head—him breaking down, confessing everything. The shame in his voice when he admitted leaving her there. Part of me understands he was just a kid faced with something horrific. But another part...

The image of Sunny's face when she described that night— feeling him hold her, hearing him call 911, only to have him walk away—haunts me. Makes me question everything I thought I knew about the man I've followed for years.

The safehouse is almost completely done. Ready for permanent crew to move in. It's amazing that we've managed to accomplish as much as we have in a few weeks. It's not going to be long before I don't have an excuse to keep from going home.

I keep thinking about how Sunny looked that evening in her kitchen—so hurt, so worn down. The trust she placed in me weighs heavy in my mind. I know she only let me in out of sheer exhaustion, but the fact that she let me make breakfast for her while she showered, and then ate every last bite speaks volumes.

As a bartender, even one without her history, it had to take a huge leap of faith to accept food and drink from someone she didn't know and didn't watch prepare it. It required a level of trust that maybe she didn't even recognize at the time. Her vulnerability in that moment, choosing to believe I wouldn't hurt her, conscious or not, makes me feel oddly protective.

It's a strange feeling, this satisfaction. Like I passed some test I didn't even realize I'd been taking until it was over. Usually, I measure success in fear or respect, not in whether someone trusts me. But somehow, that small gesture of faith means more than I would've imagined.

My phone buzzes again. This time it's Wolf with an update about a potential warehouse space near the port. Business should be my priority. It's what I'm good at. What I know.

Instead, I find myself pulling on my jacket and heading for my car. The evening air is cool as I step outside, stars just starting to appear in the darkening sky.

I tell myself I'm just going to check on her, make sure she's okay. That's what friends do, right?

Are we friends?

The truth is, I'm not sure what I'm doing anymore. I feel off-balance. Everything has shifted and I can't find my footing. The past few weeks have changed everything and I'm not sure I can make any of it make sense.

But as I slide behind the wheel, I realize I have to try. For her sake. For mine. Maybe even for Levi's, though I'm not ready to examine that part of it all too closely yet.

The neon signs lining the entrance to Sirens cast their familiar glow across the parking lot as I pull in. It takes a few minutes to find a spot. It's busy for Tuesday night. Somewhere inside, Sunny's working her shift. As Angel.

I sit in my car, the engine idling, caught between going in and driving away. Between loyalty to an old friend, someone I consider my brother, and something new I don't have a name for yet.

I kill the engine and step out into the night air. The neon bathes everything in a harsh red glow. Stepping inside is like stepping into a different universe.

Inside, the music pounds and throbs with fierce intensity. My eyes scan the room, finding Sunny behind the bar. She's wearing a white crop top and short white mini skirt. Her hair is pulled back from her face and tied with a white ribbon. She's beautiful.

She spots me and freezes for a split second before recovering her composure. I watch her shoulders square as she steels herself. Even from here, I can see the shadows under her eyes that makeup can't quite hide.

I take a spot at the end of the bar, away from the main crowd. Sunny approaches, professional mask firmly in place.

"What can I get you?"

"Whiskey, neat." I study her face. "You look tired."

Her fingers tighten on the glass she's holding. "I'm fine."

"It would be understandable and okay if you're not."

"Actually, no. It wouldn't be okay." She sets my drink down with more force than necessary. "This is my job, Z. I can't afford to be anything but fine right now."

I take a slow sip, letting the whiskey burn. "When do you get off?"

"Why?"

"Because you need to eat something, and I know a place that makes decent food at two a.m."

A ghost of a smile touches her lips before vanishing. "I don't need you to take care of me."

"I know. But maybe *I* need to do something besides sit and stare at the walls and overthink everything."

She studies me for a long moment. "Two-thirty."

"I'll wait."

The next few hours pass slowly. I nurse my drink and watch Sunny work. She moves with practiced efficiency, dodging wandering hands and deflecting crude comments with a smile. It never quite reaches her eyes though. Every so often, she glances my way like she's making sure I'm still here.

Jade appears around midnight, sliding onto the stool next to me. "You're back."

"Apparently."

"She told me what you did. Feeding her, listening to her..." Jade's voice softens slightly. "You left that part out. Thank you for taking care of her."

"How bad's it been?"

"Bad enough." She sighs. "Look, you seem like a good guy. Colt tells me you are. But when it comes to Angel, I don't trust anyone or their intentions completely. She needs someone right now who knows and can understand what she's been through. She loves me, but I think there's things she doesn't want me to know. She needs someone who isn't me."

"I'm not trying to—"

"Save it." Jade cuts me off. "Just... if you're gonna stick around for a while, be good to her. She's been through enough. Okay?"

Before I can respond, she's gone, disappearing into the crowd heading for the VIP section. I check my phone—several missed calls from Colt and one more from Wolf about the warehouse. Business can wait.

At two-fifteen, Sunny starts her closing routine. I watch her count tips, wipe down the bar, stack glasses with mechanical precision. When she emerges from the back room at two-thirty-five, she's changed into jeans and an oversized sweater.

"Ready?" I stand, offering my arm out of habit.

She hesitates before taking it. Her hand is small and cold against my sleeve. "Where are we going?"

"Place called Mary's. Best pancakes in the Valley."

The drive is quiet. I can feel her tension, see how tight she grips her hands in her lap. When we pull into the parking lot of the small diner, she finally speaks.

"Why are you doing this?"

I turn off the engine but don't move to get out. "I don't know."

I see her wring her hands in her lap. "That's... honest. As long as you know that you don't owe me anything. You don't have to feel sorry for me."

I meet her gaze, searching for understanding in her eyes. "I know I don't. There's a lot I'm trying to figure out right now, same as you."

She nods slowly, a flicker of appreciation crossing her face.

The air between us feels heavy, charged with a sense of loss, the weight of the past, and the uncertainty of the future. Her grip relaxes a little on her lap.

"Sunny," I say softly. "I'm here because I care, and even if I'm a little lost right now, I'm here because I want to be."

"Okay then," she says decisively. She lets out a breath with a long sigh, a tentative smile tugging at her lips. "Let's get those pancakes you promised."

Inside, the diner is nearly empty. The fluorescent lights are harsh against the early morning sky, making everything feel too bright, too exposed. We slide into a booth near the back. Sunny orders coffee and pancakes. I order the same.

"Tell me something," she says after the waitress leaves. "Did you know? Before? About what happened that night?"

"No." I grip my coffee mug tighter. "Levi only told us a small part of the story. He told us that he thought you were murdered. That he believed Garrett killed you and his mother and that it had been a random attack. Everything we've done since then—building the business with him in the ways we have—it was all about finding Garrett. Getting revenge for taking the people he loved away from him."

"Do you believe him?"

"I don't know what to think. Or what to do."

She traces patterns in the condensation on her water glass. "That makes two of us."

Our food arrives, and I watch her pick at her pancakes. She's lost weight since that morning in her apartment. Dark circles under her eyes suggest she's not sleeping well.

"You should eat more than that."

She gives me a weak smile. "Sure thing, *Dad*."

"I'm serious. You look exhausted."

"Yeah, well, finding out the guy you loved didn't only break up with you badly, but actually thought he was leaving you to rot tends to mess with your sleep schedule."

The bitterness in her voice makes me wince. "Have you thought about what you want to do?"

"Besides hide in my apartment forever?" She sighs. "I don't know. Part of me wants answers. Part of me wants to run as far away as possible. But apparently I'm really bad at not being found."

"You don't have to decide anything right now."

"Don't I?" She meets my eyes. "He knows where I am now. You all do. Everything I've built here—my job, my life—it's not just mine anymore, which means it's not safe for me. I don't know what to do with that."

I reach across the table, stopping just short of touching her hand. "We can protect you."

"Yeah. I've heard that one before." Her voice cracks slightly. "Look how well that turned out."

Chapter Thirty-One

Zane

I heave another dusty box onto the growing pile in the living room, my muscles protesting after hours of hauling junk up from the basement. The safe house's musty underground has become my personal version of hell today. Who knew one basement could hold so much history?

A cloud of dust explodes as I drop the latest box, making me sneeze. "Shit." I itch my nose with the back of my hand, leaving a grimy streak across my skin. My white T-shirt is now more gray than white, and my suspenders are hanging loose at my hips.

The basement stairs creak under my boots as I head back down. The bare bulb swinging overhead casts weird shadows in the corners. Dozens more boxes sit stacked against the far wall, their cardboard sides bulging with who knows what.

I grab the top one, lighter than the others. The side splits as I lift it, spilling old papers across the concrete floor. "Perfect." My voice echoes in the empty space.

Kneeling down, I gather the scattered sheets. Most are yellowed invoices and receipts from years ago, but a few photos mixed in catch my eye. One shows a younger version of Levi's father standing in front of this house, arm around a woman who must be Levi's mom. They're both smiling, no hint of the darkness that would come later.

I shove the photos back in the box without looking at any more of them. The past needs to stay buried, especially right now with everything so fucked up between me and Levi.

My phone buzzes in my pocket. Another message from Wolf about the warehouse viewing later. I ignore it like I've been ignoring Colt's texts about making peace with Levi. Some things can't be fixed with a few apologetic words.

The next box is heavier, packed with old ledgers and account books. The leather covers are cracked and faded, but the numbers inside might still mean something. I'll have to go through them later, see if any of the old business information is worth saving.

Sweat trickles down my back as I carry the box upstairs. The AC is working overtime against the September heat, but it's losing the battle. I drop the box with the others and pull my shirt off, using it to wipe my face before tossing it aside.

The final box feels different when I lift it. Metal clinks inside, and something that sounds like chains shifts. My gut tightens. This house has seen some ugly business over the years. Some things are better left undiscovered.

But I can't leave anything unchecked. Not when we're trying to make this place operational again. I set the box on an old workbench and pry open the top.

Chains, along with bundles of brittle, old zip ties, duct tape, and other restraints fill the bottom of the box. Standard equipment for our line of work, but these are old. Rusty in places. Covered in dark stains I don't want to think about too hard.

Under all that, I find a small leather case, engraved with the letters *A.R.* Inside is a set of knives, well-maintained despite their age. The handles are worn smooth from use. I recognize the maker's mark—same guy who crafted my favorite blade.

My phone buzzes again. Wolf, getting impatient about the warehouse. I check the time and curse. Been down here longer than I meant to be.

I close the knife case and return it to the box. Everything goes upstairs. The sorting can wait until later.

Dusting my hands off on my pants, I head for the stairs. The are more piles of boxes in the living room, patiently waiting their turn. So much history in this house, so many secrets. And now we're adding our own to the mix.

I grab a clean shirt, set the alarms and climb into my car. I check my reflection in the rearview. Still covered in dust and cobwebs, but I don't have time to clean up.

The air conditioner blasts cold air as I pull out of the driveway. My mind drifts to Sunny, wondering if she's working tonight. We've fallen into a comforting routine of late-night diner visits and phone calls after her shifts. She's still guarded, but sometimes I catch glimpses of who she must have been before everything went wrong.

I force those thoughts away. Got enough complications without adding more. The warehouse needs checking, security systems need a final upgrade, and somewhere in all those boxes might be information we can use.

I pull up to the warehouse, spotting Wolf's black SUV already parked out front. He's leaning against the hood, cigarette dangling from his lips. His dark clothes blend into the shadows of the building, making him look more like his namesake than usual.

"Took your sweet time," Wolf drawls as I step out of my truck. He eyes my dusty appearance. "What happened to you?"

"Been clearing out the basement. Place is a damn museum." I stretch, my back cracking from all the heavy lifting. "Show me what we're working with here."

Wolf flicks his cigarette away and pulls out a ring of keys. "You're gonna love this place. Previous owners went bankrupt, but they left everything in good condition."

The metal door groans as he pushes it open. Stale air hits my face as we step inside. Wolf flips some switches, and industrial lights flicker to life overhead, revealing the massive space.

"Holy shit." I whistle, my voice echoing. The warehouse stretches far back, with high ceilings and multiple loading bays. "How many square feet?"

"Twenty thousand." Wolf's boots echo on the concrete as he walks ahead. "Got office space upstairs, security system already wired in—needs upgrading but nothing we can't handle. Loading docks can handle four trucks at once."

I run my hand along a support beam. Solid construction. "Storage capacity?"

"More than enough for what we need. Could triple our usual inventory and still have room." He gestures to the far wall. "Climate controlled section over there for the sensitive stuff."

We walk the perimeter, Wolf pointing out features while I mentally map security camera placement and access points. The location is perfect for storing and inventorying the black-market goods we deal in. It's close enough to the ports that it allows for easy transportation, but isolated and far enough away to avoid unwanted attention or suspicion.

"Levi's getting antsy," Wolf mentions casually as we check out the office space. "Wants to see things moving forward faster."

I grunt in acknowledgment. Of course he does. Levi's never been good at waiting once he sets his mind to something.

"Talked to that contact he sent me," Wolf continues. "Says if you green light this place, we can have steady shipments coming in from the ports within two weeks. Get the old operations running again, maybe even expand."

"Two weeks seems ambitious." I peer out the office window, surveying the main floor below.

"Guy's connected. Has all the right people in his pocket already." Wolf pulls out another cigarette but doesn't light it. "Just needs your okay to start moving pieces into place."

I drum my fingers on the windowsill, considering. The warehouse is perfect— almost too perfect. But we need a base of operations if we're going to rebuild what Levi's father had here.

"What's your read on the contact?" I ask Wolf.

"Solid. Did some digging—he's got history with Levi's old man. Kept his mouth shut when things went south back then. Loyalty like that's hard to find."

I nod slowly. "And the price?"

"Higher than before, but reasonable considering the risk. Plus, we get priority routing through his channels."

More pieces falling into place. Maybe too neatly, but we can't afford to be overly cautious right now. Not with Levi pushing for progress.

"Alright." I turn to face Wolf. "Lock it down. But I want our people to handle the security setup, not local contractors. And I want background on everyone involved in the shipping chain."

"Already started the checks." Wolf finally lights his cigarette. "Figured you'd want that."

"Good man." I take one last look around the office. "How soon can we get the paperwork started?"

"Can have it ready for signatures tomorrow. Previous owners are motivated sellers."

I check my phone—no new messages from Levi or Colt. They're probably buried in all the meetings and paperwork I usually handle. Or maybe they've decided to finally give me some space. Either way, this decision is on me.

"Do it," I tell Wolf. "But keep it quiet for now. Don't want anyone getting curious about why we're setting up shop here."

Wolf nods, already pulling out his phone to make calls. I head back downstairs, mind racing with plans and contingencies. Twenty thousand square feet of possibility—or twenty thousand square feet of potential problems.

The empty warehouse echoes with my footsteps as I walk the floor again. In two weeks, this place will be humming with activity. Shipments coming and going, inventory stored, money flowing. Just like the old days.

I pause at one of the loading bays, staring out at the gathering dusk. Somewhere across town, Sunny's probably getting ready for her shift at Sirens. I wonder if she'll call tonight.

Wolf's voice drifts down from the office as he makes arrangements. I push thoughts of Sunny aside and focus on the task at hand. We've got a warehouse to secure and an operation to rebuild. Everything else will have to wait.

I walk out of the warehouse, leaving Wolf to handle things. My boots crunch on loose gravel as I head toward my black Dodge Charger.

Something white catches my eye, fluttering under my windshield wiper. My steps slow. Every instinct screams danger. No one should know I'm here except Wolf.

I scan the area, noting the empty parking lot, the tall weeds and thick trees behind the building, and all of the dark corners where someone could hide. Nothing moves except plastic bags and other trash blown by the wind.

The note is plain white printer paper, folded once. No fingerprints visible on the crisp edges. "Actions Have Consequences" printed in basic Times New Roman. Professional. Clean. Threatening.

My hand moves automatically to the gun at my hip as I continue scanning. The message could mean anything, but the timing…

Someone's been watching. Waiting.

Could be about the warehouse deal. But that feels too fresh—no one outside our immediate circle knows yet. Wolf's contact testing us maybe? No—too risky, too much money on the line for them to fuck with us.

My thoughts turn to Sunny. Few people know I've been seeing her after her shifts. Jade. Benny. The security guards at Sirens. But they have no reason to threaten me. Unless...

Unless someone else found out. Someone who thinks they're protecting her. Or someone who wants to use her against us. Or...

I take a photo of the note before carefully folding it into a bag from my glove compartment. The paper feels expensive under my fingers. High-quality. The kind used in professional offices, not cheap copy shops.

Back in my car, I sit for a moment, letting scenarios play out. Could be about the safe house cleanout. Maybe there are things buried in those boxes that are supposed to stay buried. Maybe I found something I wasn't supposed to. Or this could be about splitting me, Levi and Colt up, right when we should be the most solid. Or maybe we aren't the only ones who found Sunny.

Too many possibilities. Too many enemies. And someone bold enough to walk right up to my car before the sun was even set.

I start the engine, watching my mirrors. No tail as I pull out of the lot.

I drum my fingers on my steering wheel, debating. The note sits heavy in my pocket, its message burning in my mind. "Actions Have Consequences."

My phone feels like lead as I pick it up. Colt's number stares back at me. Three weeks of avoiding his calls, and now I'm the one reaching out. Fuck.

The line rings twice before his voice bursts through, way too cheerful. "Z! Man, I was starting to think you'd fallen off the face of the earth!"

"Hey." I clear my throat, already regretting this. "Got a minute?"

"For you? I've got all day. Hold on—" There's shuffling, a door closing. "Okay, I'm alone. What's up?"

I grip the steering wheel tighter. "Something happened at the warehouse viewing. I need you and Levi to be aware."

"Warehouse viewing? The one Wolf set up?" Papers rustle in the background. "Thought that was just routine."

"It was. Until I found a note on my car after." I describe the message, the paper quality, the timing. Keep my voice neutral, just facts.

"Shit." Colt's enthusiasm dims slightly. "You think it's about the expansion? Someone trying to muscle in?"

"Could be. Could be nothing." I watch a stray cat slink past my car. "I wanted you both in the loop though."

"Want us to head back? We can—"

"No." I cut him off. "Not yet. Give me some time to figure out what we're dealing with first."

"But—"

"If we mobilize everyone now, we'll show our hand. Better to keep it quiet until we know more."

Colt sighs, and I can picture him running his hands through his blonde hair, messing it up like he always does when he's thinking. "You talked to Levi yet?"

"You're first call."

"He's gonna be pissed you waited."

"I don't care." The words come out sharper than intended.

"Z..." Colt's voice softens. "You know he's beating himself up about everything. The whole Sunny situation—"

"Don't." My knuckles go white on the wheel. "This isn't about that."

"You sure? Because—"

"It's about business. That's all." I force my grip to relax. "Keep your eyes open on your end, yeah? And tell Levi. I'm not up for that yet."

"Fine." Colt doesn't bother hiding his disappointment. "But Z? We miss you, man. Both of us."

I end the call without responding.

My mind circles back to Sunny, to late-night conversations, and to the strength it must have taken to rebuild her life from nothing.

But there's no logical connection between her and this note. None that makes sense, anyway. Better to focus on the obvious threats—rival organizations, old enemies, ghosts drifting up from the safehouse basement.

I check my mirrors again out of habit. No tail, no suspicious vehicles. Just me and my paranoid thoughts.

The note crinkles in my pocket. "Actions Have Consequences." Someone's making a move. I just don't know from what direction.

Chapter Thirty-Two

Zane

I wake to my phone vibrating against my chest where I fell asleep with it. Sunny's name flashes on the screen and my stomach drops. I already talked to her this morning while she was finishing up her shift and getting ready to leave work.

"Z?" Her voice comes through shaky, barely controlled. "I think... I think someone followed me home."

I'm already up, grabbing my keys and gun from the nightstand. "Tell me what happened."

"I ended up sticking around a little bit later to help one of the other bartenders. I was fine leaving the club, but as soon as I got out of my car it felt like I was being watched. The whole walk up the stairs, I felt like there was someone behind me. And now..." She takes a shallow breath. "I swear I can hear someone on the other side of my door."

"Stay on the phone with me. I'm a little more than five minutes out." I'm grateful now for our morning routine. Our daily phone call. Early morning breakfasts and coffee and conversations have given me more than just the pleasure of her company—they've gotten me used to functioning on her schedule. I'm up, dressed and out the door in under a minute.

The streets blur past as I push my car harder than I should. "Keep talking to me, Sunny. Are all your windows locked?"

"Yes." Her voice is barely a whisper now. "Z, I'm scared."

The vulnerability in her voice hits me hard. Sunny would never admit to fear unless she was overwhelmed by it. Our time together has shown me how carefully she guards herself, how rare it is for her to let anyone see below the surface.

"I'm almost there. Two minutes." She gasps and I hear rustling through the phone. "What was that?"

"Someone's definitely out there. I can hear them moving." Her breathing quickens. "What if it's..."

She doesn't finish the thought, but she doesn't need to. Garrett's shadow still looms large over her life—I've seen it in the way she startles at sudden movements, how she always positions herself with clear sight lines to exits.

I screech into the parking lot of her complex, not bothering to find a proper spot. "I'm here. Coming up now. Stay away from the door."

Taking the stairs two at a time, my hand stays close to the gun tucked into my waistband and hidden under my jacket. The hallway leading to her apartment is empty and silent, but something feels off. There's a faint smell of cigarette smoke that gets stronger the closer I get to her apartment.

I reach her door and notice a few scratches and scuff marks on the frame. They aren't very noticeable, but I know they weren't there yesterday when I dropped her off after breakfast.

"Sunny," I whisper into the phone. "I'm right outside. Going to knock three times, okay?"

I hear her small sound of acknowledgment and rap my knuckles against the door in our now-familiar pattern. The lock clicks and the door opens just enough for me to slip inside.

Sunny stands there in one of the oversized hoodies she wears to work, face pale but composed. I do a quick sweep of her apartment while she resets all the locks.

"It's clear," I tell her, holstering my weapon. "No one's here."

She nods but doesn't relax. "I know what being watched feels like, Z. Someone was following me."

I believe her. Sunny's survived too much to ignore her instincts. "Tell me everything you noticed. Any details."

She sinks onto her couch, pulling her knees up to her chest. "I don't know. I got off work a little late, like I said, but I didn't notice anything unusual. I didn't notice anyone pulling into the garage after me. The garage was deserted, like it always is this time of night. But I swear, as soon as I got out of the car, I knew I wasn't alone."

I sit beside her, careful to leave space between us. Spending time with her has taught me the dance of proximity—how to be close enough for comfort without triggering her need for distance.

"The feeling got stronger in the stairwell," she continues. "And then..." She glances at the door. "I swear someone was right there, Z. Just... standing there."

"I believe you." I pull out my phone to text Wolf, asking him to check the club's security cameras. "You can come back to the safehouse with me and stay until we figure this out."

"No." Her response is immediate, firm despite her lingering fear. "I can't run every time I get scared. This is my home."

I recognize the hardness in her voice—it's the same tone she gets when she insists on paying for her own breakfast and giving me money for groceries on days I cook for her. It's pointless for me to argue, so I don't.

"Then I'm staying here."

She starts to protest but I cut her off. "It's non-negotiable, Sunny. Someone was here. Until we know who and why, you're not alone."

The silence stretches between us, filled with all the things we don't say about why someone might be watching her. About who it could be and what it means.

Finally, she nods. "The couch is yours. It's going to be uncomfortable though."

"I'm sure I've slept rougher."

"No doubt." She unfolds herself from the couch, some of the tension leaving her shoulders. "I'm going to change. There's extra blankets in the hall closet."

I watch her disappear into her bedroom, listening for the click of her lock. Our morning routine has shown me this side of her too—how she needs these small barriers, these moments of complete privacy to feel secure.

While she's gone, I do another sweep of the apartment, checking windows and sight lines. I position myself on the couch where I can see both the door and the hallway leading to her room. My phone buzzes with a response from Wolf—he'll have the camera footage for me by morning.

When Sunny emerges in sleep clothes, her hair damp from a quick shower, she pauses in the hallway. "Thank you, Z."

I meet her eyes, seeing the sincerity behind those simple words. Thank you for coming. For believing me. For staying.

"Anytime," I tell her, and we both know I mean it.

I sit with my arms stretched out on the back of the couch, listening to the quiet sounds of Sunny settling into bed. She was right. The couch isn't very comfortable to sit on and I can't imagine what it'd be like to sleep on. Good thing I have no intention of trying it out. I rest my gun within easy reach on the coffee table.

Every small noise from outside draws my attention—a car door slamming, footsteps on the stairs, the hum of the building's ancient cooling system. I check my phone periodically, but Wolf hasn't sent any updates.

My mind keeps circling back to the scuffs and scratches on her doorframe. Someone was here, watching, waiting. The thought makes my jaw clench. I've seen too much in this life to believe in coincidences. With what went down at the club with Levi there's no way to know who heard 'Angel's' real name or where that information ended up. There's no way to know who's taking an interest in Sunny suddenly or why.

Levi made sure everyone in the place knew she was connected to us. That could make her very valuable to some people. Or it could be completely unrelated to us at all. It could be something as simple as a customer from the club not understanding boundaries.

The hours crawl by. I scroll through work emails, coordinate with Wolf about more issues with the warehouse, anything to stay alert. Around six, I hear Sunny's door open softly. Her footsteps pad down the hallway—I recognize the slight hesitation in her gait, the way she favors her left side when she's tired.

"Can't sleep?" I keep my voice low.

She shakes her head, curling up on the other end of the couch. "The monsters are hungry tonight."

I know better than to offer empty reassurances. Instead, I decide a distraction is in order. I pull up a stupid game Colt installed on my phone. "Want to help me beat this level? I'm stuck."

She slides closer to see the screen, and we spend the next hour taking turns trying to solve increasingly difficult word puzzles. Her commentary gets progressively more sarcastic—and hilarious—as fatigue sets in, making me bite back smiles.

I must doze off at some point because the next thing I know, bright late morning light is filtering through the windows and there's a soft warmth along my side. I freeze, barely daring to breathe.

Sunny is curled up tight against me, her head resting on my shoulder, one hand tucked under her cheek. Her face is completely relaxed in sleep, with all the careful guards she maintains stripped away.

She looks younger like this, unburdened by the stress she carries when she's awake.

I don't move a muscle, afraid to startle her awake, or worse, disturb this moment of pure trust. My chest feels tight watching her breathe deeply, evenly. In all our shared breakfasts and late-night diner runs, this is the first time she's ever truly let her guard down. I'd dismiss it as nothing more than exhaustion on her part, but there's no way she'd let herself be this vulnerable completely on accident. She's too careful for that.

And just when I thought she couldn't get any more beautiful, the edges of her lips curl up in a slight smile and she sighs.

A realization hits me square in the center of my chest—I want this. I want to be this for her. The person she trusts enough to fall asleep with. The one she calls when she's scared. I want to be her safe place. Her safe person.

It's a dangerous want. Between what I do for a living, where my loyalties lie, and her past, there are a lot of sharp edges to navigate. For both of us. But watching her sleeping so peacefully, I know it's already too late for me. Whatever any of this is, I can't stop it.

My phone vibrates in my pocket. Carefully, moving with glacier-like slowness, I extract it without disturbing her. A message from Wolf about the security footage. But for now, it can wait. This moment—holding Sunny's complete trust, giving her a few, small moments of real rest—feels too good and too important to disturb.

I rest my head back against the couch, keeping perfectly still, and let myself be the guardian of her peace a little longer.

Chapter Thirty-Three

Sunny

Warmth. That's the first thing I register as consciousness slowly returns. I feel safe, comfortable, and completely at peace. The sensations are so foreign they take a moment to identify. There's a gentle weight on my shoulder, and I'm curled up against something solid and warm. I snuggle into the blanket a little deeper.

In the space of a breath, reality crashes in.

My eyes snap open and I bolt upright, my heart thundering against my ribs as I realize I'm not alone. I scramble across the couch, dragging the blanket with me trying to remember why I'm not in my room, who's here with me. The room spins as panic claws its way up my throat. My chest constricts painfully, and I can feel tremors starting in my hands. I squeeze my eyes shut tight against all of it.

"No, no, no…" the words are frantic, pleading as they pour out of my mouth.

"Sunny." A voice I recognize cuts through the static roaring in my ears. "Look at me."

I can't. I'm frozen. Stuck in place. My breath comes in sharp, hitching gasps that make my lungs hurt, make me dizzy. I think I'm going to be sick.

"Sunny." The voice is firmer now, but still gentle. It's Z. Zane is here with me. "Focus on my voice Sunny. Match my breathing."

He takes my hand and gently places it against his chest, letting me feel the steady rise and fall of each measured breath he takes. "In through your nose, out through your mouth. With me."

I force my eyes open, force myself to look at him, anchoring myself in the calm blue of his eyes. He breathes deeply, deliberately, and I struggle to match his rhythm.

"That's it," he encourages. "You're safe. Nothing bad is happening. Just breathe with me."

Gradually, the vice grip around my chest loosens. The room stops spinning, and my breathing evens out. Z keeps holding my gaze, his hand pressing mine to his chest, until the worst is over.

"I'm sorry," I whisper. Shame and embarrassment replace the frantic need to get away. I pull my hand away. "I've never... no one's ever..." I wiggle my toes in between the cushions of the couch. "You must think I'm crazy."

"I don't think you're crazy Sunny. And you don't have to apologize." He shifts subtly, leaning back to give me more space. "There's nothing to be ashamed of."

"It's not that." I wrap my arms around myself, trying to hide how badly my hands are still shaking. I remember coming out here and sitting next to Zane. I remember playing the stupid game on his phone, and then there's nothing. "I shouldn't have come out here last night. I don't know what I was thinking."

"You were exhausted." His voice is even, with no judgment or pity. "I thought about waking you up, but you looked so peaceful. I thought you could use a few hours of good sleep."

I risk glancing at him, expecting to see discomfort or awkwardness, but his expression is open, understanding. I relax a tiny bit.

"It's still embarrassing," I mutter.

"We all have ghosts, Sunny." His tone is quiet.

He stands, stretching. "I'll make us some coffee."

I watch as he moves around my small kitchen with familiar ease, pulling out mugs and starting the coffee maker. It should bother me how comfortable he is here, how naturally he's slipped into my space. But, it doesn't. It feels better than it probably should.

"You should eat something too," he says, dropping bread into the toaster. "Even if it's just a few bites."

"I'm not hungry."

He gives me a look I've come to recognize—the one that says he's not buying my bullshit. "Humor me."

The coffee maker gurgles to completion, and he fixes our cups—mine with way too much cream and sugar, just how I like it. He sets both mugs on the coffee table along with a plate of toast.

The comfortable silence stretches between us as we sip our coffee, but there's something I need to ask.

"How did you know that doing that thing you did would work?" I trace the rim of my mug with my finger. "That breathing thing."

Z's expression shifts, something raw and painful flickering across his face before he masks it. "My sister. She would get panic attacks sometimes. They were horrible for her."

The past tense hangs heavy in the air. I don't push, but I can't help noticing how his hands tighten around his mug, the way his jaw clenches slightly.

"She's gone now, but maybe someday I'll tell you about her," he says with a sadness I can feel.

I nod, understanding both the offer and its limits. We sit in comfortable silence, the morning light growing stronger through my windows. It strikes me how comfortable this feels—sharing space with someone, not having to fill every moment with words. I've never had this before.

Z's phone buzzes. His expression darkens as he reads the message.

"Shit," he mutters, then looks at me. "Someone just triggered the warehouse's security."

I can see him wrestling with the decision to leave.

"Go," I tell him. "I'll be fine. The doors are locked."

"Ty's already outside, right at the bottom of the stairs. Wolf sent him over this morning," he says finally. "He'll keep watch. I'll be back in two hours, tops."

The thought of him leaving me alone makes my stomach clench, but I try not to let it show.

"When I get back, will you please consider coming to the safehouse with me?" His eyes meet mine, serious and concerned. "At least until I can get some answers about who was watching you last night. You'd have your own space, complete privacy. And all the security you need."

"Z..." I start to protest.

"I know you don't want to run," he cuts in. "But this isn't running. It's being smart."

Part of me wants to say yes, if only to ease the worry I can see in his expression. But the larger part of me remembers what happened the last time I let someone convince me they'd keep me safe.

"I can't," I say softly. "I need to be here. In my own place."

He nods like he didn't really expect any other answer.

"Alright," Z says finally, though he doesn't look happy about it. "But I'm coming back as soon as I'm done. And until then..." He fixes me with an intense look. "Keep your doors locked. All of them. And keep your phone on you at all times—even if you're just going to the bathroom."

"Yes, sir," I say, trying to lighten the mood, but his expression remains serious.

"I mean it, Sunny. This is serious."

"I know." I wrap my arms around myself. "I promise I'll be careful."

He stands reluctantly, gathering his jacket. At the door, he waits while I slide the locks into place, then I hear him testing the handle from the outside—once, twice. His footsteps pause in the hallway, like he's second-guessing leaving, before finally fading away.

I drag myself back to the couch, exhausted despite having slept more hours at a time than I'm used to. The blanket Z used is still there, and I pull it around myself as I lay down. The fabric smells like him—warm spice and leather. It's comforting. I know I should probably get up, maybe try to be productive, do some laundry or clean, but the events of last night and this morning have left me drained.

I burrow deeper into the blanket, creating a cozy cocoon, and let my eyes drift closed. Just five minutes, I tell myself. But as I start to drift off, I can't help the small smile that curves my lips.

When I wake, something feels wrong. The apartment is too quiet. My eyes fall on my coffee table and my blood turns to ice.

Sitting there, perfectly centered, is my set of spare keys. The ones I keep hidden in my dresser drawer.

I lift my head off the couch and look around slowly, trying to be quiet. Nothing else looks disturbed or out of place.

I slide my hand down, grabbing the phone out of my pocket. With trembling fingers, I dial. Z answers on the first ring.

"Sunny. You okay?"

I struggle to keep my voice a low whisper. "Someone's been here. Inside."

His tone shifts instantly. "Are you alone in the room right now?"

"I... I think so. I don't know."

"Don't move. Stay exactly where you are." In the space of a breath his voice becomes controlled, precise. "Tell me what you see without getting up."

"I'm lying on the couch. My... my spare keys are on the table." My breath starts coming in ragged gasps. "Z, those keys were hidden in my—"

"Focus, Sunny. I need you to tell me what you can hear?"

I strain to listen. "Nothing. It's quiet."

A beat of silence. "Is your phone on silent?"

"No."

"Put it on silent now. But don't hang up." I hear him barking orders to someone in the background.

"Good. Now, very slowly, I want you to slide to the floor between the couch and the coffee table. Stay low. Tell me when you're there."

I do as he says. My heart is hammering so hard I worry that if someone *is* here with me they can hear it.

"I'm down."

"Good. Now listen carefully. I want you to move to the door as quiet as possible. Stay against the wall if you can and keep down. If you hear anything, anything at all, you freeze. Understand?"

"Yes."

"When you reach the door, don't open it. Listen first. Three seconds minimum. You copy?"

"Copy." The military precision of his instructions helps to keep the panic at bay.

"I'm four minutes out. Ty's not responding but I've got Wolf coming. You ready?"

"Ready."

"Move. Now."

I slither along the floor, keeping my head down, fighting the urge to stand up and run.

Once I'm at the door, I press my ear against it. One Mississippi. Two Mississippi. Three—

A floorboard creaks somewhere in the hallway outside.

"Z," I breathe into the phone. "Someone's out there."

"Sunny, run. Get into the bathroom. Now. Lock the door." His voice is tight. "I'm almost there."

I turn towards the bathroom, but freeze at a sound that makes my blood run cold—the scratch of a key in the lock.

There's a loud click and the door starts to open.

"Sunny, move. NOW." Z's voice is steel in my ear.

I bolt for the bathroom, slamming and locking the door behind me.

"Talk to me," Z demands. "Are you secure?"

"Yes." My voice is barely a whisper. "The door's locked."

"Good. Get in the tub. Stay low. Keep your head down."

I climb into the bathtub, pressing myself as flat as possible against the cold porcelain. Heavy footsteps move through my apartment—slow, methodical. Searching.

The bathroom doorknob rattles.

I clamp my hand over my mouth to stifle a whimper.

"Hurry Zane," I breathe into the phone. "Please."

"Fuck!" I hear him slam his hand into the steering wheel. "I'm almost there Sunny. Stay down. Whatever you hear, whatever happens don't move until you hear my voice. My actual voice, not through the phone. Understand?"

"Yes."

The doorknob rattles again, harder this time. I scream as something heavy slams into the door. It gives, but holds.

Another slam.

The wood splinters.

Somewhere in the apartment, I hear the front door crash open.

"SUNNY!" Z's voice booms through the apartment.

The pounding on the bathroom door stops. The heavy footsteps retreat. Glass shatters—from my bedroom, I think.

"Clear!" An unfamiliar voice shouts.

"Clear!" Another voice.

"Bathroom's secure," Z calls out. "Sunny? It's me. I'm coming in."

Z slams his shoulder into the door, forcing it. When it opens, Z fills the frame, gun drawn but pointed down. His eyes are cold, deadly. Behind him, I glimpse other men moving through my apartment, checking corners, securing rooms.

"Are you hurt?"

I shake my head, not trusting my voice.

Z holsters his weapon and reaches for me. I fall out of the tub into his arms.

"I've got you," he murmurs against my hair. "You're safe."

But we both know that's a lie. Someone got past Ty. Got into my apartment.

"Wolf found Ty," one of the men reports from the doorway. "He's unconscious but alive. Looks like he was drugged."

Z's arms tighten around me. "You're coming to the safehouse." he says, his tone leaving no room for argument.

This time, I don't protest.

THE ACTION

Chapter Thirty-Four

Sunny

THE SAFEHOUSE ISN'T WHAT I expected. Nothing like anything I've seen on TV. From the outside, it's unassuming—a sprawling two-story home sitting on a large plot of land, with a couple outbuildings and well-maintained carefully designed landscaping. But watching Z's team move through it, I can see that every part of the house and land has purpose. Clear lines of sight to the entire area, secure fencing, security cameras disguised as outdoor lighting.

I stay in the corner of the living room, trying to make myself small as men move around me with military precision. My fingers won't stop trembling with leftover adrenaline from the apartment.

Z hasn't let me out of his sight since we arrived, even while directing his team. He keeps himself positioned between me and the door, or me and anyone else. He does it effortlessly. If I weren't so on edge I probably wouldn't have noticed. Every time someone new enters the room, his hand twitches toward his weapon.

"Perimeter secure," Wolf reports from his position by the window, his kind eyes a stark contrast to the weapon still holstered at his side. Just an hour ago, he'd been the one to find Ty unconscious outside my apartment. Now he's adjusting his glasses and setting up surveillance feeds. Like it's all just part of a day's work. Which I suppose it is for him.

Z nods, his deep voice filling the room. "My team's the best at what they do, Sunny. I trust every single man under this roof with my life." He pauses, his jaw tight. "I know that doesn't mean shit to you right now, but I need you to trust me, trust them. If there were any other way..."

The raw honesty in his voice makes me look up. He knows how much he's asking of me.

Chase emerges from the kitchen, his massive frame filling the doorway. He's the one who helped me to the car after Z got me out. He's huge. Easily the biggest man I've ever seen. His gentleness surprised me. "House is clear," he reports. "Security system upgrades are online. Added motion sensors to all entry points." He gives me the same reassuring smile he'd offered when Z handed me off to him.

Ty's set up at the dining room table with multiple laptops open in front of him. The bruise on his temple is a stark purple against his pale skin. The guilt hits me again—he was protecting me when that happened. From what I understand, all these men have agreed to protect each other with their lives if necessary. I was never part of that agreement.

He catches me staring at him through the doorway and gives a slight nod, as if reading my thoughts. "I'm fine," he says in a voice loud enough to carry through the room. "It wasn't your fault."

"Something smells amazing," I manage, trying to change the subject.

"That would be Jayce," Z explains.

"Making pasta tonight—an old family recipe. It's going to be delicious." A warm voice calls from the kitchen.

I freeze for a moment, my brain struggling to reconcile the domesticity in those words with everything going on around me. Less than an hour ago, they'd moved through my apartment like a tactical unit, weapons drawn, voices clipped and professional. I give up on trying to make it make sense and stretch out in the chair I'm sitting in.

Through the kitchen doorway, I can hear Jayce humming while he cooks. Wolf and Chase are discussing camera placement in low voices. Ty's fingers click steadily on his keyboard.

I sink deeper into the chair, the adrenaline crash hitting me hard. My clothes still smell like fear-sweat from being trapped in that bathroom, and my hair feels stringy and gross. Z must notice something in my expression because he straightens from his spot by the door.

"Come on," he says, offering me his hand. "Let me show you to your room. You look like you could use a shower and some space to breathe."

The thought of being alone makes my heart rate spike, but the idea of washing away the last couple hours is too tempting to resist. I follow him through the house, noting how the others subtly shift their positions as we move. Even heading up the long wooden staircase, they're protecting me.

"This one will be yours." Z opens the third door on the right.

The room is simple but comfortable. It holds a queen-sized bed with crisp white sheets, a dresser, nightstand, and a cushioned window seat overlooking the backyard. I can tell from here the window is the same thick plexiglass convenience stores hide their clerks behind.

"It's not much," Z says, leaning against the doorframe. "But it's secure. This is one of the only rooms with a private bath. You'll be safe here Sunny. Nobody knows about this place except for us."

I walk to the window, taking in the view of the well-maintained yard surrounded by tall trees and fencing. It feels isolated, protected.

"Once I finish debriefing the guys and we come up with a plan, we can head back to your apartment to let you get some things." Z's voice is steady, reassuring. "Clothes, personal items, anything important to you."

I wrap my arms around myself, trying to process everything that's happened in the last few hours. "Z, I-"

"I wish there was a way to make it easier for you." He cuts off my protest before I can voice it. "I know this isn't ideal, and I know you've got every reason not to trust us. But right now, this is the best option."

Seeing him standing there, his eyes so sincere, I want to believe him. After years of taking care of myself, of not letting anyone get close enough to help, it's terrifying to put my trust in someone else. But, he's right. For now, this is my best option.

"So those guys downstairs?" I ask, my voice smaller than I'd like. "They're… good?"

Z's expression softens slightly understanding what I'm asking. "The best. Each one of them has their own story, their own reasons for being here. But they're family. And now, for as long as you need it, they'll do everything they can to make sure you're safe."

I nod, sinking down onto the window seat. "What happens now?"

"Now, you get settled in. Lock your door, take a shower if you want, try to rest. I need to talk to the guys, figure out our next steps." He straightens up from the doorframe. "Jayce really is making pasta—he's actually a great cook. I'll have him bring you up a plate when it's ready."

"Thank you," I whisper, even though the words feel inadequate for everything he's done today.

Z just nods, his expression unreadable. "Get some rest, Sunny. Make yourself at home. We'll handle everything else."

He steps out, pulling the door closed behind him. I listen to his footsteps fade down the hallway, then get up and turn both the locks. The click as they slide into place is comforting.

I sit on the edge of the bed, running my hands over the cool blankets. The house is quiet except for the muffled sounds of conversation downstairs.

How did things manage to get so fucked up?

CHAPTER THIRTY-FIVE

SUNNY

I WANT TO CURL up and take a nap, but the thought of sleep is terrifying. A shower sounds like a much better alternative.

The bathroom is bigger than two rooms of my apartment. A pristine white claw-foot tub sits against one wall, with a separate glass-enclosed —shower in the corner. The counter holds neatly folded towels and basic toiletries—another surprise.

I turn the shower on as hot as I can stand it, letting steam fill the room. As I step under the spray, I close my eyes and try to let the water wash away the tension in my shoulders. It feels wonderful. The shower gel and shampoo smell clean but decidedly masculine—it makes me wonder whose room this is normally.

My mind drifts back to my apartment—I'm already regretting not having some of my own things. My sketchbook. My pillow. The few photos of me with my dad I managed to save and keep tucked away. I hope they're still there when we go back. The thought of someone in my space, going through my things, makes my skin crawl.

After drying off with what must be the softest, most luxurious towel I've ever used, I start opening drawers in search of a brush. The bathroom cabinets are meticulously organized—razors, shaving cream, deodorant, all lined up with military precision. I finally find a brush in the bottom drawer, barely used by the looks of it.

Standing there in a towel, I stare at the heap of clothes on the floor. I nudge the pile with my toe and can feel that at least the hoodie I was wearing is still damp with sweat. The thought of putting any of it back on sounds horrible.

The dresser in the bedroom beckons. I push down feelings of guilt as I start opening drawers and rummaging through them. Everything is perfectly folded and organized by color, each stack neat and precise.

In the third drawer, I find a collection of T-shirts. One catches my eye—faded black and soft from countless washes, with bright red lettering advertising "Lucy Lou's Bar & Grill, Old Bridge—Serving Cold Beer & Hot Wings Since 1981."

I pull it on, and it falls to mid-thigh. I can't imagine any of the men I met downstairs wearing it. It seems too... blue-collar.

I catch my reflection in the mirror and hesitate. It looks like I'm drowning in the soft material. I take a minute to weigh out my options—but one more look at the discarded pile of clothes in the bathroom and clean wins out.

After combing through my damp hair, I feel better. Cleaner. But the room feels too quiet, too still. The voices from downstairs have only gotten louder, rising and falling in a steady soothing rhythm.

My curiosity gets the best of me. Besides, the smell of bread wafting up from the kitchen makes my stomach growl.

I have a moment of hesitation about being seen in nothing but this shirt, but I remind myself that these men met me at Siren's. They've seen a hell of a lot more of me than what this T-shirt covers, even if it doesn't feel like it.

I pad down the stairs quietly, following the voices into what looks like a dining room. The guys are gathered around a large wooden table, heads bent together in discussion. Wolf has a laptop open in front of him, and there are papers spread across the table.

They all look up when I enter, conversation dying immediately. Z's eyes slide up my bare legs and stop at the front of the shirt. Recognition flashes in his eyes, followed by something dark and intense. His gaze lingers a beat too long before he looks away, his jaw tight. I realize this must be his shirt I'm wearing—he gave me his room. The silence is thick, awkward. I shift my weight from foot to foot, suddenly feeling like an intruder.

Chase looks from me to Zane getting a read on the situation before clearing his throat and breaking the tension. His voice is deep and surprisingly gentle when he speaks. "Perfect timing. Jayce is just about done with dinner." He pulls out the empty chair next to him. "Come, sit. We were just finishing up anyway."

I hesitate for a moment before taking the seat offered. Wolf closes his laptop, sweeping a stack of papers into a folder. Whatever they were discussing, they clearly don't want me involved.

"Hope you like garlic," Jayce calls from the kitchen. "Because I might have gone a little overboard."

"Like we'd ever expect anything less," Ty snorts.

"Ha. Ha." Jayce retorts, emerging with a huge pot of pasta. The rich smell of tomatoes and herbs fills the room.

Chase gets up to help, returning with a basket of garlic bread and a bowl of salad. It's surreal, watching these intimidating men move around each other in perfect choreographed movements.

"Wine?" Z asks, holding up a bottle of red.

I shake my head no, watching as he pours generous glasses for everyone. The normalcy of what's happening around me is throwing me off balance.

"So," Chase says as we start passing dishes around. "You're an artist?"

I nearly choke on the drink of water I took. "How did you"

"Z told us about your drawings," he shrugs. "Says you have some hung up on your walls. I draw too." He nods toward the sketchbook I noticed earlier.

"Oh." I twirl pasta around my fork, oddly touched that he noticed. "Yeah, I guess."

"She's being modest," Z cuts in. "Her work is incredible."

Heat creeps up my neck at his words. I didn't realize he'd paid that much attention.

"You should see Chase's work," Wolf says, tearing into a piece of garlic bread. "Guy could be selling in galleries if he wanted to."

Chase ducks his head, embarrassed. "It's just a hobby."

"Show her the one you did of Wolf sleeping at his desk," Jayce grins. "Drool and all."

"I do not drool," Wolf protests, but he's fighting a smile.

Just like that, the tension breaks. The conversation flows easy, punctuated by laughter and good-natured ribbing. They tell stories about each other, share inside jokes. I find myself relaxing despite everything. They make it easy to get drawn in.

Zane wasn't lying. Jayce is a brilliant cook. The pasta is perfect, the sauce rich and flavorful. I'm on my second helping before I realize it.

"Thank you," I say quietly to Z while the others are arguing about some movie I've never seen. "For everything you did today."

He meets my eyes, his expression serious. "You don't have to thank me. We take care of our own."

"Is that what I am now? One of your own?"

"You're under our protection," he says simply. "So, yeah. You're family."

Family. The word sits heavy in my chest. I'm not even sure what that word means.

"More wine anyone?" Chase offers, already reaching for the bottle.

I let the warmth of the food and conversation wash over me. For the first time since this afternoon, I feel my shoulders relax.

Maybe, this won't be as bad as I was imagining it.

After dinner, everyone drifts to their own corners of the house. Chase returns to his book, Wolf disappears into what looks like an office, and Jayce starts cleaning up the kitchen with Ty's help. It's how I imagine a family operates.

Z touches my elbow lightly. "Can we talk for a minute?"

I follow him to a small study off the main living room. Books line the walls, and a leather armchair sits in one corner next to a reading lamp. Z closes the door behind us, and my heart rate picks up slightly.

"First," he says, leaning against the desk, "I want you to know I'm glad you're here."

I wrap my arms around myself, suddenly cold despite the warmth of the room. "Did I have a choice?"

"There are always choices, Sunny." His gaze is locked on mine.

"Choices and options are worlds apart."

He nods slowly. "About that... Wolf pulled the security footage from around your apartment building."

My stomach drops. "And?"

"Someone's definitely been watching you. Following you." He runs a hand through his long black hair, frustration evident in the gesture. "We don't know who yet, but the cameras have shown cars entering the parking lot outside your building right after you pull into the garage. When you leave they leave. I had Wolf check and they always park so they have a clear view of your front window and door. It appears to be the same person, but it's hard to tell."

The room suddenly feels too small. I sink into the leather armchair, my legs unsteady. "How... how long?"

"That's the thing—we can only access footage from the past ten days." He leaves the sentence hanging.

"Could it be..." I can't bring myself to say Garrett's name.

"We don't know. But whoever it is, they know what they're doing. They keep themselves far enough away from the security cameras to make ID'ing them almost impossible. They change cars, change plates every other day. They aren't an amateur. The only reason you knew they were there was probably because they wanted you to know." Z pushes off from the desk and crouches in front of my chair, bringing himself to my eye level. "Which is why I need to tell you something else."

I meet his gaze, dreading what comes next.

"I can't keep this to myself anymore. I need help if I'm going to keep you safe. Sunny, I need Levi and Colt here."

The sound of Levi's name sends a jolt through my system. "No."

"Sunny—"

"No." I stand up abruptly, forcing him to step back. "I can't... do that."

Z's voice remains steady, calm. "I can't imagine how any of this feels, but this is about keeping you safe. Whoever's watching you is serious and they know what they're doing. We need resources, manpower. That means Levi and Colt and the rest of the guys."

"You said *you'd* protect me." My voice comes out smaller than I intend, accusing.

"And I will. That's exactly why I need to bring them in." He steps closer but doesn't touch me. "Look, I know what Levi did. I know he left when you needed him most. But right now, we need his help."

I pace the small room, feeling trapped. "Does he already know I'm here?"

"No. I haven't told him anything yet." Z watches me move, his expression unreadable. "But he needs to know. We're dealing with something bigger than just you and him."

The logical part of my brain knows he's right. If someone's really watching me, if they have the kind of determination that Z is talking about of course he should do whatever he needs to.

But the thought of seeing Levi again, of being in the same house as him is unbearable.

"I won't let him come here," Z says, as if reading my thoughts. "Not unless you agree. But you need to know that I can't keep you as safe as you would be with him here. We need his help, his connections. And Colt? Colt's the best at what he does. If anyone can figure out who's watching you, it's him."

I stop pacing, pressing my forehead against the cool glass of the window. Outside, the sky has turned dark, and I can see the shadowy outline of motion sensing security lights lining the fence around the property. Somewhere out there, someone is looking for me.

"What if..." I swallow hard. "What if it's him? What if Garrett found me?"

"Then we'll deal with it." Z's voice hardens. "But we need to know what we're up against."

I turn back to face him. "You really need them here?"

"I do." He steps closer, close enough that I have to tilt my head back to meet his eyes. "I wouldn't suggest this if it wasn't absolutely necessary. You know that, right?"

And I do know that. In the short time I've known him, Z has never given me any reason to doubt anything he's said.

"Okay," I whisper. It feels like a surrender in the worst possible way. "But I don't... I can't..."

"I'll be here with you the whole time," Z promises. "None of this has to mean anything more than just pooling our resources to keep you safe."

I nod, exhaustion crushing in on me. "When will you tell them?"

"Tonight. The sooner we get started, the better." He studies my face. "You should get some rest. It's been a long day."

I push away from the window. "Z?"

He pauses with his hand on the doorknob. "Yeah?"

"Thank you. For being honest with me. About all of it."

Something softens in his expression. "I will never be anything less than that to you. That's a promise."

CHAPTER THIRTY-SIX

SUNNY

I JOLT AWAKE, HEART hammering against my ribs. The sheets tangle around my legs like restraints, and for a moment I'm back there—pinned down, helpless, Garrett's breath hot on my neck.

No. I'm at the safehouse. In Z's house.

My T-shirt—Z's T-shirt—clings to my skin with cold sweat. The digital clock on the nightstand blinks 2:47 AM in harsh red numbers. Sleep feels impossible now, the nightmare still clinging to the edges of my consciousness.

I swing my legs over the side of the bed, pressing my feet against the cool hardwood floor. The contact grounds me, helps push back the lingering panic. I need to get out of this room.

The hallway is dark but there's light spilling up from downstairs. Voices drift up—low, male voices that make me freeze for a split second before I recognize them as Wolf and Chase.

I pad down the stairs, careful to avoid the creaky third step I noticed earlier. The kitchen light spills into the hallway, and I can see them hunched over laptops and papers spread across the kitchen table.

"No, look—" Wolf points at something on the screen. "Eddie and Jake will be here tomorrow evening. If we put them here and here during the night shift..."

"Hey Angel—sorry, Sunny." Chase notices me first, his massive frame straightening. "Everything okay?"

"Yeah, just..." I wave vaguely at nothing. "Couldn't sleep. Thought I'd come down and get some water."

Wolf immediately stands. "Here, let me—"

"I can get it." I move to the cabinet I saw Z take glasses from earlier. "Don't let me interrupt."

"You're not interrupting." Chase pushes back from the table. "We're just going over security protocols for when the boss gets here in a couple days."

My hand trembles slightly as I fill the glass. The boss. Levi.

"Want something to eat?" Wolf asks. "Z went out earlier and got some of those protein bars you said you liked."

The offer catches me off guard. I mentioned them in passing. A week ago. "Sure, thanks."

Chase pulls out a chair. "Join us."

I settle into the chair, accepting the bar Wolf hands me. The papers spread across the table are blueprints of the property, guard rotation schedules, security codes.

"I don't want you to get in trouble. Isn't this all super-secret, or something?" I say, taking a bite and waving my hand over the stacks of papers.

"Are you a spy?" Wolf says, his tone serious.

"No."

"Then no worries, right?" His face breaks into a wide smile, and Chase chuckles.

"So, Eddie and Jake, from Sirens? They're coming?" I ask.

"Yeah, Z called them earlier. He seems to trust them, and they jumped at the chance to make some real cash. It doesn't hurt that they seem to have kind of a sweet spot for you. They'll be part of the night shift rotation." Wolf taps the schedule. "Day shift will be mainly us and the guys coming with Levi and Colt."

"How many..." I clear my throat. "How many people are coming?"

"About a dozen." Chase's voice is gentle, like he understands why the question's important to me. "All good guys. But most of them will be sleeping in the bunkhouse out back. There's only going to be a few more guys in here. With us. You're gonna love Rex. He's hilarious."

I manage a small smile at that.

The casual conversation helps ease some of the tension in my shoulders. I watch as they continue working out the schedule, pointing out different access points on the property.

"Main gate code changes daily," Wolf explains, making notes while Chase listens. "Secondary gates every three days. Emergency override stays the same."

Chase scribbles a number down on a piece of paper with a long list of numbers written on it.

7726. I memorize the number and a few of the locations they discuss on the blueprint. Just in case.

"These motion sensors," Chase points to red X's on the paper. "They'll be live 24/7 except during shift changes. Anyone tries crossing that line, the whole place goes into lockdown."

"The kind of lockdown where you need that override code?" I ask before I can stop myself.

Wolf's eyes crinkle at the corners. "Smart girl. Yeah, exactly that kind."

We fall into comfortable silence as they continue working. The protein bar settles my stomach, and the nightmare feels further away with each passing minute.

"You know," Chase says after a while, his deep voice surprisingly soft. "It's good having you here. Place feels less... I don't know. Heavy."

"What he means is it's nice having someone around who can put Z in a good mood," Wolf adds with a grin.

I find myself smiling back, genuine this time. "Well, thank you. I guess."

Their easy banter washes over me as they finish up the schedules.

"You should try to get some more sleep," Chase says eventually, gathering up the papers. "A lot going on over the next few days."

The reminder of what's coming sends a fresh wave of anxiety through me, but I nod. "Yeah, probably should."

"Hey." Wolf's voice stops me as I stand. "We've got your back, okay? No matter what happens."

I swallow hard against the sudden tightness in my throat. "Good night."

I climb back upstairs, my feet dragging against the carpet. The conversation with Wolf and Chase left me feeling oddly lighter, despite everything. My bed welcomes me back, sheets cool against my skin, and before I can spiral into thoughts about Levi's arrival, sleep claims me.

Sunlight streams through unfamiliar curtains when I open my eyes. The clock reads 12:07 PM and I bolt upright. I never sleep this late. Ever. Never more than a few hours at a time. But here, in this strange house full of dangerous men, I've somehow managed the deepest sleep I can remember.

The house buzzes with activity when I venture downstairs. Voices and footsteps echo from different rooms, along with the occasional power tool whirring. The smell of something amazing cooking draws me toward the kitchen. Again.

Z and Jayce work in perfect sync, moving around each other like they've done this a thousand times. Z chops vegetables while Jayce stirs something on the stove that makes my mouth water. They're mid-conversation, both grinning.

"Man, you should've seen his face when Wolf told him the security system was voice-activated." Jayce laughs, adding spices to whatever he's cooking.

"Chase actually believed that?" Z shakes his head, sliding diced peppers into a bowl.

"For like ten solid minutes. Kept trying different voice commands."

Something in my chest aches watching them. Their easy friendship, the inside jokes, the comfortable silence between words—it's something I've never really had. Even Jade, as close as we are, only knows the carefully edited version of my life I've allowed her to see.

Z spots me hovering in the doorway and his whole face lights up. "Look who finally decided to join the land of the living."

"Sorry, I didn't mean to sleep so late."

"Are you kidding? I'm glad you finally got some rest." He waves me over. "You've got to try this soup Jayce is making. He thinks he's some kind of master chef."

"I *am* a master chef, thank you very much." Jayce holds up a spoon. "Here, taste this and tell Z he's wrong."

I take a careful taste. The soup explodes with flavor on my tongue—rich and spicy and perfect. "Oh wow."

"See?" Jayce points the spoon at Z triumphantly.

"Speaking of cooking," Z says in a serious tone, "did I mention that you are standing in the presence of someone who burned water?"

"Z!" My cheeks heat up. "That was one time."

"She set off the smoke alarm. Boiling water. Just water."

"How do you even..." Jayce stares at me in mock horror.

"I got distracted! And anyway, I do just fine without cooking."

"Oh yeah?" Jayce raises an eyebrow. "How's that?"

I pull out my phone, showing them my favorites list. "I have an excellent relationship with every delivery place in town. Speed dial and everything."

"That's it." Jayce shakes his head. "No way. You're learning to cook. This is unacceptable."

"I'm really good at microwave meals too," I offer, which makes them both groan.

"Basic life skills, Sunny." Z bumps my shoulder with his. "You can't live on takeout forever."

"Watch me." But I'm smiling, caught up in their playful energy.

"Nope. Starting tomorrow, you're getting cooking lessons." Jayce points the wooden spoon at me. "Non-negotiable."

"Will you teach me how to make your soup?"

"If that's what it takes?" He grins.

Z watches our back and forth with something soft in his expression that makes my heart do a funny little flip. For a moment, I can almost forget why I'm here. Almost.

Chapter Thirty-Seven

Levi

Colt and I pull up to the house as the first rays of light start creeping over the hills surrounding the property. I'm gripping the steering wheel so hard my fingers ache. The call from Z the other night left me with a lot more questions than answers. There's so much he hasn't told me and it pisses me off.

Colt sits shotgun, silent. He gave up a few hours ago trying to get me to talk. He knows my temper's resting on a hair trigger. It took a full day and a half to get things settled, and ready for us to clear out, and another ten hours of driving. I'm tired and ready to get some sleep and answers.

"Take it easy," he murmurs as I kill the engine. "Whatever's going on, you have to remember you trust Z. He's your brother. I'm sure he has a good reason for doing things the way he has."

I grunt in response, too wound up to form words. I toss him the keys and he hops out of the truck and starts directing the guys who followed us into parking spots. Most of them have never been here before and I want to make sure they're familiar with the place and settled in as quickly as possible.

The house is quiet, only a few lights coming from the back of the house are visible, but as I let myself in the back door I catch the sound of voices. And then—a high pitched, musical laugh.

Sunny.

The sound strikes a chord inside me. It's a sound I never thought I'd hear again. I follow it into the kitchen.

I freeze when I hit the doorway, gut-punched by the scene in front of me. Sunny's leaning against the counter, arms crossed over her chest, wearing nothing but an oversized white T-shirt with a familiar logo emblazoned across the chest. It's one of Z's favorite band shirts. Her long blonde hair falls in messy waves around her shoulders and down her back. She's barefoot and seems completely at ease.

She laughs again. My breath catches as I watch her eyes crinkle at the corners as she grins at Ty. Fucking *Ty*. The guy I hired three years ago and have never heard string more than five words together at one time unless absolutely pressed. But here he is, standing center stage like some wind-up toy with no off switch. He's so invested in being the morning's entertainment he doesn't even notice me standing here.

And then there's Z...

Standing next to the sink, dumping an ungodly amount of sugar into a cup of coffee with a stupid grin on his face. He's shirtless, wearing a pair of grey sweatpants and looks like he just rolled out of bed. He drops a spoon in the mug and offers it to Sunny. "Here you go, your morning cup of sugar. Just the way you like it," he says.

It feels like I'm intruding—getting ready to walk into a private moment I have no right to disturb. It's intimate. It's cozy. It's making my blood boil.

"Morning, Levi." Z says without turning, without taking his eyes off Sunny.

Of course he knew I was here.

"We were wondering what time you guys would get here."

The smile slides off Sunny's face the second he says my name. Z leans in and murmurs something into her ear I can't quite hear. Whatever it is, she rewards him with a soft, sweet smile.

When she turns toward me, the smile is gone and her face is shuttered and unreadable. The guarded look she wears twists something deep inside my chest.

Realization slaps me in the face. This is her new normal. Here. With him.

"You've got to be kidding," I spit out.

Z turns his gaze to me, arching his brow. His expression is otherwise neutral. "About?" His voice is calm, steady.

He knows exactly what I'm talking about.

"This." I open my arms and sweep them around the kitchen. "All of this. I thought—" I sneer, curling my lip in disgust. "Is this why I haven't heard anything from you in weeks? Too busy playing house?"

Zane's eyes narrow and his voice drops dangerously low. "I would choose your next words very carefully, if I were you. You have no idea what you're talking about," he warns.

Ty takes the opportunity to slip out of the kitchen, brushing past me without a word.

"I'm not a fucking idiot you know. Is this why you were so anxious to get me out of town?" The words taste like acid on my tongue. "You wanted her all to yourself."

Sunny's mouth drops open in shock. She stays silent but takes a step, positioning herself so she's standing slightly behind Z as my voice escalates. He shoots me a glare as he moves himself closer to her. The protective gesture only feeds my building rage.

"How long?" My voice thunders through the kitchen, and Sunny's whole body jerks as if I've struck her. I see her hands start to shake, her chest rising and falling as her breath comes in quick, shallow breaths. Her eyes are still focused on me, but they're clouded with fear.

I hate myself for the words, but I can't make them stop.

"I said how long," I hiss through gritted teeth. There's a far away voice somewhere in the back of my mind, screaming at me to stop. To walk away before it's too late. Before I say something I can't take back. But I don't. I can't.

"Levi," Zane's voice is calm, but full of warning as he speaks, "I won't warn you again."

Sunny cringes, letting her forehead fall against Zane's arm. My brain is flooded with the memory of a terrified seventeen-year-old Sunny stepping behind me that way—letting me put myself between her and the monster, between her and Garrett. Except this time, I'm the one she's afraid of. I'm the one she wants protection from. The realization does nothing to stop the words from pouring out.

"How long has this been going on?" I snap, my voice turning into a roar.

Sunny visibly flinches at each word as it leaves my mouth. The sight of her in Z's shirt, the easy way she was laughing, the way she trusts him—it's all too much.

Her face is hidden, but I can see her toes digging into the wooden floor. A nervous habit she never grew out of apparently. "Since he isn't going to answer me, maybe you will. How long Sunny? How long have you been fucking my best friend?"

She sucks in a sharp breath. Good, I hit a nerve. Maybe now I can get some answers.

"Is this how you've both decided to hurt me? To get revenge?" I let the words land, giving them time to sink in and find their mark.

The color drains from her face. Her eyes well with tears as she shakes her head.

"You owe me an answer. You both owe me at least that."

Those are the words. The ones that snap her out of whatever place she was stuck in. She lifts her head, looks at me, and everything shifts. Her expression hardens and the fear dissipates. Her hands curl into tight fists clenched at her sides.

She steps out from behind Z, shoulders squared, chin lifted. The frightened girl is gone, replaced by a woman who looks ready to tear me apart with her bare hands.

"Just who the fuck, do you think you are?" she questions. Her voice trembles with rage.

Fury blazes in her eyes, pinning me in place. She moves forward, each step deliberate and charged.

"*I* don't owe you anything Levi. Not one damn thing. How dare you come in here and demand anything from me." Her voice, razor-sharp cuts through the kitchen.

Z moves to step between us, but Sunny raises her hand, stopping him cold. He backs down and she advances.

"You gave up any rights you had with me the night you left me."

The sight of her standing there, arms crossed, body trembling with anger, shatters a part of me. I made a mistake. I wish I could take it back. Start over.

"You want honesty Levi? Wanna hear my secrets?" Her laugh is bitter, nothing like the sweet sound from moments ago.

She takes her final step forward, jabbing her finger into my chest looking up at me, defiance shining bright in her eyes as she continues. "Let's start with an easy one."

Sunny leans in, her voice little more than a whisper. "That night? I remember everything, Levi."

The room tilts and I feel dizzy. A tiny, sad smile curves her lips as she watches the weight of her words settle. *That can't be true. There's no way that's true.*

"For one stupid, stupid moment I thought you'd come to save me. Rescue me. But that's not what happened, is it? You called the cops, then stepped over me like I was a piece of trash and walked out."

She blinks back tears but doesn't look away. "You left me there to die, Levi. By myself."

"Sunny," my voice cracks as I speak. "No. That's not what I—I'm sorry, I didn't—" The words tangle in my throat, getting caught on the lump forming there.

"Here's a little more truth for you since you want it so bad." She cuts through my stammered apologies.

"I laid in that hospital bed for twelve days, Levi. Twelve. Fucking. Days. Two surgeries on my hand, dressing changes. Pain you can't even imagine. And no one was there. Not a single soul. Not you. Not my mom. No one." Her voice splinters and she forces a deep shuddering breath into her lungs before continuing.

"Oh, but don't worry. I still made plenty of excuses for you though. For quite a while actually. I could *not* believe that I'd been so wrong about you. I thought, there's no way he'd abandon me. He loves me. He promised. But, that's exactly what you did isn't it?"

She pauses, waiting for a response, but I have nothing. There are no words.

"I waited, Levi. I begged and prayed and hoped for just one phone call. One visit. Anything to let me know that I hadn't made it all up. Anything to let me know that I wasn't alone. That you weren't a liar."

Tears stream down her cheeks now, but it's the hollow whisper her voice becomes that guts what's left of me. "But you never came back. And that's where the biggest truth of all is, isn't it? After everything we went through—after all of your pretty words and promises—when it came right down to it—it didn't matter enough to you. *I* didn't matter enough to you."

Each word drives another nail into my chest. For the first time I feel the full weight of what I did and what I failed to do and it threatens to bring me to my knees.

"Holy fuck, Levi," Colt breathes from behind me. I hadn't even heard him come in from outside.

"And now, now you want to pretend that you care? That I matter to you?" She shakes her head. "You're the one who isn't being honest, Levi."

"I'm so sorry, Sunny." The words feel pathetic, but I force them out anyway. "I thought you were gone. I truly believed that. I never would have left if—" I swallow hard. "I couldn't face it, couldn't face living without you. Please, please forgive me."

"It looks like *you* found a way to manage just fine." She looks at me for a long moment, her expression carved from stone.

"One last little piece of honesty. Something I hope you think about for a long time. You always thought you were the good guy, so proud to be my savior. But the truth is, you Levi, are so much worse than Garrett ever was. At least when he was hurting me, using me, he didn't lie about it. He knew what he was doing, what he was and never pretended to be anything but that. You though…" she says quietly.

The words steal the air from my lungs and leave me reeling. My legs nearly buckle beneath me as the full weight of her accusation crashes over me. The truth of it—being compared to Garrett, being told I'm *worse*—shatters something down in the very core of who I am.

I lower my eyes to the floor. I can't look at her, can't bear to see the truth of her words reflected in eyes that used to look at me with so much love and trust.

"You don't deserve an answer to your question, but I'll give you one anyway." She lowers her head and stares at the floor, the tension draining from her body.

"After that night… after you left…"

Her breath hitches and she wraps her arms around herself. "There hasn't been anyone. No one's touched me, Levi. Not once in the past seven years. Garrett was the last. You know why?"

Her voice is thick with grief and pain and barely more than a whisper as she continues. "Because you destroyed any chance I ever had of being able to trust anyone again. I hate you for that. And I will never, ever forgive you."

Before I can respond, she turns and runs up the stairs. The sound of her door slamming echoes through the house, followed by the decisive click of a lock.

I stand frozen in the kitchen, her words replaying in an endless loop. The magnitude of what I've done—the depth of pain I've caused—crashes into me and steals my breath.

My legs give out and I sink to my knees, barely registering Z and Colt's presence anymore.

Chapter Thirty-Eight

Sunny

I SLAM THE DOOR behind me and slide down against it, my legs giving out. The wood is cool against my back, grounding me as violent tremors wrack my body. My hands won't stop shaking.

I can't believe I did that. I can't believe I just laid everything bare in front of everyone. The shame burns hot in my chest, knowing that now they all know. Every single person downstairs heard exactly what happened to me. What Garrett did. What Levi did.

Levi.

His face when I told him I hated him more than Garrett...

God, I'd wanted to hurt him. I wanted him to feel even a fraction of the pain I felt lying in that hospital bed day after day, hoping he'd walk through the door. Praying he'd come explain why he left me there broken and bleeding.

But seeing him break like that—it didn't feel like I thought it would. There was no satisfaction in it.

I pull my knees to my chest and press my forehead against them, trying to steady my breathing. The rage that fueled me downstairs is draining away, leaving me hollow. Empty. Exhausted.

I tuck my legs into Z's shirt and wrap my arms tighter around myself, grateful for the comfort of it even as guilt gnaws at me. Not for what I said, but for how it must have looked to Levi. Seeing me like this. In Z's shirt, acting like this is my home or something.

Not that I owe him anything.

Seven years. Seven years I've carried this weight, these questions, this pain. And now it's just... out there. Everyone knows. Chase. Wolf. Ty. Jayce. The others I haven't even met yet. Complete strangers know my darkest moments, my deepest shame.

But oddly, I feel lighter. Like finally speaking the truth, finally confronting Levi, loosened something that's been coiled tight inside me since that night.

I drag myself up off the floor on shaky legs and move to sit on the edge of the bed. The morning sun streams through the window, catching dust motes dancing in the air.

How will I ever walk out of this room and face anyone again?

I catch a glimpse of myself in the mirror across the room. I barely recognize the woman staring back at me. She looks lost. Scared.

The sounds of voices drift up from downstairs—muffled but loud. Very loud. I should feel anxious about what they're saying since there's no way they aren't about me. I'm sure everything that I said is getting discussed and dissected.

My fingers trace absently over the tattoo on my chest and the scars underneath. Physical proof of survival. At least there's that. Lucky me.

I lie back on the bed, staring up at the ceiling. The trembling in my hands is starting to ease. The numbness spreading through me feels almost peaceful after the storm of emotions. It feels a lot like trying to breathe underwater.

The double locks Z installed on the door make me feel secure enough to close my eyes. To let the exhaustion of the morning's confrontation wash over me. I don't sleep—I'm too wired. I let myself drift instead, away from the chaos downstairs.

For now, in this room, in this moment, I just... am.

Eventually, I do drift off into an uneasy sleep, but voices outside my door drag me awake. The hushed but heated tones make my eyes snap open.

"You need to leave her alone, Levi." Z's voice, firm and protective.

"Move Z. Get out of my way. I have to talk to her." Levi's desperation bleeds through the door. "I have to explain—"

"Explain what? Why you acted like such an asshole this morning? Or how you didn't mean—"

"You don't understand!"

"No, you don't understand. She's been through hell the past couple of days. She's finally starting to feel safe here. I won't let you destroy that."

My chest tightens at Z's words. The bed creaks as I sit up, every muscle tensed.

"That's not your call to make," Levi growls. "You don't know what we had—"

"Had being the operative word. She trusted you, and you broke it."

"I was a kid! I panicked—"

"She was a kid too! A kid who needed you, who counted on you, who believed what you told her."

Their voices rise slightly before dropping again into a low hiss.

"She's not yours, Zane."

I freeze, my breath catching in my throat.

"She's not yours either, Levi." Zane's voice is calm, but there's an unmistakable bite to it.

There's a pause, the kind that's heavy with meaning, and I inch toward the door, my heart pounding.

"She said it herself. She doesn't owe you a damn thing," Zane says, his voice low but firm. "Whatever you think you had with her, you ruined it. You gotta know there's no going back. Especially after this morning."

"I was wrong. I get it. I shouldn't have assumed—"

"You think?" The disappointment and hurt is clear in Z's voice.

"I have to try and fix things. I can't let her go again without trying to make things right. You have to see that." Levi snaps, the crack in his voice unexpected.

I press my ear to the door, listening to every single word.

"She's not some prize you can earn," Zane says, softer now. "She's been through enough without *either* of us turning this into some sort of pissing match."

Levi doesn't respond immediately, and when he does, his voice is quieter. "I know that. But I can't just walk away. Not again."

There's another long silence, and I can almost picture the two of them staring each other down, opposite sides of the same coin.

"She deserves better," Zane says finally.

"I know," Levi replies, his voice heavy. "But I'm going to prove to her that I'm not the same person I was. I have to. Even if she never forgives me, she has to know that I never stopped thinking about her. Never stopped loving her, and I will never stop looking out for her now that I know she's alive."

Something shifts in Zane's tone, a hint of resignation. "Good luck with that, *brother*," he mutters. "Because she already has someone looking out for her. And it's not you."

I pull away from the door and sit on the edge of the bed, my fingers twisting in the hem of Z's borrowed shirt. Everything's too bright, too sharp. Too much.

The words echo and blur together in my head. *Never stopped loving her.*

I remember feeling so beautiful, so loved with him. I'd felt safe for the first time in my whole life. Until I didn't.

Z understands silence. Knows when to push and when to wait. His presence is solid, steady. No expectations. No demands. Just... there.

God, that raw break in Levi's voice. The pain. Real pain that he didn't know I was hearing.

My chest aches, hollow and full at the same time. Relief mingles with fear, with shame. There's no way that the men in this house didn't hear every word of what I said.

And, to top all of it off, somewhere out there, someone's watching. Someone good enough to slip past Z's defenses is waiting for an opening to get to me.

I press my palms against my eyes until colors burst behind my lids. A month ago, my biggest worry was making rent. Now...

My stomach growls, reminding me I haven't eaten since last night. The memory of the dinner last night feels like it happened in another lifetime. I'm not ready to leave this room though. To face anyone. Not yet.

I don't know how much time passes before I hear footsteps coming down the hall. My breath catches and I stay silent.

"Sunny?" Z's voice is soft, careful. "I brought you some dinner. It's good. Jayce insisted on baking you some fresh bread and more of the soup you like."

I stay silent, my throat too tight to speak. Part of me wants to open the door, to let him in. But I can't. Not yet. Not when everything is so raw and confused.

"I just, I want to make sure you're okay," he continues. "You don't have to talk. You don't have to open the door. I'll leave it right here for you."

I hear the gentle clink of a tray being set down, followed by Z's quiet sigh.

"Take all the time you need, Sunny. I'm here when you're ready."

His footsteps retreat down the hall, and I wait until they fade completely before moving to the door. My hand hovers over the locks, trembling slightly.

The scent of fresh bread and herbs seeps under the door, making my stomach clench. I unlock the door as quietly as possible, opening it just enough to slide the tray inside.

Steam rises from the bowl of soup, carrying memories of easy laughter in the kitchen. The bread is still warm, golden-brown and perfect. Such a simple gesture of care, but it makes my eyes burn with fresh tears.

I carry the tray to the small desk by the window, sinking into the chair. The soup is exactly what I need—warm, comforting.

But it does nothing to stop the questions I can't let go of. How am I supposed to face either of them? How do I reconcile the Levi I knew, the Levi who left me, and the man who claims he never stopped loving me? How do I trust the things I feel about Zane when everything is such a mess?

For now, I don't have to decide anything. For now, I can just exist in this room and let tomorrow's problems wait until tomorrow.

But I know I can't hide forever. Eventually, I'll have to face them both. Face these feelings. Face myself.

The sun sets outside my window, painting the room in soft shadows. I finish every drop of soup, every crumb of bread, grateful for a small bit of comfort in the middle of all the chaos.

Chapter Thirty-Nine

Sunny

I'M SITTING IN THE window seat watching a couple men work on fixing a stretch of fence in the distance. It's been more than twenty-four hours since Levi got here. Since I told him I hated him. I still haven't worked up the nerve to leave my room.

The words still taste bitter in my mouth.

Sleep comes in waves, dragging me under then spitting me back out. My dreams blur with memories until I can't tell which is which anymore. Levi finding me. Levi leaving me. Z's quiet knock on the door every few hours pulls me back from both.

This room feels both too small and too big. Four walls closing in on me while the space between them stretches out endlessly. I hate being trapped here, but where else can I go? My apartment isn't safe. The club isn't safe. Nowhere is safe.

I roll over, pulling my—Z's— shirt tight around me. It's comforting and I hate that it helps.

A sketchbook that Chase slid under the door for me sits unopened on the desk along with the pencils he gave me. I should draw, lose myself in the familiar motion of pencil on paper. But my hands feel empty, useless. Like they belong to someone else.

Footsteps approach my door again. Not Z's usual quiet tread—these are heavier, purposeful. A knock follows.

"Sunny." Z's deep voice carries through the wood. "I know you're probably not ready to come out yet."

I stay silent, curled on my side.

"Wolf and I were working in the basement, bringing up some boxes." He pauses. "We found some… things. Things you need to see."

My heart stutters. What could they have possibly found that I need to see? I can't imagine anything good coming up from a basement in a place like this.

"I won't push," Z continues. "But it's important. When you're ready, come find me. I'll be in the office down the hall."

His footsteps retreat, leaving me alone with the weight of his words.

I close my eyes, trying to sort through the chaos in my head. Part of me wants to stay here, locked behind a door where nothing can touch me. Where I don't have to face Levi or my past or whatever Z found in that basement.

My fingers trace the wildflower tattoo wrapping around my ribs. The artist who did it said flowers represent rebirth. Growth from decay. Beauty from pain. I wanted so badly to believe that.

Z's words echo in my head. Things you need to see.

Need, not want. Z chooses his words carefully. If he says I need to see something, he means it.

I drag myself up, muscles protesting after hours of stillness. My reflection in the mirror shows a stranger—hollow eyes, tangled hair, borrowed shirt hanging loose on my frame.

This isn't me. This isn't who I am.

I splash water on my face, run fingers through my hair until it looks less wild. I grab another T-shirt from the drawer and slide it on. It'll have to do for clothes, I'm not ready to face anyone long enough to ask for anything else.

The hallway stretches endless before me when I finally open the door. Voices drift up from downstairs—Wolf and Chase discussing the last shift change, Ty's laugh, the clatter of dishes. Normal sounds that feel anything but normal right now.

I pad silently down the hall to the office, bare feet silent on worn wood. The door stands half-open, warm light spilling out. Z sits at his desk, head bent over something I can't see.

He looks up as I hover in the doorway, face unreadable. "You came."

"You said I needed to see something."

He nods, pushing back from the desk. "Come in. Close the door."

I do, though every instinct screams to keep an escape route open. Z has never given me reason not to trust him, but old habits die hard.

"Sit." He gestures to a chair across from him.

I perch on the edge, ready to bolt. "What did you find?"

Instead of answering, Z pulls open a drawer and sets a manila envelope on the desk between us. It's old, edges worn and frayed with time. No labels or markings to hint at what's inside.

"Before you open this," he says carefully, "I need you to understand something. What's in here—it's going to hurt. But you deserve to know the truth. And we all could use some answers."

I STARE AT THE envelope, hands shaking as I reach for it. After every-thing—seeing Levi again, reliving that night, spilling my hatred at him— what could possibly hurt more than that?

"Go ahead," Z says softly.

I slide my chair closer to his desk, the legs scraping against hard-wood. The envelope feels heavy in my hands, weighted with more than just paper. Taking a deep breath, I upend it over the desk.

Photos spill out first, scattering across the polished surface like fall-en leaves. Behind them tumble what look like letters, paper yellowed with age, creases worn soft from repeated folding and unfolding. My heart stops as I pick up the first photo.

It's me. In a hospital bed.

The image is grainy, clearly taken from a distance, maybe through a window. I'm unconscious, tubes and wires everywhere. Bandages wrap my chest, peek out from under the thin hospital gown. Dark bruises mottle every visible inch of skin.

My hands shake harder as I pick up another. And another. More photos of me in the hospital, tracking my recovery day by day. Some are closer—taken from inside the room while I slept. The thought makes me shudder.

"There's more," Z says quietly.

I shuffle through the stack. Photos of me leaving the hospital. Getting on the bus. Arriving in Oak Valley. My first day working at Sirens. Years of surveillance, documenting every move I made.

"Someone's been watching me. All this time?" My voice sounds strange to my own ears.

"Look at this first," Z says. He's holding a stack of photos, separate from the rest. He takes the first one and passes it to me. Three men stand arm in arm outside what looks like a warehouse. "Do you recognize everyone in that photo? It was taken about a year before your father died."

"Umm. That's my dad. And that's Garrett?" My stomach lurches. "What the hell is this Zane?"

Zane reaches across the desk and points to the man in the middle. "That is Alexander Reeves. Levi's father."

"Wait." I grab Z's wrist as he reaches for another document. "My father knew Levi's father? That's... that's impossible. I would have known."

"Would you?" Z's voice is gentle. "You were young, Sunny."

I stare at the photograph again. My father—the man who taught me to draw, who'd sing off-key while making me sundaes—standing there with Alexander Reeves like they were old friends. And Garrett. The same Garrett who...

"No." My voice breaks. "My father would never associate with someone like Levi's dad. Or Garrett. He was good. He was..."

But was he?

The words die in my throat as Z slides another photo across the desk.

A birthday party. I instantly recognize myself and my old backyard. I'm maybe five or six, sitting at a picnic table, wearing a shiny party hat, getting ready to open a brightly wrapped gift. In the background, my father and Alexander Reeves sit at the patio table, heads bent close in conversation. Garrett stands behind them, eyes focused on me.

"This was at my house." Bile rises in my throat. "All this time. Garrett. He was there, waiting."

"I don't understand any of this Zane." I swallow hard over the lump in my throat.

Z lays down a series of documents next to the photo. "Your father was apparently Alexander's accountant. These are transaction records he signed off on—millions of dollars in income. Illegal weapons sales, money laundering. He was in deep Sunny."

"That night. With Garrett. He told me he killed my father." I blink away the tears and take a deep breath. "But, I still don't understand."

"I don't know everything yet, Sunny. But, here." Z unfolds a letter, Alexander's precise handwriting stark against yellowed paper:

Garrett - The situation with Kent has gotten out of hand. It requires your immediate attention. Upon confirmation of removal, payment will transfer as discussed. Additional compensation to include all rights and control over his family assets and dependents. No police involvement. - A.R.

My hands shake as Z places bank statements beside the letter. Offshore accounts. Regular deposits spanning years, all into accounts with variations of Garrett's name.

"This letter is dated within weeks of when your father disappeared. The only thing I can think of is he wanted out. Or he was skimming. And there was no way either of those things would be allowed." Z's voice is gentle. "Then this."

Another letter. Written in a messy scrawl I recognize immediately as Garrett's.

It's done. Confirmation enclosed. Moving in with the widow and girl next week as agreed. They won't be any trouble.. - G

"He gave us to him," I whisper. "Alexander Reeves paid for my father's murder with *us*."

"Sunny, I think that everything that's happened since the night Garrett tried to kill you was all designed to make sure that Levi wouldn't find out you were alive. If you'd have ever met Alexander you'd know how important keeping Levi close to him was."

"And if Levi knew I was alive he'd have come for me."

"Levi's father was very single-minded. The only things that ever mattered to him were his money and his son. I think he kept you hidden by giving Garrett the resources to pull the strings that kept you apart. He made sure Levi believed you were dead. Made sure he had no reason to ever leave again."

The final photo shows Alexander and Garrett together, dated just weeks before Alexander's death. The same offshore account numbers are scrawled on the back.

"When Levi killed his father..." I start.

"He unknowingly cut off one of the only ways he could've found you," Z finishes.

I stare at the evidence of decades of manipulation. My father's murder. My mother's pain.

"We have to tell him, tell them." My words surprise me.

"Are you sure?" Z studies me carefully.

"This is too big Z," I admit. "But at least now I understand why. Why Garrett always acted like he owned us. Why he could never be caught." I pick up the first bank statement. "He literally bought us."

Z reaches for the intercom. "I'll call him up."

"Wait." I grab his hand. "Just... give me a minute with this before you do that. To process it."

He nods, settling back in his chair. Waiting while I try to make sense of how my entire life was shaped by the three men staring at me from the old photo I'm holding.

And somewhere in this house, Levi is about to learn that everything he thought he knew about his father, about Garrett, about me, is even worse than he imagined.

I take a deep breath, steadying myself. "Okay, I'm ready."

Z nods, gathering the photos and letters. "I'll call everyone in."

Minutes later, all of the men who make up the inner circle are crowded into the office. Wolf and Chase lean against the wall while Ty perches on the windowsill. Colt sprawls in a chair, but his usual relaxed posture is tense. And Levi stands in the corner furthest from me, arms crossed, face unreadable.

My fingers twine through my hair nervously as Z lays out what we found. The surveillance photos are spread across his desk like a grotesque collage of my life. Seven years of me being stalked and documented.

"Jesus," Colt breathes, picking up a photo of me at Sirens. "This is..."

"Sick," Chase finishes, his deep voice rumbling with anger.

I force myself to look at Levi. His jaw clenches as he walks up to the desk and picks up one of the photos. It's one of me in the hospital, taken from the end of my bed while I sleep. He stares at it, his fingertips white where they grasp the shiny paper. The muscle in his cheek ticks—a tell I remember from before. A sign of him trying to keep himself in check.

"The letters are worse," I say, my voice steadier than I feel. "You need to read them."

I watch as Levi picks up the first letter, his eyes scanning the page. His face drains of color. He grabs another, then another, moving through them with increasing urgency. The photos scatter as he searches.

"Everyone out," he says, his voice a low growl. "Except Colt, Z, and..." His eyes flick to me, then away. "Sunny."

Wolf and Chase exchange glances before filing out silently. Ty and Jayce follow, closing the door behind them with a soft click.

"Is this—" Levi's voice cracks. He looks at Z, green eyes wild. "Tell me this isn't what it looks like."

The muscles in his jaw work, that familiar tick becoming more pronounced. His hands shake slightly as he picks up the photo of our fathers together.

"Z. This can't be right." Levi's voice cracks.

Z meets his gaze. "It is. Your father has been behind everything that's happened. He paid Garrett to kill Sunny's father. Then gave him the means to..." He glances at me, hesitating.

"To own us," I finish quietly. "Me and my mom. We were part of his payment."

Levi makes a sound like he's been punched. He braces himself against the desk, head bowed. "The accounts. The properties. All this time, it's been my father's money protecting him?"

"He knew the whole time." Levi's voice is barely a whisper. "He knew she was alive."

"Yes." Z's voice is gentle. "He used Garrett to keep her hidden from you. Used your belief in her death to keep you close."

"And my mother?" Levi asks, though I can see in his eyes he already knows the answer.

"On your father's orders." Z confirms. He picks up another sheet of paper, stapled to a faded polaroid, and offers it to Levi. "Proof pic, and a confirmation letter."

Levi reaches out his hand but yanks it back before he touches it. He shakes his head. "I can't..."

Instead, he picks up another photo—one taken of me getting off the bus in Oak Valley. His fingers trace the edges of the bandages visible in the image.

"I left you there," he says, not looking at me. "I left you, and he knew. He knew you were alive and he..." His voice breaks. "He let me think..."

The silence stretches between us as Levi absorbs each horrible revelation. His eyes move from photo to photo, letter to letter, piecing together the twisted web his father wove around all of us.

I watch his face as each new connection clicks into place. The way his father used Garrett. Used me. Used him. The way everything—every moment of pain and loss and grief—was carefully orchestrated by Alexander Reeves.

The enormity of the moment fills the room. Z looks to me and then to Levi before standing. Colt follows his lead.

"You two need some time to sit with this. We'll be downstairs if you need us," he says quietly.

I want to beg Zane to stay, but I know this conversation needs to happen. Has needed to happen since Levi walked back into my life.

The door clicks shut behind Z, leaving me alone with the man I once loved. The man who left me for dead.

CHAPTER FORTY

SUNNY

THE SILENCE STRETCHES BETWEEN us like pieces of shattered glass—sharp and dangerous. Levi hasn't moved from where he collapsed in the chair behind the desk, one of his father's letter still clutched in his hand. I can see the paper trembling.

"I killed him," Levi finally says, his voice hollow. "I killed my father thinking I was breaking free. But all I did was make sure Garrett would always have..." He stops, swallowing hard. "Everything. Everything he needed to keep hurting you."

"You couldn't have known." The words surprise me. After everything I said to him in the kitchen, about my pain, about hating him, I didn't expect to be the one offering him comfort.

"I should have though. I knew my father. I knew what he was capable of." His eyes meet mine, raw with a pain that matches my own. "I should have looked deeper. Should have found these before." He gestures at the scattered evidence of our shared nightmare.

"Like I should have known my father was mixed up with yours?" I trace the edge of the old photograph. Three smiling men who destroyed everything. "We were both collateral damage Levi. Stuck trying to survive the messes our fathers made."

"I don't know how to fix this Sunny." He hangs his head, his voice filled with defeat.

"I don't think it can be fixed." I stand, needing to move, to breathe.

"Sunny—"

"But maybe," I cut him off, turning to face him, "maybe it's time we stop letting their choices control what happens next. Your father. My father. Garrett. They've done enough damage. Don't you think?"

Something shifts in Levi's expression. Not hope exactly—we're not there yet—but understanding. An agreement to stop the bleeding from our shared wounds.

"Whatever comes next," he says carefully, "whatever we do about Garrett—it needs to be your choice. Not his. Not mine. Yours."

It's a long way from trust. It's even further from forgiveness. But it's a place to start.

I sit quietly at the opposite end of the leather couch from Levi, watching Z pace in front of the whiteboard. He's scribbling strategies, ideas, plans—creating a layered overview of... nothing. Nothing with any substance.

The room feels crowded. Wolf and Chase are in the chairs by the fireplace, Colt perched on the desk, others scattered across the room. Levi leans against the wall, arms crossed, brooding.

My mind keeps drifting to those photos spread across Z's desk upstairs. Seven years of my life documented in grainy surveillance shots. Every move I made, every attempt at building something good for myself, Garrett was there in the shadows. Watching. Waiting.

"We'll need teams of at least three rotating shifts..." Z's deep voice fades into background noise as I study the complex web of notes and arrows he's drawn.

None of this feels real.

"The warehouse gives us a good staging area..." Z continues, but I barely hear him.

I can't stop thinking about Alexander Reeves orchestrating all of this from the beginning. Paying Garrett to murder my father. Offering up my mother and me like we were property to be traded. Making sure Levi never found out I survived that night.

"We'll need to get—" Z marks another point on his diagram.

My fingers absently trace the wildflower tattoo where it covers my collarbone. All these years thinking I was free, building a new life, and Garrett was right there. Close enough to reach out and grab me anytime he wanted. But he didn't.

"Stop." The word bursts out of me. Every head in the room swivels toward me.

"This won't work." I stand up, my legs shaky but my voice steady. "None of your planning matters. You're all missing the point."

"Sunny?" Levi's looking at me with a confused expression on his face.

"He's had seven years to come after me. Seven years of watching my every move. But he didn't. I never had any clue I was being watched. He waited until Levi showed up at the club that night."

I gesture at the photos Z brought down. "Look at the pattern. Everything he's done since Levi came into my life is about keeping us apart. Keeping me for himself."

"That's exactly why we need to..." Z starts but I cut him off.

"No. That's exactly why we need to give him what he wants. If I'm what he wants, that's what we need to give him."

The room erupts in protest. Levi surges to his feet beside me. "Absolutely not."

I force myself to meet his blazing green eyes. "This is the only way that makes sense. He wants me. Has always wanted me. But more than that, he wants to hurt you through me."

"You can't seriously be suggesting—" Colt pushes off the desk.

"I am. Set me up. Have Levi there too. Provoke him. He won't be able to resist." My heart pounds but my voice remains steady. "You'll never find him otherwise. He's too good at hiding. Too patient."

"No." Levi's voice is hard. Determined. "It's too dangerous."

Z nods his head in agreement. "I won't let that happen Sunny."

"You just got done telling me it was my choice." I spin to face Levi.

He scrubs his face with his hands.

"Sunny's right." After a moment, Z's voice cuts through the noise. "We've been trying to track Garrett for years with no success. He's careful. Patient. The only time he's slipped up was when his obsession with keeping you away from Sunny overrode his common sense."

Z voice is confident. "She's right. We've been chasing shadows. Garrett only ever slips when his obsession overtakes his training. Sunny changes the equation."

"So, we dangle her like bait?" Wolf snaps.

"No," I say. "You set the stage. I write the script. I'm done hiding. We get to choose how this ends."

The room goes still.

Colt nods slowly. "It's our best shot."

Z studies me. "We'll need layers of security. Backups. Traps."

They all look at me like I've cracked. Maybe I have.

The silence stretches as they absorb my words. I can see the calculations happening behind their eyes, weighing risks against rewards.

"She's right." Colt finally breaks the quiet. "It's the best shot we have at drawing him out."

Z studies me for a long moment before nodding slowly. "We'll need to plan this carefully. Set up multiple layers of security. Make sure nothing can possibly go wrong."

"I know." I meet his intense blue gaze steadily. "But it has to be me. I'm tired of being afraid."

CHAPTER FORTY-ONE

SUNNY

I WATCH, LEANING AGAINST the kitchen counter next to Jade as she directs Colt with the precision of a drill sergeant. She's been spending a lot of time here, and I must admit, it suits her.

Despite her sharp instructions, Colt's grin never wavers, glancing back at her often with puppy-like devotion etched into his face.

"You know," I say, accepting a mug from Jade, "for someone who claimed to have sworn off men for good, you sure seem to be enjoying yourself."

Jade smirks. "Well, I mean look at him. He's kind of adorable."

I glance over at Colt who is happily stirring a heaping spoon of sugar into a fresh cup of coffee. The look on his face when he turns and extends two full cups of coffee to me and Jade, is undeniably… adorable. Just like she said.

It hasn't taken long for things here to feel comfortable. Domestic. Safe. The stack of surveillance photos on Z's desk upstairs tells a different story—years of candid shots of my life, of Jade's life. A catalog of our friendship. Our different routines and shifts at Sirens. Her tiny little house at the edge of town, and my apartment. Garrett had been watching, waiting, probably laughing at how oblivious I'd been. It had never occurred to me that Jade would ever be a target because of me.

Z enters the kitchen, his thick black hair tousled from sleep, his gray sweatpants slung low on his hips and Jade nudges me with a small, quiet giggle when she sees my expression.

He's become a steady constant in the chaos, someone I find myself gravitating toward without thought. His kindness has made him even more beautiful. He squeezes my shoulder as he passes—a gesture that has become familiar over the past few days—before grabbing his own coffee.

"Levi's running perimeter checks again," Z announces, though no one had asked. The tension between Z and Levi has become a living thing, crackling whenever they occupy the same space. They maintain professional courtesy, but the strain shows in tight jaw muscles and clipped conversations.

"Third time today," I note quietly. I understand Levi's restlessness. This house holds ghosts for him too—memories of his father's influence lingering in every shadow. The fact that Garrett knows the layout as well as we do keeps everyone on edge.

"We're as secure as we can be," Z assures me, but his eyes flick to the windows. We all know better than to settle into that thought too comfortably.

Jade takes a sip of her coffee and lays her head on my shoulder. "At least the company's good," she says, watching as Colt and Z sit at the kitchen island and start discussing the plans for the day. "Even if the circumstances suck."

I nod, grateful that Jade is here, even though I hate that my best friend has been dragged into this mess. The photos made it clear—Jade is as much a target as anyone, whether as leverage against me or out of Garrett's twisted sense of revenge.

Through the large window over the sink, I catch sight of Levi talking to a small group of the men he brought with him. Our eyes meet briefly, and I manage a small smile. We still haven't spoken more than a few words to each other, but we'll get there. At least now the weight of our fathers' sins aren't suffocating us. But watching him turn away, I can't help but notice how his gaze travels from me to Z and back again. *It's going to take time*, I remind myself.

Z calls us into his office later that afternoon. The tension in the room is immediate—Levi leaning against the wall near the window, Colt perched on the edge of Z's desk, while Jade and I take the chairs opposite Z. His expression is grim as he spreads out a timeline of photos across his desk.

"We need to talk about the club," Z says, his voice tight. "About what needs to happen to make this believable enough to draw him out."

"Garrett's been content to watch from the shadows for years," Z continues, his eyes meeting mine briefly before shifting to Levi. "Until you showed up."

"What are you suggesting?" Jade asks.

My breath catches. I already know where this is going.

Z's jaw tightens. "If we want to force his hand, we need to give him what he's waiting for. The thing that's always made him act—Levi and Sunny together."

Levi pushes off the wall, taking a step closer. He runs his hand roughly through his hair. "Us, together?"

"I think," Z says carefully, "Sunny was right. Garrett's entire pattern revolves around keeping you two apart. The threats started when he found out you had seen Sunny. He's escalating because he sees history repeating itself."

"And you think us being together will make him snap?" I ask, my voice barely above a whisper.

"I think it's our best shot," Z admits, though I can see how much it costs him to say it.

Levi's eyes find mine across the room, and suddenly I'm seventeen again, feeling that same electric pull that used to exist between us. Maybe it never really went away.

Jade clears her throat. "So, what exactly are we talking about here? How *together* are they supposed to be?"

"Enough to be convincing," Colt answers, his usual playfulness absent. "Enough to make him believe it's real."

I force myself to look away from Levi, catching the new tension in Z's shoulders as he outlines the rest of the plan. He's right—it all makes tactical sense. But watching him deliberately avoid looking at either me or Levi as he speaks, I realize that logical doesn't mean painless.

"We'll start tomorrow night," Z concludes. "Levi and I will both be at the club. Colt will run all of the surveillance from the van."

As everyone files out of the office, Levi catches my arm gently. The contact sends a jolt through my system that I'm not prepared for. When our eyes meet again, I know he felt it too.

"Are you going to be okay with this?" he asks softly.

"Does it matter?" I counter, but there's no bite in my words. Just the weight of everything we once were, everything we lost, and everything we might have to pretend to be again.

The tension lingers after everyone else leaves Z's office. I'm still caught in that strange space between Levi's touch and Z's carefully controlled expression.

"There's one more thing," Z says, making both Levi and me turn back. "You two look like you're about to break out in hives at the thought of touching each other. That's not going to work."

I feel the heat rise in my cheeks, but Z continues, his voice professional. "You've got eighteen hours before we put this plan in motion. Use them. Get comfortable with each other again. If you flinch every time he reaches for you, Sunny, or if you hesitate before touching her, Levi— Garrett will see right through it."

"What exactly are you suggesting?" Levi asks, and I hear the edge in his voice.

"I'm suggesting you figure out how to act like two people who were in love with each other and are working on rekindling things," Z replies bluntly, his voice tightly controlled. "Because that's what will get his attention. That's what will make him act."

Z's words settles over us. He's right, of course. The awkward distance between Levi and me might be real, might be earned, but it won't serve the purpose we need it to.

I catch Levi's eye and see my own resignation mirrored there. We both know what needs to be done, even if neither of us is quite ready to admit how dangerous this game might be—and not just because of Garrett.

EVERYONE ELSE HAS GONE to bed, but I can't sleep. I find myself in the kitchen, sitting on one of the barstools with a mug of hot tea in my hands, when Levi makes an appearance. He hesitates in the doorway, and I wonder if he'll leave when he sees me. Instead, he leans against the counter opposite me.

"Couldn't sleep either?" he asks softly.

I shake my head. The moonlight through the window casts long shadows that seem to fit the mood. We sit in the awkward silence between us, until I can't stand it anymore.

"I don't know how to do this," I admit. "How to pretend that everything that happened... didn't."

"I don't think we need to," Levi says, his voice gentle in a way I haven't heard since before. "We just need to find a way to exist in the same space without the pain of it standing between us."

"You think that's possible?"

He's quiet for a long moment. "Do you remember that first day? Under the tree?"

"It's hard to forget being called a fish." The memory brings an unexpected smile to my lips.

"Yeah." He moves closer, slow and careful, like I'm a wild thing that might bolt. "I was such an ass to you that day. But God, Sunny, you were so beautiful. Even crying. So beautiful, I couldn't think straight. I have a lot of memories of you like that."

"Me too," I admit reluctantly. "Can I ask you something?"

"Hm? Sure." His face breaks into a gentle smile and he reaches out and places his hand softly over mine.

"I've always wondered why you decided to step in that day. I know I said at that time I didn't care, but I did. I was just so afraid of what your answer would be. We never really talked about it," I whisper.

"Truth?"

I nod at him. "Please."

"Okay, so I don't know how to tell you this without it sounding creepy."

Levi laughs at the concerned look I get on my face. "No, no. It's nothing bad. I just—"

He lets out a big sigh and drops his eyes to our hands. "It took me almost three weeks to work up the nerve to talk to you. On the day we moved in, I walked out onto my balcony, and saw you. You were sitting under that damn tree, your nose in a book, twirling a strand of hair around your finger and... it made my heart stop. You were just so perfect. Lost in your own little world, completely unaware and unbothered by anything.

I watched you read for hours that day. Kept making excuses to go out on that balcony every single day hoping to catch you outside again. But every time I tried to go down and talk to you, the words wouldn't come." His voice breaks slightly.

"Sunny, there was no decision for me to make. Not after I saw your shoulder. Not after I heard the things he said to you. About you. I couldn't have walked away and pretended I didn't see. Didn't care."

We sit in silence, letting the memory fill up the space between us. I slide my other hand on top of his.

"Levi, if this is going to work, I need you to tell me about that night. I need to hear it from you. Maybe it will help me understand."

He's quiet for a long moment before he starts tracing tiny circles over my knuckles. I can feel the tension building in him.

"I had this great idea on how to get even with Zack. On making sure he couldn't hurt you anymore." he finally says, his voice rough. "It was such a stupid, petty thing. I ignored your calls because I was riding the high of finally putting him in his place. I didn't want you to see that side of me. When I got home..." He swallows hard. "When I found my mom, everything kind of stopped for me. And then I found you, and in that moment I swear the biggest and best part of me died."

His free hand comes up to cup my cheek, and this time I don't flinch. "I was positive that you were gone. That I'd lost you both. I couldn't... I couldn't handle it. So, I ran. Got in my truck and starting driving to the only place I thought I had left."

"Your dad?" I ask quietly.

Levi nods. "He cleaned it all up. Made everything go away. I never even talked to the cops." His thumb brushes my cheekbone. "I believed him when he said I couldn't go back. That it looked so bad for me—taking off the way I did, what I'd said on the 911 call about it being my fault. I didn't know you were alive. God, Sunny, if I'd known..."

"But you didn't," I finish for him, believing the words for the first time, realizing how awful it all had to have been for him. "You really didn't know."

He nods, and I can see the guilt still gnawing away at him. But there's something freeing about finally having it all laid bare between us.

"Can we start here?" I ask. "I don't think we can go back and undo anything, but maybe we can start building from here?"

"Yeah," he breathes. "I'd like that."

We stay like that for a long time, sharing space and silence, Levi's hand covering mine, our fingers entwined. It's not forgiveness, not yet. But it's a beginning. And maybe, for tonight, that's enough.

CHAPTER FORTY-TWO

Levi

I fiND Z iN his office, hunched over his desk where blueprints of Sirens and security plans are spread out like a paper maze. The familiar smell of coffee and gun oil hangs in the air. The lighting in here makes the dark circles under his eyes more obvious. He pulled an all-nighter planning this thing.

"Everything set?" I drop into the chair across from his desk, trying to ignore the tension that's been building between us for days.

Z doesn't bother looking up from his papers. "Almost. Since Eddie and Jake can get into the club without raising any suspicions, they're there already getting things prepped. Wolf's team will be scattered throughout, as customers." He slides a paper across to me. "These are your positions. You'll need to stay visible, make it obvious you're with Sunny."

"That won't be a problem." I can't help the slight smirk that plays at my mouth. "Sunny and I spent most of the night... uh, working things out."

I watch as Z's pen stills mid-sentence. His eye twitches—a tiny tell that most people would miss, but I know him well enough to spot it. The temperature in the room seems to drop several degrees.

"Working things out?" His voice is carefully neutral, but I can see his knuckles turning white where he grips the pen.

"Yeah," I continue, knowing I'm acting like a jerk. "It was really, really good for both of us." I let the implication hang in the air.

Z finally looks up, his eyes flat. "As long as you remember this isn't about you getting what you want. This is about keeping her safe."

"Like I'd forget," I shoot back. "Don't worry. She's in good hands. I'll make sure she's *very* well taken care of."

The pen in his hand snaps, and I feel a surge of satisfaction that I've gotten under his skin.

The silence stretches between us, heavy with words we're both holding back. I know Z is thinking about Sunny wearing his clothes, sleeping in his room. Just like he knows I'm thinking about our shared history, about how she was mine first.

"Look," Z says finally, his voice tight. "We both know this isn't the time for... complications."

"Complications?" I laugh, but there isn't any humor in it. "That's what we're calling this?"

"She needs space. To figure out who she is without either of us pushing for more." He meets my eyes steadily. "You know I'm right."

I know. It doesn't make it any easier to watch her gravitate toward him, though. "Doesn't mean I have to like it."

"I don't like it either," Z replies, and for a moment I hear the strain in his voice that matches my own.

Before I can respond, movement at the door catches my attention. Sunny stands there, drowsy and rumpled from sleep, wearing another one of Z's damn shirts that hangs almost to her knees. Her hair is a mess of honey-blonde tangles, and she blinks at us sleepily.

My chest tightens at the sight of her, both from want and from the knowledge that Z's the one she came looking for first this morning.

"Morning," she mumbles, seemingly oblivious to the tension in the room. "Is there coffee?"

I watch Z's expression soften as he looks at her, and my jaw clenches. Yeah, we're both stuck alright. Stuck watching each other watch her.

After Sunny leaves to shower and change, I head downstairs to wait. My mind keeps circling back to last night—how much it took for her to let me hold her hand, how hard she has to work to relax with me. A lifetime of hurt doesn't disappear overnight, no matter how much I wish it would. Every small victory feels huge, but we have a long way to go, and not much time to get there.

The living room feels too small for my restless energy. I pace, trying to figure out how we're going to make this look convincing without pushing things too far, too fast. Everything in me wants to protect her, but here I am, about to ask her to put herself in harm's way. The irony isn't lost on me.

When Sunny appears in the doorway, hair damp and wearing her own clothes for once, my chest tightens. I stop my pacing and sink onto the couch, relaxing and trying to make my posture less threatening. She looks smaller today. More vulnerable.

"Hey," she says softly, hovering uncertainly at the edge of the room. The distance between us feels loaded with everything we've been through, everything we still need to work through.

I hold out my hand, palm up, letting her choose whether to take it. "Come here?"

She studies my face for a moment, then my hand, before crossing to me. Her smaller hand slides into mine, and the trust in that simple gesture makes my heart clench.

"Just this for now?" I ask quietly, running my thumb over her knuckles. "We can take it slow."

"Yeah," she whispers, and I feel her fingers relax in mine. "This is nice."

"You're shaking a little," I murmur, giving her hand a gentle squeeze. "We don't have to do any of this if it's too much. We can figure something else out."

She shakes her head, taking a small step closer. "No, I want to try. I trust you here."

That damn qualifier at the end. What she meant to say, but didn't, is that she trusts me as long as she knows Z isn't too far away. Fuck.

I tug her hand gently, drawing her closer until she's standing between my knees. "Tell me if you want to stop, okay?"

My free hand moves slowly to her waist, barely touching, giving her time to pull away. Instead, she lets out a shaky breath and leans slightly into my touch.

"Is this alright?" I ask, my thumb making small circles against her hip.

She nods, then surprises me by placing her free hand on my shoulder. "I remember..." she starts, then stops herself.

"What do you remember, Angel?"

Her eyes meet mine, full of something that makes my chest ache. "How safe you used to make me feel."

I swallow hard. "I want to make you feel safe again. Always."

She moves closer, and I can feel her trembling slightly. "Can I...?" She glances at my lap, then back at my face, uncertainty written across her features.

"Whatever you want," I assure her. "Whatever feels right."

That's when I notice Z in the doorway, but I keep my focus on Sunny. This moment feels too precious to break.

Slowly, carefully, she settles herself sideways across my lap. I keep my movements gentle, predictable, as I wrap one arm loosely around her waist.

"Okay?" I whisper against her hair.

She nods, gradually relaxing against me. "Yeah. This is okay."

"You can lean back if you want," I tell her softly. "I've got you."

She hesitates only a moment before letting herself sink against my chest, her head finding the spot between my neck and shoulder like it's where she's always belonged.

From the doorway, I hear Z's sharp intake of breath, and Sunny turns slightly at the sound. Their eyes lock, and I watch something unspoken pass between them.

My hand slides to her lower back, steadying her, and she turns back to me with pink-stained cheeks. The moment stretches out between the three of us, silent.

"We should plan to be out of here in two hours," Z says finally, his voice professional despite the intensity in his eyes. "That'll give us time to get everything in place."

Sunny nods but doesn't move from my lap. If anything, she seems to settle more firmly against me, like she's finally allowing herself to remember how we used to fit together.

This thing between the three of us is far from simple, but for now, she's here, letting me hold her. It feels like reclaiming something I thought I'd lost forever, even as I recognize that nothing about this situation is what I expected it to be.

Chapter Forty-Three

ZANE

Everything is exactly where it should be. I've run through the security positions a dozen times in my head, checked every camera feed, and confirmed everyone's placement. Still, I can't shake this feeling in my gut. All my experience in security has taught me to trust my instincts, and right now they're screaming that we're missing something.

From my spot at the main bar, I have clear sightlines to both exits. Chase's voice comes through my earpiece, confirming the van's position out back and that the camera's are up and running. Wolf's team is scattered throughout the crowd—Rex at a corner table with a clear view of the emergency exit, Ty playing pool near the main entrance, all the others blending perfectly with the usual Thursday night crowd.

The club pulses with energy. Music throbs through the speakers, forcing everyone to have to focus on what comes through their comms. It's exactly how Benny runs it every night. Without him none of this would be possible. Sunny is lucky she's had someone like him looking out for her all these years.

Colt lounges in Jade's section, playing his part flawlessly. To anyone watching, he's just another customer captivated by her. But I know his eyes never stop scanning the room, cataloging every face, every movement. He's already flagged three customers who seem off.

And then there's Angel.

She moves behind the bar with practiced grace, all professional smiles and efficient movements. It's jarring to see this version of her after watching the way she curled up on Levi's lap this afternoon. The contrast between who she has to be here and who she is with us is stark. Every time she passes close to me, I catch the faint tremor in her hands that betrays her nerves. But her smile never wavers, her act never slips.

Levi catches my eye from his spot at the corner of the bar. He's been there for an hour, nursing the same whiskey, watching Angel like he can't quite believe she's real. I get it. Seven years is a long time to think someone's dead. The muscle in his jaw ticks every time another customer calls for her attention, but he maintains his composure. Barely.

"Another club soda?" Angel asks, appearing in front of me with that carefully crafted smile. But there's something different in her eyes now, a depth of emotion that wasn't there before. It makes this whole plan feel even more dangerous.

"Please." I keep my voice neutral, professional. We're working. This isn't the time to think about how she looked at me from Levi's lap this afternoon, or what that look meant. Not when we know Garrett's watching. Waiting for his opportunity.

Jake's voice crackles in my earpiece. "All clear out front. Third sweep complete."

Eddie confirms the same from his position by the back entrance. "Loading dock secure. No unusual activity."

Angel drifts back toward Levi, and I watch him lean in to whisper something that makes her smile. She runs her fingers through his hair, and then trails them down his arm. He cups her cheek in his hand and kisses her forehead before she disappears behind the bar again.

She smiles at him over her shoulder. It's genuine—not the practiced one she gives customers. The sight stirs something I can't let myself get distracted by right now.

"Anything unusual on the cameras?" I ask Chase, needing the distraction.

"Nothing yet, boss. Seems pretty normal. Though that guy at table seven keeps checking his phone."

I spot the man Chase mentions. Mid-fifties, expensive watch, nervous energy. I make note but don't signal the others. We can't jump at every shadow. We have to remember, we might be in this for the long haul. There are no guarantees Garrett will show up tonight. Or any night.

I take another sip of club soda, ice clinking against my teeth. Everything is in position. We've planned for every contingency we could think of. We know that we've made Sunny as safe as she can be. There's no way Garrett would be dumb enough to try anything inside. But watching Angel move between Levi and me, seeing how naturally she fits in this space while staying alert for danger, I can't help but wonder if we've missed something obvious. Garrett's had years to study her routine, her habits. He's patient, calculating. The kind of man who waits for the perfect moment.

"You're thinking too loud," Jade says as she passes behind me with a tray of drinks. She's right. I need to focus on the job, not on the way Angel's eyes keep finding both Levi and me across the bar. Not on how vulnerable we've made her.

It's going to be a long night. Every minute that passes ratchets up the tension another notch. Angel serves drinks, laughs at jokes, plays her part perfectly. Levi watches her like a man dying of thirst. I monitor every movement, every shadow, trying to predict where the strike will come from.

All we can do now is wait. And hope that when Garrett makes his move, we're ready. Because if we're not—if we've miscalculated even slightly—I'll never forgive myself for putting her in harm's way. None of us will.

Chapter Forty-Four

Sunny

I HAVE TO PEE. The bass thrumming and vibrating up through the floor, isn't helping. I've been holding it for the last hour, but I'm getting kind of desperate. No one told me the plan for this.

On top of that, something feels off tonight. The energy is wrong, like the air before a storm. I keep trying to tell myself it's nerves, but it doesn't feel like that. At all.

"I need a quick break," I finally tell Levi, trying to keep my voice casual as I wipe down the bar for the hundredth time. His eyes narrow immediately. "The bathroom."

"I'll come with you." He's already standing, that muscle in his jaw ticking.

"To the bathroom?" I arch an eyebrow at him, channeling Angel's confidence even as my bladder screams at me. "Really? I'm a big girl you know."

Z appears beside Levi, his presence solid and reassuring. "She needs to maintain normalcy. A bouncer escort to the bathroom isn't normal."

"The dressing room bathroom," Levi argues. "Not the main one. And I'll wait outside. No big deal."

I want to argue more, but honestly, I just need to pee. And something about tonight makes me willing to compromise. "Fine. But you're being ridiculous."

Levi's hand slides over my shoulder and down my arm. It's a touch that anyone watching wouldn't be able to miss. "Humor me, Angel."

The walk to the dressing room feels longer than usual with Levi trailing behind me. Every instinct I've developed over the years of being Angel prickles at having someone follow me, even if I know them. Even if I know why.

"Five minutes, tops," I tell him at the dressing room door. "I promise."

He nods, but I can see the tension in his jaw. "Five minutes."

"Hey, it's going to be okay. I'm going to be okay. We got this." Thankfully the words come out sounding more confident than I feel at the moment.

He looks at me, trying to believe what I just said. I stand up on my toes and place a kiss on his cheek, smiling at his shocked look when I pull back. "Really."

The dressing room is empty when I get inside. It's late enough that everyone is either on stage or working the floor. The silence feels heavy after the throbbing bass of the club. I hurry to the back where the stalls are, relieved to finally have a moment alone.

Just a normal bathroom break, I tell myself. Just a normal night.

Now, if only I can convince myself to believe it.

Levi

I CAN STILL FEEL her lips on my cheek.

Five minutes. I check my watch again. Three minutes have passed.

The hallway feels too narrow, too confined. Every laugh and shout from the main floor sets my nerves on edge. The earpiece crackles with routine check-ins—Jake at the front, Eddie by the back door, Chase in the van. Everything's normal. Everything's fine.

I hate this plan. Hate being this exposed. Hate using her as bait.

A crash from the main floor catches my attention. Raised voices follow, then Jade's voice, sharp with anger. More crashes. The earpiece erupts with voices talking over each other.

"Situation in section three—"

"Colt, stand down—"

"Need backup—"

My feet shift toward the noise instinctively, but I force myself to stay put. Whatever's happening out there—Sunny is safer away from it. Three minutes and counting. She said five minutes.

The comms are chaos now. I catch fragments about Jade, about a customer getting physical. Colt's voice rises above the others, furious. Z's barking orders.

"Status on Angel?" Chase's voice cuts through the noise.

"Still in dressing room," I respond, my voice tight. "Three minutes."

More crashes from the main floor. The sound of breaking glass. Someone screams.

"Levi," Z's voice is strained. "We need—"

The earpiece goes dead.

Two minutes.

I pound on the dressing room door. "Angel? Time's up."

Nothing.

"Angel?" Louder this time.

The silence on the other side of the door makes my blood run cold.

Zane

THE SITUATION SPIRALS OUT of control in seconds. One minute Jade's pushing away a handsy customer, the next she's stumbling backward with blood pouring from her nose. The customer grabs her arm hard enough to bruise.

Colt moves before I can stop him, all pretense of cover forgotten. His fist connects with the guy's jaw just as three more men stand up from different tables. How did we miss this?

"Chase, I need eyes on those exits," I bark into my comm, already moving toward the fight. "Jake, Eddie, lock it down."

Glass shatters. Someone screams. Wolf and his team converge on the new threats, but it's chaos. Too many bodies, too much movement.

"Status on Angel?" Chase's voice crackles through.

"Still in dressing room," Levi responds. "Three minutes."

My gut twists. This is wrong. All wrong. The timing—

"Check the camera feeds," I order Chase, ducking under a thrown bottle. "Dressing room, now."

Static fills the comm line.

"Chase? Chase, respond." Nothing but white noise.

"Levi," I try, fighting my way toward the back hall. "We need—"

The comms go dead.

Everything clicks into place too late. The fight. The strategic positioning. The disabled communications.

We played right into his hands.

Sunny

THE BATHROOM DOOR CREAKS as I push it open, the sound oddly loud in the empty dressing room. Muffled chaos filters in from the main floor—crashes, shouts, the heavy thud of bodies hitting tables.

It's all wrong.

I move faster, reaching for the dressing room door. My hand wraps around the handle just as a familiar cologne hits my nostrils. A scent that still haunts my nightmares.

"Hello, Princess." His breath is hot against my neck. "It's been a while."

My body freezes—I can't move. Behind me, Garrett chuckles – that same awful sound I remember from all those nights I tried to forget.

"I've missed you."

I try to scream, but his hand clamps over my mouth. Something sharp pricks my neck. The room starts to tilt.

"Shhh," he whispers, and I feel his smile against my ear. "He couldn't stay away could he? You're mine Sunny. Always have been. It's gonna be just like old times."

Through the spreading darkness, I see the dressing room door burst open. Levi's face, twisted in rage and horror. Z behind him, reaching for his gun.

The emergency exit behind us crashes open, the alarm adding to the chaos. Two men in security uniforms—not club security—rush in. There's a loud bang and smoke fills the room, thick and disorienting. I hear shouts, gunshots, the sound of bodies colliding.

But they're too far away. Too late.

The last thing I see as consciousness fades is both of them fighting through the smoke, their shouts muffled like I'm underwater, while Garrett drags me backward through the emergency exit. Levi's voice breaks through the haze, screaming my name—my real name. "SUNNY!"

Then nothing.

Levi

THE SMOKE BURNS MY lungs as I fight through it, but I can't see her anymore. Can't reach her. The emergency exit slams shut with a finality that stops my heart.

"NO!" The word tears from my throat, raw and desperate. I slam into the door, throwing my shoulder against it with enough force to make the hinges groan. It gives way to a empty alley and the sound of squealing tires.

Gone. She's gone.

Z appears beside me, gun still drawn. "Chase! Status on the alley cameras!"

Only static answers.

My legs give out. I slide down the wall, the brick rough against my back. Seven years ago, I walked away thinking she was dead. Now I've watched her be taken, alive and terrified, and I couldn't stop it.

"I promised her," I whisper, my voice breaking. "I promised I wouldn't let him touch her again."

The sound of fighting still echoes from inside. Colt shouting orders. But all I can hear is Garrett's laugh, see Sunny's eyes as they closed, feel the weight of another failure crushing my chest.

We never had a chance. He played us like a fucking conductor.

And now she's gone.

Stay Connected

Scan the QR code or head to **jennichris.com** to join my mailing list. Get exclusive bonus content, sneak peeks, and regular updates on future projects!
You can also find me on Instagram/Facebook/Tiktok @jennichrisauthor

READY FOR MORE?

The story is far from over...

THANK YOU FOR READING BEAUTIFUL SCARS: BREATHLESS

If you can't get enough of Sunny, Levi, and Zane...
If you're wondering what happens next...
Turn the page to enjoy the first chapter of the next book in the
Beautiful Scars Duet.

BEAUTIFUL SCARS: UNSHAKEABLE

It hits harder and burns hotter.
Happy reading!

Beautiful Scars Unshakeable

Chapter One

The darkness is absolute. It presses against my eyes like a physical weight. My head throbs with each beat of my heart as consciousness creeps back in. Cold metal bites into my wrists and ankles and the concrete underneath me steals what little warmth I'm struggling to hold on to.

Sharp fragments of memory flash through my mind. Levi's face contorting in horror. Rough hands dragging me through the club's back door. The sharp sting of a needle. Then nothing but darkness.

I want to scream, call for help, but my throat feels like sandpaper and my tongue is dry and swollen. Thoughts drift in and out, none staying, making it impossible to piece together how long I've been here.

A metallic click echoes through the room. Harsh fluorescent lights blast on, flooding the entire room, searing my retinas. I squeeze my eyes shut against the assault.

"Well, well. Look who's finally awake." The voice sends ice through my veins. "Did you miss me, Princess?"

Heavy boots scuff across the floor and stop in front of me. I force my eyes open, blinking against the glare. Garrett looms over me, his blonde hair longer than I remember, his face harder. But those cold, dead eyes—they're exactly the same.

"Seven years is a long time to play look, but don't touch, baby." He crouches down, reaching out to brush my hair back. I jerk away but the chains leave me nowhere to go. "You've grown up so pretty. But then, you always were beautiful. My beautiful, sweet princess."

"Don't touch me." The words come out as a croak.

"Aw, you think you have a choice. That's cute. You thirsty?" He produces a water bottle, unscrewing the cap and squatting down in front of me. "Open up."

Pride wars with desperation. Thirst wins. I let him tip the water into my mouth, hating how good the liquid feels sliding down my raw throat.

"See? You still need me to take care of you." His fingers trail down my cheek. "We were doing just fine before those assholes showed up, weren't we? You got the chance to build up your little life, just the way you wanted. Did I interfere? Nope. Not once. I let you believe you had all the freedom in the world."

My stomach churns. "But I didn't. You were always there. Watching."

"Of course I was. You're mine Sunny. That's never changed." His grip fastens on my jaw. "But they just couldn't leave you alone, could they? Trying to take what belongs to me."

"I don't belong to anyone."

"Still so stubborn. Don't you remember? You're mine or you're dead." He laughs, the sound sharp and cruel. "You know, when I got the call and they told me you were in the hospital, alive, I knew I'd been given a second chance. A chance to do it right. I was content to keep you in my glass jar, safe on your little shelf. But..."

"They'll find me." The words lack conviction even to my own ears.

"Oh, I'm counting on it." Garrett stands, towering over me. "But, by that time, you're going to remember exactly where you belong. Who you belong to."

Fear claws up my throat as memories of the past surge forward—nights spent trying to disappear into myself while his hands moved over my body. The same hands that killed my father. That almost killed me.

"You're crazy." I struggle to keep my voice steady. "I'm not that scared little girl anymore. I don't belong to you."

"We'll see." He kneels, face inches from mine. His breath reeks of whiskey. "You might start to feel differently after a couple weeks."

His fingers trail down my neck and graze over the ink at my collarbone, tracing over the scar there. I want to scream. To fight. To show him how wrong he is. But my body betrays me, and I freeze.

"We're gonna have so much fun making up for lost time." He stands again, heading for the door. "And when your knights in shining armor finally show up? Well... I've got plans for them too."

The lights click off, plunging me back into darkness. His laughter echoes off the walls as the door slams shut.

I twist in on myself as much as the chains allow, trying to control my ragged breathing. Tears slip down my cheeks silently and I close my eyes—refusing to let them become sobs, refusing to give him the satisfaction. He's right—it's just like before. Except now there's more at stake.

Levi. Zane. The thought of them walking into whatever trap Garrett has planned makes my chest constrict. But the alternative—being left here alone with him with no hope of ever being rescued—is a terror that threatens to swallow me whole.

The darkness presses in close again, bringing with it memories of every touch, every violation I'd tried so hard to forget over the years.

I open my eyes hoping it will stop, but the blackness keeps going on and on and on.

TIME BLEEDS TOGETHER. MINUTES, hours, days—they all feel the same. My muscles scream from being forced into and held in the same position by the chains, and thirst claws at my throat again. It feels like a lifetime ago that Garrett gave me the water.

The door creaks open, and the lights flick on. Fluorescence stabs at my eyes. Two silhouettes fill the doorway.

"Get up." A gruff voice commands.

My legs shake as they unlock the chains from the floor. Rough hands haul me up to my feet, and I bite back a cry as blood rushes back into my limbs bringing sleeping nerves back to life. They drag me forward, not waiting for my feet to find purchase.

Cold air hits my bare skin as we move through the building. It looks I'm being held in some sort of abandoned warehouse. Metal rafters stretch high overhead, and moonlight filters in through dirty windows. Our footsteps echo off concrete walls. I try to memorize the path—left, right, down a long corridor—but everything looks the same.

The grip on my arms tightens as we approach another door. One of the men fumbles with the keys attached to his belt, while the other holds me in place. His fingers dig into my flesh hard enough to bruise.

Once the door is open, they shove me into a room that stinks of bleach and other cleaning supplies. I stumble, catching myself against the wall. A queen size bed sits in the middle of the room, its metal frame bolted to the floor. There's a small table with a lamp, and through another doorway I glimpse a bathroom—toilet, shower—no door, no privacy.

"Boss said you need to get yourself cleaned up." The taller guard's eyes rake over me. "Don't try anything stupid. There's cameras everywhere."

The door slams shut. The lock clicks.

I slide down the wall, wrapping my arms around my knees. The room is warmer, more comfortable than the concrete floor, but I can't stop shaking. Memories of Easton Creek flood back—of all the lessons and time it took for me to learn to be quiet, to be small, to obey. And I still never got it right.

"They'll come for me," I whisper to myself, but the words sound hollow spoken out loud in the empty room. Levi and Zane will tear this place apart looking for me. I have to believe that.

But will there be anything left for them to find?

My gaze drifts to the bathroom and my stomach does a flip. I should welcome the chance to take a shower, to get warm, to get clean. But going in there and turning on that water means accepting this situation. It means following orders.

I press my forehead to my knees, fighting back tears. I spent seven years thinking I was free, only to discover Garrett had been pulling strings the whole time. Now, I'm right back where I started — naked, afraid, and completely at his mercy.

I wasn't lying when I said I'm not that scared teenager anymore. My body may remember, part of me may want to curl up and disappear, but I refuse to let him break me.

Forcing myself up, I stand on shaky legs. One step at a time. Clean up. Gather strength. Watch for opportunities. I may have to play his game for now, but I won't make it easy. Not again.

The bathroom light flickers as I turn it on. No mirror, thank God. I don't want to see the bruises I can feel forming. The water runs ice cold before turning warm, and by the time I step under it, it's steamy hot. It feels good. Much better than I want to admit. It helps clear my head, and centers me here in the present instead of letting me drift away in memories.

A towel hangs on a hook—small mercy that it is. As I dry off, I hear movement outside the door. My heart rate spikes. It's too soon. I'm not ready.

But ready or not, I know what's coming. I fight the panic working its way into my head, into my body.

I wrap the towel around myself, backing into the corner.

Levi and Zane are coming. I have to survive until then. That's all I have to do.

Breathe. Stay present. Don't disappear.

The lock clicks and the door opens.